A Hodder Children's Books two-in-one special edition

Jill's Riding Club
Challenges for Jill

Jill's Riding Club

Ruby Ferguson

Hodder
Children's
Books

a division of Hodder Headline plc

This special edition first published in Great Britain in 1995
by Hodder Children's Books

ISBN 0 340 64641 1

Jill's Riding Club
Copyright © 1956, 1993 Hodder and Stoughton Ltd.

First published as a single volume in Great Britain in 1956
by Hodder and Stoughton Ltd.
Revised editions 1969, 1993 by Knight Books

A Catalogue record for this book is available from the British Library

Typeset by
Hewer Text Composition Services, Edinburgh

Printed and bound in Great Britain by
Cox & Wyman Ltd, Reading, Berkshire

Hodder Children's Books
a division of Hodder Headline plc
338 Euston Road
London NW1 3BH

Contents

1 Who wants a riding club?

It was one of those wet Saturdays when you argue for a long time about what you are going to do and in the end you do nothing.

'Everybody thinks it would be an awfully good idea if we had a riding club here in Chatton,' said my friend Ann Derry.

'Who's everybody?' I said.

'Oh well, everybody, really. And everybody thinks it would be a jolly good thing if you started one.'

'I like that!' I said. 'Why pick on me?'

'Well, you do more or less start everything round here, don't you?'

'I'm not starting a riding club,' I said. 'It's too much bother. If anybody else wants to start one I wouldn't mind joining.'

'Oh, yes you would,' said Ann, with a flash of insight into my character which I can only describe as supersonic. 'I can't see you joining a riding club that Susan Pyke started, or that your cousin Cecilia started. You know you wouldn't like any riding club that you hadn't started yourself.'

'There's something in that,' I said. 'What does a riding club do, anyway?'

'Well, everybody joins, and you get a paddock – '

'Where from?'

'Oh gosh, I don't know. Don't interrupt. There must be millions of paddocks lying around doing nothing. You get one, and you have a meeting once a week or as often as you want, and you get somebody who knows all about equitation to come and lecture to you; and then you school everybody like mad; but the point is, that in the end you can have your own one-day event. Don't you think it would be marvellous to run a gymkhana, for instance, ourselves?'

I thought this over, and admitted it wouldn't be bad at all. In fact it appealed to me very much. It might be worth starting a riding club to run one's own gymkhana, and perhaps it wouldn't be too much of a bind. Perhaps we could get hold of some worthy types of people who would do the actual work.

'How do we begin?' I said.

'You mean, you'll really do it? Nice work!' said Ann.

'If we don't like it we can always give it up,' I said.

'Who do you think would join?'

'Oh, crowds of people. You needn't worry about people not wanting to join.'

'But we don't want a lot of drips,' I said.

Ann thought a bit and said, 'I expect we'll have to have *some* drips. I mean, you can't say "drips not admitted to the riding club", because nobody actually thinks that he or she is a drip. That is only apparent to other people. I mean, there might be people who thought that you and I were drips.'

'Don't be silly,' I said. 'You know what drips are. There are two types; people who can't ride and won't bother to improve, and people who can't ride and think they can. I don't know which are worse. You can't teach either lot anything.'

'You might be able to do something with the first lot.'

'I'd rather not do anything with either lot,' I said. 'But from what I know about riding clubs – which isn't much – you've got to put up with anybody who wants to join. You get an awfully mixed entry.'

'That's the whole point, I suppose,' said Ann. 'People join riding clubs to learn as well as have fun. But if you're a properly organised riding club, really important experts are willing to come and teach you because they think they are doing something noble for the cause of equitation.'

'I think you'd better run this show yourself if you know so much about it,' I said.

'Oh no, Jill, you do it, and I'll back you up.'

'That's what you think,' I said.

We didn't talk any more about the idea of the riding club, as at that moment Mummy came in and said she would take us to the pictures, seeing it was such a beastly wet Saturday afternoon; but during the evening I thought the idea over.

If you have read my previous books you will realise that I had done quite a lot since I came to live in Chatton five years ago, in fact there seemed to be very little in the local world of equitation that I hadn't had a stab at at one time or another. My adventures, in fact, had already made four books, and I didn't think there was much else that could happen to me. I had one more year at school ahead of me, and that would be mainly marred by swotting for my GCSEs after which I had a wild and woolly dream of going to work as a groom at Captain Cholly-Sawcutt's stables, if he thought I was good enough. I hadn't planned anything for the approaching holidays, beyond trying to win a spot of Grade C jumping – if anybody would be rash enough to lend me a horse to do it on – and I thought it would just be the usual round of events. And now Ann had to crash in with this riding club idea.

The one thing I hadn't thought of was a riding club, and I could see that it would be quite something for

Chatton to have one. Everybody rode, of course. They learned at various riding schools, or taught themselves, or 'grew up on a horse' like farmers' children, or were taught by their adoring but occasionally misguided parents who had themselves learned to ride in the dark bygone ages of about 1932. The only time all these people had the chance to meet one another and exchange ideas was in the show ring, where as you know, what with having the needle and thinking how much better turned out everybody looks than yourself, you haven't much time for exchanging anything at all but nervous glances.

So the more I thought about a riding club the more it seemed to be a useful thing, as well as good fun; only I still kept thinking, why pick on me to run it? Now if somebody like Susan Pyke had chosen to run a riding club I could have understood it, except that I couldn't imagine anybody in their senses joining a riding club run by Susan Pyke. But there were also jolly decent people like the Heath twins. Why couldn't they start a riding club? Oh well, I thought, if it's got to be me, then it's got to be me, and that's all there is to it. Probably nobody will join and it'll all fizzle out, but nobody in Chatton can say we didn't try a riding club while we had the chance.

So the next morning I rang Ann up, and the minute I heard her answer, 'Chatton 92', because all the Derry family answer the telephone in this correct and proper way instead of the usual Hello, I said, 'How do you start a riding club, anyway?' Immediately I realised I had got the wrong person, as instead of Ann's voice I heard Mrs Derry's rather nervous and milk-chocolaty one saying, 'Oh dear, is that you, Jill? What on earth are you going to start now?' I felt like saying, 'Measles', but I said, 'Please can I speak to Ann?'

I heard her say to Ann, 'It's Jill, for you, and I don't know what she's talking about.'

I said to Ann, 'You'd better come round here,' and she said she would. Mrs Derry, Ann's mother, lives in a perpetual state of thinking there is going to be a disaster, and it isn't much good having anybody like that hovering around when you are planning to do anything.

In the end we went to our orchard and sprawled under the trees, and my ponies Black Boy and Rapide nuzzled us and tried to chew our hair, and it was all very pleasant, especially as Ann had brought some chocolate.

'About this riding club,' I said. 'How would we start it? I don't mean to say I'm going on with the idea, but one might as well know.'

Ann said the thing to do was to tell everybody at school to tell everybody who was interested, and get them to come to a meeting.

'Where do we have the meeting?' I said.

'We can have it at our house on Wednesday, because Mummy's going to London for the day.'

'Couldn't we have it here in our orchard?' I said, but Ann thought an orchard wasn't a very dignified or impressive place to have a meeting and we might find that we suddenly wanted to be dignified and impressive. So we decided to have it at her house.

Then before the riding club was even started we began to plan all the things we could do. Schooling and jumping in the paddock, and games and competitions, and perhaps cross-country riding. Perhaps somebody with horsy instincts and large grounds might be interested and invite the club for a field day and tea. And then of course we would be able to run a gymkhana.

Ann said, we'd have to have some rules; and I said,

why not let all that kind of thing work itself out as we get to it? I felt a few qualms about having rules because if you have rules you have got to enforce them or it is chaos, and really only a grown-up can enforce rules. As there would be a number of people in the club my own age or older I could see nothing but endless arguments if anybody tried to lay down the law, so I thought it was the best thing to deal with details as they cropped up and not make regular rules to be fought over. Ann said she thought I was a mass of brains and ought to go into the Diplomatic Service.

'You could get round it,' she said, 'by not having anybody as old or experienced as us in the club, but then it would be a kids' affair and there wouldn't be any competition for us.'

I agreed that we wanted competition and people of our own age or older, because the riding club wouldn't be any fun if it just meant coaching kids.

'And I tell you here and now, Ann,' I said, 'if I don't like the way the club is turning out I shall wash it all up. The summer holidays are short enough without rushing about doing things you don't care about doing.'

'Leave it all to me,' said Ann. 'We'll have a meeting on Wednesday and see who turns up and how keen they are. Other people make a success of riding clubs and I don't see why we shouldn't. It's about the only thing we *haven't* tried in Chatton.'

This made me think more than ever that Ann was better qualified to run this affair than I was, but Mummy was by now calling us for tea and we galloped into the cottage.

2 A noisy meeting

We didn't mention the riding club during tea, as we both felt it was still on the secret list, but I was getting rather excited about having something definite to do in the holidays and couldn't keep it all to myself, so next morning which was Saturday I said to Mummy, 'What do you think is the latest? I'm going to start a riding club.'

'How interesting,' she said in a rather cool way. I knew at once that for some reason or other she was taking a dim view.

'What's the matter?' I said. 'I fed the hens.'

Mummy said, if I really wanted to know what was the matter, my room was a disgrace, and every single garment I owned wanted darning or hooks putting on or elastic through.

I thought a bit, and then said, 'OK, I suppose I'd better do something about it,' and she said that that would be a useful idea, only don't let it interfere with the ponies, which I suppose was justified but rather soulless of her.

So all the time I was getting my cotton knotted and sewing hooks on upside down, only to tear them off again with muttered oaths, I was thinking about the riding club and wondering who would join. I thought perhaps Ann had been a bit optimistic and nobody would join, in which case we would be back to where we were; or we might only get a few small kids like Ann's sister Pam, and spend literally millions of glowing summer hours hoisting them on and off their unfortunate ponies, in which case Ann could do it alone.

I then went to the other extreme, and wondered what I would do if a lot of frightfully superior people joined, and expected the riding club to be run in a frightfully superior way, far beyond my humble capacities. This gave me such a jolt that I accidentally sewed the buttons on my white shirt with the same black cotton that I had been using for my navy-blue skirt, but it was dinner time by then and too late to do anything about it.

I went on thinking vaguely about the riding club all through dinner, though in a dim sort of way I realised that Mummy was asking me what sort of bulbs we should get for the garden borders. This sort of thing naturally makes one's parents think one is half-witted.

Meanwhile Ann must have been spreading the news and arousing a lot of what might prove to be misplaced enthusiasm, because when I got to school on Monday morning everybody was pouncing on me at once and asking, 'Are you really starting a riding club? Where is it going to be? What are you going to do? Can anybody join?'

I simply didn't know what to say.

As I was coming out of the Art Room I bashed into Susan Pyke, now quite out of my class and in the sixth form. She looked at me in quite a friendly way and said, 'What's this about a riding club? Good gracious! You *are* coming on!'

I said, 'Coming on what?' and she laughed in a sort of tinkly way, and said, 'It should be quite fun for the little ones.'

This didn't cheer me up; it wasn't my idea of a riding club at all. I found Ann and said, 'Something's gone wrong with your publicity. People seem to have got the idea that this riding club is a sort of nursery class. What happens if we get the whole of the junior school turning up on Wednesday, and nobody else?'

'It'd be jolly noble of us,' she said, 'to do something for the tinies. We could pat ourselves on the back and feel we were helping the cause of equitation no end.'

'I'm not as noble as all that,' I said grimly, 'especially in the holidays.'

So we left it at that, and wondered what would happen on Wednesday.

When I took the ponies their water that night I told them about the riding club. Black Boy hadn't much to say; he looked at me in a rather gratifying you-know-best kind of way. But Rapide made four different faces at me; then he gave a very dramatic whinny and blew thoughtfully into the bucket. A lot of water went over my jodhpurs. I told Rapide what I thought of him, but as usual he couldn't care less.

Ann was having spasms of a different nature, wondering what would happen if Mrs Derry suddenly decided *not* to go to London on Wednesday; but nothing so awful happened, and she went off early. I decided to ride Rapide to the meeting, so after I had taken the stains out of the knees of my jodhpurs and put on a clean blue shirt I set off. It was a very hot day and Rapide was in a sauntering mood. I suggested that he might trot up the drive to Ann's house so as to look keen if anybody was looking out of the window – as they might well be – but he wasn't having any, in fact he began to do his downtrodden pony act as soon as we got in sight of the house. I was ashamed of him.

I expected to find about six people at the meeting. Instead of that the room was crammed. Quite a lot of the people I had never seen before in my life, but my eye went unfailingly to two points of horror, Clarissa Dandleby and my cousin Cecilia. Nothing could have been worse. Obviously Cecilia was spending the holidays with her friend Clarissa, and if I had known I would have run twenty miles before I'd have started this riding club, only I couldn't know.

I had a cold feeling inside.

'Aren't there a lot of people here?' Ann said proudly.

'There are only two so far as I'm concerned,' I said. 'Why on earth did you let them in?'

'Oh, you mean Clarissa and Cecilia. I couldn't very well turn them away, could I? I don't know how they heard about the riding club, but they must be keen or they wouldn't have come.'

'I don't know half the people here,' I grumbled, and Ann said, surely that was the whole point of the riding club, to bring strangers together in the cause of equitation.

I said, 'You've got an answer for everything.'

'Oh, hello, Jill,' said Cecilia, catching my eye. 'We've ridden all the way from Clarissa's house for this, so it had better be good.'

'It isn't meant for experts,' I said, knowing what she was like on a pony at the best of times. 'Unless you'd like to give us a lecture. We shall want some people to give us lectures.'

'I wouldn't mind,' said Cecilia, and my eyes nearly shot out of my head, as what Cecilia knows about riding would go on a postage stamp.

'When you two have done arguing –!' said Ann, coming to my rescue. 'Now let's get on with the meeting. I expect you people have come here because you've heard we want to start a riding club these holidays and you must think it's a good idea or you wouldn't have bothered to come. Most of us belong to one or another of the local riding schools, and others are possibly taught by their proud parents or uncles, but the point is we usually never meet except in the show ring. It seems a pity, because I feel that if we could all get together occasionally we could probably teach each other a lot. So the idea is, well – just to get together.'

'When I lived at Camberley,' said one of the boys, 'I belonged to a riding club. We used to have jolly good rallies, and some smashing people came and lectured to us and inspected us. It was terrific.'

'I don't know if this will be as terrific as all that,' I said. 'But the point is that anybody who doesn't like it or thinks they aren't getting any good out of it can always buzz off. I don't know how it is, but as soon as I start anything it gets too big before it even starts, if you know what I mean. Our idea was first to get a paddock to hold our rallies, and then to have a rally at least every week in the holidays.'

'Where?' said Clarissa Dandleby. She would!

'I don't know yet,' I said. 'There must be plenty of paddocks lying around.' My one hope was that she wouldn't feel inclined to come ten miles every week, but she dashed my wild hopes to the ground by saying, 'Cecilia is staying with me for the whole of the holidays, and we shall be able to come over in the horsebox.'

Seeing I was rendered speechless by this idea, Ann said, 'The first thing to do is to take the names of all those who think they'd like to join. Stick your hands up, and we'll make a list of the names.'

Everybody stuck their hands up, and we started putting their names down. Fortunately there were quite a lot of decent people that we knew, like Diana Bush and the Heaths and other people from school.

'How much is it going to cost?' asked a first year kid called Brookes.

'I dunno,' I said. 'I never thought of that.'

We thought a bit, and then decided that we'd make

it five pounds to be a member, and see how it worked out according to what we had to pay for.

'Don't you think there ought to be an age limit?' said Cecilia.

Diana Bush said, 'Why? It would be rather nice to have some older people, even twenty-ish ones.'

Cecilia gave her a withering look, and said, 'What I meant was, we definitely don't want any kids.'

Clarissa said, 'Hear, hear. I bar the under-twelves.'

I was furious, and wanted to ask who she thought she was to bar anything, but just then Val Heath butted in – and she was the right person to do it, as everybody knew she was jolly good and had won prizes at Richmond Horse Show – and said, 'Surely you know that a riding club is meant for all ages, so long as people are keen. Anyone who doesn't like that needn't join. But if anybody of four wants to join they can, and even if they're forty they can join if they want to, though I don't suppose anybody would.'

'Hear, hear,' somebody said.

'What do we do at the rallies?' somebody asked. 'Just have competitions?'

'No,' said Ann. 'We improve the standard of our riding, that's the main thing. We help each other with anything we know. And we get people to come and school us.'

'Schooling!' said Clarissa in tones of utter disgust. 'Some of us got past that stage long ago.'

'That's what you think,' said Val. 'No rider ever ought to say a silly thing like that, and you know it.'

A boy said, 'Even schooling's good fun when you do it together. But I suppose we'll have plenty of games and competitions too. And what about a gymkhana?'

Everybody shouted out, 'Oh, yes, do let's have a gymkhana.'

'If we ran our own gymkhana,' said another boy, 'we

could make our own rules, and not have such stuffy judges, like the ones at Lyneham last week who were more or less unconscious all the time and kept rushing off to the refreshment tent instead of looking keen. I do think the least judges can do is to look interested in the competitions.'

Another boy said that perhaps the standard of horsemanship at Lyneham had been enough to make any judges unconscious or send them fleeing to the refreshment tent, and as a matter of fact his own uncle often judged at pony shows and wondered why he wasted his time on such a hopeless crowd.

I said, 'Look, can't we get back to the point? We've got to convince our parents and other people that this riding club is going to be a good thing and a useful occupation for the holidays. The first thing they'll ask is, what are our aims and objects.'

'Well, what are they, anyway?' said Cecilia, and somebody else murmured, 'Help! Do we have to have aims and objects? I thought we were going to enjoy ourselves?'

'I should say the chief aim and object,' said a boy called John Watson, 'is to improve the standard of horsemanship in this district. If we tell people that, it ought to fetch them.'

'Oh yes, and to promote a spirit of what-do-you-call-it among pony owners,' said Diana Bush. 'My father says we ought to learn to compete without rivalry. Some people are bad losers, and if we get any of those in the riding club we can knock it out of them. My father says – '

'We might get your father to come and give us a lecture,' I said. 'If we could get some older horsy people to come and talk to us it would be a help.'

'Oh, we don't want to listen to lectures, we can read it all in books,' said Cecilia, rather rudely. 'And we haven't decided yet where we're going to hold these rallies. Perhaps Jill can suggest some place.'

'I don't know yet,' I said rather miserably. 'I expect something will turn up.'

'It's not going to be much good if you haven't got a field,' said Cecilia.

'You shake me to the teeth,' I said.

'It would be rather nice if we could get some expert to come and instruct us in jumping,' somebody said.

'There's no reason why we shouldn't. If people see we are keen they might be glad to help us.'

'They might even be glad to give us a field,' said Cecilia sarkily.

'All right, all right,' I said. 'Aim number one then, to improve the standard of horsemanship all round. Aim two, to work for a gymkhana of our own – '

'Aim three,' somebody chimed in. 'To have some fun. I'm sick and tired of hearing about work, work, work.'

'Of course,' I said. 'Aim three, to have a lot of fun. Any more aims?'

'I think we've got more than enough,' said Clarissa.

'Enough, anyway,' said John Watson, glaring at Clarissa, 'to convince our parents and local experts of the horse world that we're a keen and sincere riding club. Everyone in favour, hands up.'

Everybody put their hands up, and I said, 'To get on to the next point, what are we going to call the riding club?'

'Do we have to call it anything?' said Ann.

'Well, all good riding clubs have a name,' I said; and John Watson said, 'What about the Chatton Riding Club? There isn't another one.'

'I don't think we can do that,' said Val Heath. 'It sounds so sidey, as if we owned the village. Couldn't we have something that suggests a serious aim, like Perseverance?'

There was an absolute yell of protest, and somebody said, 'I think we ought to have an imaginative sort of name. What about the Pegasus?'

'I think that name's been used already somewhere,' said Diana; and one of the boys said, 'Couldn't we go all western and call it the Buckaroo Riding Club? I think that sounds smashing.'

'I should call it the Stinkaroo and have done with it,' said Clarissa crushingly, and Cecilia said, 'Oh, you are a scream!' and they both went into a fit of giggles.

'Shut up, you two,' said Ann. 'What name would you like for the club, Jill?'

'Oh, she'll want to call it Jill's Riding Club,' said Cecilia. '*Cela va sans dire.*'

'Quite, quite!' said John Watson. '*Avez-vous trouvé la plume de ma tante*? Let's call it La Cecilia Riding Club.'

'You're not a bit funny,' said Cecilia, and John said, 'Strangely enough, neither are you.'

'I've got an idea,' said Val Heath. 'I know where there's a paddock, if we can get hold of it. It's on the Greenlee estate, old Miss Durdon's place, and if she would let us have the land we could call the club the Greenlee Club. It's a pretty name and dignified too.'

Everybody agreed that this was a good idea, and Ann said, 'How do we get this business of the paddock fixed up? Would you be able to do that, Val? I mean, see this Miss What's-her-name and ask her if we can use the land?'

'Oh gosh, no,' said Val. 'I was only making the suggestion. Somebody else will have to see about it. My father and Miss Durdon have been having rows over land for about the last forty years. The Heaths and the Durdons have always been at daggers drawn. If she even knew that I was behind this she wouldn't let you have a paddock for untold gold.'

'That does sound hopeful!' I said.

'There's no reason why she should know the Heath family are interested,' said Val. 'One of you ought to go along and see her. I suggest you go, Jill. You've got plenty to say, and you're not terrified of old people.'

'Help!' I said. 'Is she awful?'

'She's probably not bad if you approach her the right way. I mean, she's keen on horses – that's a point. And it's a perfectly serious business deal. I don't see why she shouldn't let us have the land. It isn't being used for anything else.'

'If we rent it, how are we going to pay for it?' said Ann. 'The five pound subs may not be enough.'

'What I was thinking,' said Val, 'was that she might be induced to charge just a nominal rent of about twenty pounds for the eight weeks of the hols. I mean, anybody with horsy instincts ought to be proud to have their land used for a thing like a riding club. In her palmy days she used to ride to hounds, and though she's about a hundred now she must have some decent feelings left about equitation. If I was a rich old woman with land I'd practically go down on my knees and beg people to use it for a riding club. She probably only needs asking.'

'All right,' I said gallantly. 'I'll go and ask her. Only somebody will have to come with me.'

'I'll go with you,' said Clarissa promptly.

'That's torn it,' muttered Ann.

'We'd better vote for who goes with me,' I said.

'I'll go,' said Diana, 'if anybody will vote for me.'

I told everybody to put their hands up for Diana, and then for Clarissa, and when we counted the votes were even.

'Right,' said Clarissa. 'We'll both go.'

I looked at Diana, and she put her hand on her heart and rolled her eyes up.

I first met Clarissa at a garden fête which a person called Mrs Whirtley was getting up; that is to say, Clarissa and I were both on the committee and went to the meetings. She was sixteen and considered herself a hard woman to hounds, and was always muttering darkly about having ridden in her first point-to-point when she was only eleven, in fact she gave you the impression that she belonged to the higher realms of horsemanship, until you saw her on a pony. How that girl kicked, bounced, and shoved was an eye-opener.

'We'll go and see Miss Durdon tomorrow,' said Diana. 'That's settled.'

'And if she lets you have the paddock,' said Val, 'couldn't we all meet there on Saturday for the first rally?'

Everybody agreed that that would be marvellous, and that was actually the end of the meeting, though everybody was by now talking at once, as if getting the paddock from Miss Durdon was a foregone conclusion and all we had to do was to ride round there and enjoy ourselves.

When I got home and thought things over there seemed to be a lot of 'ifs' about the riding club. If we could get the paddock. If we had enough money to pay what Miss Durdon might ask for it. If the members were keen enough about the real aims of the club and didn't just want to play about. Etc. Etc. I felt that what I needed was some expert advice. I thought I might go up to the riding school and consult Mrs Darcy, but there again the situation was tricky. She might think she should have been consulted before I called the meeting, whereas one does like to do things off one's own bat, a thing no grown-ups can understand.

In the end I went down to the library and asked the

librarian if she had got any books about riding clubs. She looked at me in a vague sort of way, and I had to repeat Riding Clubs, about four times.

In the end she said she'd go and see, so she clambered down from her stool very slowly and doodled away into the dark recesses of the library where doubtless all the dull unwanted tomes were kept, and after about ten minutes she came back and just said, 'No'. I said, could I go and look myself, and she said I could if I liked, and if there was anything it would be under Horses and Cattle on the top shelf in the far bay, but she had already looked and there wasn't anything. I went myself, and how right she was! Evidently how to run a riding club was something one had to work out for oneself by trial and error, with no aid from great literary minds.

When I got home I rang up Ann and told her about my lack of success, and asked if among all her pony books there wasn't one about running a riding club, and she said there was one, and she'd already gone through it carefully but it wasn't going to be much use to us. The children in it had boundless parkland at their disposal and were instructed by their uncle who was a famous equitation expert, and though it made a jolly good story she had chucked it out of the window in exasperation as it wasn't true to life.

I said, 'Just think, the world is full of famous literary people and nobody can write a book about how to run a riding club!'

Ann said, 'Don't be silly, there must be dozens if we could find them,' and I said bitterly, 'Go on then, find them.'

Ann said she didn't know what I was worrying about, I had got a lot of keen people and keenness was the only thing that counted. The riding club would practically run itself. I said I hoped she was right.

3 Fuss about a field

'One thing we didn't do,' said Diana Bush at school next morning, 'is to get a President for this riding club. Somebody impressive.'

I was dumb and speechless.

'My father would be it,' said Val Heath, 'though I suppose you'd not think he was impressive. What about asking Miss Durdon? She'd be flattered. You could ask her to be President first, Jill, and then when she beamed at you and was frightfully pleased you could slip in the bit about the paddock.'

I said that I thought Miss Durdon, whom practically nobody had ever heard of, was just about the least impressive person on earth, and Mr Heath was well known as an equitation expert in the district and I was all in favour of asking him to be President.

'It wouldn't be any good,' said Val. 'The first thing Miss Durdon will ask you is, who is President of the Riding Club. Grown-ups are terribly keen on that kind of thing, and if you say the name Heath you certainly won't get the paddock. She'll go up in smoke.'

'Oh blow!' I said. 'What *can* I say?'

'Tell her the committee is considering,' said Ann Derry. 'That sounds good. Tell her we haven't got round to details yet. Tell her we felt we couldn't do anything about a President until we were sure of a field.'

'You think of everything,' I said.

The afternoon was a half-holiday and Clarissa was

supposed to be meeting Diana and me at the bus stop. We both hoped she wouldn't turn up, but there she was with her specs glittering in the sun, and Diana said, 'Galloping goldfish, she's come!'

Clarissa greeted us in such a friendly way that we were quite overcome. The bus came along and we piled in. When the conductor came round for the fares it turned out that he had once worked as stableman for Clarissa's father. He said, 'Well, if it isn't Miss Clarissa! Been winning any cups lately?' Clarissa went a coy pink and said, 'Well, one can't help picking up a few here and there, though my main interest is hunting.' The conductor said he betted there was no woman in the shires faster over timber than Clarissa, and she said it was only right to hold back sometimes, it didn't look sporting to lead the field all the time. By now everybody in the bus was goggle-eyed, listening to this shame-making conversation, and Diana and I could have gone through the floor.

The bus put us down at last at the gates of Greenlee Hall, and Clarissa said, 'Well, here we are. Who's going to do the talking?'

Diana said, 'I think you've done enough talking already. All that guff about leading the field! I should think the huntsman comes out in blisters every time you turn up at a meet. Jill can do the talking. She's got sense.'

Clarissa opened her mouth to say something crushing, but I suppose she couldn't think of anything, so she shut it again, and we walked up the drive.

Greenlee Hall was a huge, grey, ugly house with bay windows sticking out all over it, and venetian blinds drawn down in case any sun got inside.

We knocked, and an aged maid opened the door and looked at us as if we were collecting for the guy.

I said, 'Can we see Miss Durdon, please?'

She said, 'What name?' and I said, 'The Greenlee Riding Club.'

She looked a bit taken back, and Diana gave me a dig and said, 'You tactless clot!'

I realised that I should not have used the name Greenlee right on its owner's doorstep; however the maid said, 'Come in, please, and wipe your feet,' which made us feel about six, unless of course she had orders from Miss Durdon to say this to all visitors.

She showed us into the drawing room which was so dark it took us about five minutes to see anything at all. It was the sort of room that makes you talk in whispers, and it was crammed with little tables and whatnots which were all covered with framed photographs of ancient and grim-looking people.

'There's one photograph of a horse, anyway,' said Diana, 'but the man mounted on it is practically sitting on its rump, there's room for another one in front of him, and he's got his hands under his chin.'

'I see you're admiring the portrait of my papa,' said a voice behind us. 'The finest cavalryman that ever threw leg over saddle. That was taken in India in 1928.'

I daren't look at the other two, and Clarissa gulped, and said, 'How smashing.'

I don't know if you are like me and always make a picture in your mind of any new person you are going to meet. Perhaps if so you are cleverer than I am, as I always seem to be wrong. I had pictured Miss Durdon as being about ninety, with snowy hair and wrapped in shawls and wearing a sweet, grandmotherly expression, but actually she wasn't very old at all, and she was rather fat and had ginger hair done in curls on the top of her head. She had on a riding shirt with a mannish collar and tie, and a tough sort of skirt. She had little round bright eyes that looked very shrewd and brisk.

'Now,' she said. 'What's all this about?'

I saw Clarissa opening her mouth, and before she could chip in, which I felt would be fatal, I managed to get started on the speech I had made up and learned by heart in the silent watches of the previous night.

'My name is Jill Crewe,' I squeaked, 'and these are Diana Bush and Clarissa Dandleby. We represent a new riding club which is just being started in Chatton. The fact is, we need a paddock for our rallies, and we thought that as you have a good deal of land you might be able to lend or rent us a bit. We are all very keen and serious, and our objects are good horsemanship and – er – good sportsmanship, which I'm sure you will agree are very important things in life. I hope you will see your way to granting our request.'

I thought this was a jolly good speech, and while I was getting it off my chest I could see Diana and Clarissa looking quite stunned with admiration.

I had made it up that Miss Durdon should then reply, 'I am very interested in the aims and objects of your riding club, and as I would do anything for the cause of equitation I shall be very glad to lend you free of charge any suitable bit of my land that you would like for a paddock.' After which we would all thank her very ardently, which wouldn't be difficult to manage once the spadework was done.

But unfortunately it didn't work out like that. Miss Durdon looked at me with her little round eyes and said, 'I suppose you think I'd like to see a lot of children stampeding round my grounds and tearing up the park? I never heard of such a thing. Absolute nonsense!'

I was so taken back I was dumb, and Diana said, 'But we are a serious riding club, Miss Durdon, and we don't tear up ground and stampede,' and Clarissa said, 'The bit of land we'd like is at the farthest end of your park, and you'd not even see us, and this is a businesslike request and we are a properly constituted deputation. You might like to know,' she added, flashing her specs at Miss Durdon, 'that I myself hunt regularly with the West Morshire, and my father has been Master of Foxhounds.'

Actually she couldn't have said anything worse or more likely to rouse blue murder in the breast of Miss Durdon, who had always hunted with the Peckhill and loathed the very name of the West Morshire.

'That rabble of monkeys!' she said coldly, and Clarissa was so overcome by hearing her beloved Hunt called a rabble of monkeys that her specs fell off, and she was then as blind as a bat and yelled, 'Oh, my specs!' and started scrabbling about for them on the carpet, and the next minute she knocked over a little table and photograph frames came raining down all over the place. Diana and I had to shove our fists into our mouths to keep from screaming with laughter, and though I was giggling I was nearly sick with disappointment because everything was going wrong, and now there didn't seem a chance of us getting any land.

'Clumsy, clumsy, clumsy!' hissed Miss Durdon, snatching photograph frames up from the floor. Diana and I tried to help her, but the frames wouldn't stand up and Miss Durdon said snappily, 'Leave them alone!'

Clarissa found her specs and put them on, and I said, 'Couldn't you really rent us some little bit of land that you're not keen on, Miss Durdon? I mean, if we go back and tell the others we haven't got a paddock it will mean we can't have a riding club.'

'And that will probably mean the end of horsemanship in this district,' said Diana, 'because if you don't encourage the young entry, what's going to happen when the old ones die off?'

'Not much fear of that,' said Miss Durdon grimly.

'Some of us are good for about another thirty years, I hope. I've already told you I don't approve of packs of children on horseback charging round the place without let or hindrance. If they want to ride they should go to a competent instructor at a riding school, like I did. Horsemanship? Pooh! You don't know what it is.'

'I'm quite sure,' said Clarissa, trying to sound haughty and aloof, 'that you'll live to regret your decision.'

'That's my affair,' said Miss Durdon. 'I'm not worrying. Good afternoon. If you'll press that bell, girl, the maid will show you out.'

There seemed to be no hope left, and yet the saying that the darkest hour is just before the dawn proved true. The door opened and a girl came in. Diana and I let out one yell.

I don't know if you remember in one of my previous books how Diana and I went into the country to visit an aunt of Diana's who had a comic little farm on which she was assisted by a weird girl called Mercy Dulbottle. We had spent an afternoon on the marshes ringing Diana's aunt's ducks, and this girl Mercy proved to be the last word in drips and let the ducks escape as fast as we caught them.

Well, here in the ancestral home of the unspeakable Miss Durdon, at this grim crisis in our careers, who should appear at the drawing-room door looking exactly the same as on that bygone day, but Mercy Dulbottle herself.

She recognised us at once, and said, 'Oh, hello, Diana! Hello, Jill! Have you come to tea?' She sounded frightfully welcoming, partly I suppose because she hadn't many friends, and partly because it must have been a relief to see anybody human in Miss Durdon's house.

'Oh, hello, Mercy,' I gasped, and Diana said, 'Golly,

fancy you turning up here. What are you doing here, anyway?'

Miss Durdon said coldly, 'Do you know these people, Mercy?' and Mercy said, 'I should think I jolly well do. How marvellous to see Jill and Diana. Let's have tea at once, can we?'

This seemed to take the wind out of Miss Durdon's sails to such an extent that before she could speak or act in any hostile manner Mercy had rung the bell and told the maid to bring tea, and was jabbering away to Diana and me as if we were her long-lost sisters. It turned out that Miss Durdon was her godmother, and she simply doted on Mercy and only lived to give her everything she wanted. Mercy had had German measles and had come to stay with Miss Durdon for several weeks to convalesce, and after that Miss Durdon was going to pay for her to learn farming at an Agricultural College. Personally I thought the Agricultural College would take one look at Mercy and blow its roof off, but that was neither here nor there.

Miss Durdon was still in a sort of trance, and by the time she came round the tea was in, and Mercy was pouring it out and Clarissa was passing round the buns.

'How's the riding these days?' said Mercy to Diana, and Diana said, 'Well, that's just the point – I mean – ' She stopped and went red, and Mercy said, 'Oh, have I dropped a clanger?'

'Well, actually,' I said, 'we've just started a riding club, only – but it doesn't – it isn't – '

'A riding club?' said Mercy. 'How smashing! Could I join, do you think?'

'No, you couldn't,' snapped Clarissa. 'We haven't been able to get a field for the rallies so the whole thing's off.'

'But that's silly,' said Mercy. 'Why, Aunt Henrietta

has got acres of land doing nothing, and there's a marvellous little bit down by the west boundary that would be just the thing for you and your riding club. I say, what luck you came here!'

Miss Durdon was by now uttering hollow groans, what with loathing the sight of us and yet not being able to deny her darling Mercy anything.

Mercy with blissful blindness then went on enthusiastically to tell the wilting Miss Durdon that so far as riding went practically nobody in England of our age was as competent as Diana and me. We were fidgeting with embarrassment at this flattering untruth, but we wouldn't have stopped Mercy for the world as she seemed to be doing our work for us so well, and even Clarissa managed to push in a bit about how long it took her every Saturday to clean all the cups she had won.

'Think of having these people riding here, in your own paddock!' said Mercy, as if she was offering Miss Durdon the Crown jewels on a plate.

Miss Durdon made one last effort. 'I really don't want them. I don't want to let any of the land. Once they get in the paddock they'll be all over the park.'

'That,' said Mercy, 'would be nicer still.' She was the sort of person you simply couldn't flatten; she had an answer for everything. I just sat there munching currant buns and letting her fight my battles for me.

'You know you're only just beginning to ride, Mercy,' said Miss Durdon, 'and I don't want to have your seat and style spoiled by a pack of children bouncing about on ponies, when I'm really getting you ready to hunt.'

I thought for a minute that Clarissa was going for Miss Durdon tooth and nail, and my heart stood still because if she had let fly at that fell moment all would have been lost for ever, but fortunately Nature took a hand and stuck a crumb right in Clarissa's throat, so she gave a few strangled hysterical coughs and was silent.

'Honestly, Aunt Henrietta,' said Mercy, 'nothing could spoil me after all your wonderful coaching, and I'm sure it will give you a terrific lift with the Hunt to be entertaining a good riding club on your land. It will look as if you Believed in Young Riders, and the Master of Foxhounds is sure to be very keen on that sort of thing. Do tell Jill it's all settled!'

Miss Durdon said, 'Really, Mercy, I don't know. You shouldn't rush me like this.'

'Oh, Aunt Henrietta, be a sport,' said Mercy, and Clarissa butted in with, 'Oh yes, Miss Durdon, do be a sport!' while the poor woman half closed her eyes and went green at the thought of anybody who hunted with the hated West Morshire prancing about on *her* land.

I said, 'Of course, if we could have the field you could join us, Mercy, and we'd call the club together and have a rally at once.'

Mercy said, 'Do you hear that, Aunt Henrietta? I'd simply love to join! Do say it's all settled!'

Miss Durdon gave a groan, which might have meant anything at all, and immediately Mercy said, 'Oh, thank you a million times!' and turned to me and said, 'There, it's all settled. When are we going to start?'

'Oh, thank you, Miss Durdon,' I said, and Clarissa and Diana also started saying thank you, Miss Durdon, so she didn't have time to back out of it.

'There's just the matter of the rent,' I said. 'I hope it wouldn't cost a lot, as actually we haven't got any money at all – yet.'

'Why, it wouldn't cost *anything*,' said Mercy. 'The land isn't doing anything, and Aunt Henrietta would be only too glad to lend it to me to amuse myself in the holidays, wouldn't you, Aunt Henrietta?'

Miss Durdon was by now past speech, but Clarissa

said, 'It ought to cost something, or we wouldn't feel
it was legal, so what about twenty pounds and call it
a deal?'

'Oh yes, that'll do splendidly,' said Mercy, 'and we're
awfully glad you came, aren't we, Aunt Henrietta?'

Miss Durdon looked as if she could cheerfully have
murdered us, but she couldn't refuse Mercy anything,
so she was in what they call a cleft stick, and we'd got
the field and it was all too good to be true.

Clarissa, who had rather a legal sort of mind, said we
ought to have it all written down, so Mercy brought
a piece of writing paper and Clarissa wrote on it, 'I,
Miss Durdon, declare that the Greenlee Riding Club
can have the little paddock on the corner of Bent
Lane and Broomstick Lane for their rallies during the
holidays for the sum of twenty pounds. Yours truly.'

'Who said you could call it the Greenlee Riding
Club?' said Miss Durdon in a warlike way.

'It's just to do you the honour,' said Diana helpful-
ly.

'Oh, all right,' said Miss Durdon. 'But please don't
ask me for anything else, Mercy, or you'll bring on
my asthma.'

She then signed the paper, and Clarissa said Thanks,
and put it in her pocket.

4 The first rally

'If it hadn't been for Mercy Dulbottle we shouldn't have got the field at all,' I explained to Ann as we were on our way to the first grand rally of the Greenlee Riding Club, 'so you'd better be decent to her.'

'Will that be an effort?' Ann asked. 'What's she like?'

'At first sight you'll think she's ghastly,' I said, 'but she's quite a good sort underneath, apart from being slightly mad.'

'Can she ride at all?'

'I wouldn't know,' I said. 'Actually I think she's a beginner. The only time I ever met her before she was on a bike.'

Ann said, perhaps Mercy thought it was a bike-riding club and we both giggled; however, when we got to the paddock the first person we beheld was Mercy sitting up stiffly on a most beautiful bay hack which I suppose Miss Durdon had lent her or bought for her.

'That's a smashing horse!' said Ann. 'Only I'm surprised Miss Durdon didn't tell Mercy to put her hat on straight.'

The field was lovely. It was level and green, about an acre and a half, bordered by a belt of trees on one side and with a low hedge on the road side, and the road itself was merely a lane that very few people used. You couldn't have imagined a more perfect bit of land for what we wanted, and I couldn't get over our luck in having it.

People were turning up all the time, and most of them I knew; but there were a few strangers. In the end there were twenty-seven of us with our ponies, and as might be expected the crowd was a bit mixed. There was Clarissa Dandleby and my cousin Cecilia both on beautiful ponies and very well-dressed. There were also the people that I might call 'our crowd', the ones from school that I had been riding with for years. There were a few farmers' children whom I had met in the show ring. These mostly rode very well, but there were also some beginners of various ages, and a number of under-twelves like Ann's sister Pam. Everybody was standing about looking self-conscious.

'You might begin by telling some of them that it's usual to come to a rally on a clean pony,' said Ann. 'It hasn't rained for a week, and some of those ponies have still got mud on them. It's perfectly disgraceful.'

I said, I didn't think it would go down very well if we started off by having a row, and perhaps if we lined the dirty ones up between the clean ones the dirty ones would take the hint.

Nobody seemed as if they knew what to do. I felt a bit awkward myself, but I thought we would have to make some sort of a start. I wished I had a megaphone, even a home-made one, because everybody was talking and there wasn't a chance of making my voice heard.

However, there was one person there who had a voice like a ship's siren, and that was Clarissa, and while I was still wondering what to do she charged in and yelled, 'Come on, let's get cracking. Everybody line up and face me!'

'There you are,' I said to Ann. 'She's going to run the show. I knew it.'

'Well, tell her it isn't her show.'

'Unfortunately, she's the only one that's got the voice.'

But even Clarissa looked stunned when she realised what she had started. The so-called lining-up took about half an hour. There were people there who you would think had never before made a pony stand in line, and there were ponies whose one idea seemed to be *not* to stand in line.

Some of us more experienced ones got down to help the others by pulling and shoving, but as fast as we got two or three into line the first ones were zigging about all over the place. After about another half-hour the line was more or less organised, though it looked like a snake's tail and liable to break up at any minute. Clarissa looked at me and said, 'What do you want done with them now?'

'Make them ride a circle, I should think,' I said.

The chaos that followed had to be seen to be believed, as about nine people started riding round the wrong way, which annoyed the people who were riding correctly. People actually whacked other people's ponies.

'Anti-clockwise, you dopes!' screamed Clarissa, but that wasn't much good as nobody could remember which way anti-clockwise was and half of them merely turned and began riding the opposite way.

'What a bunch!' said Clarissa.

'Tell them to stop,' I said. 'Let's get them sorted out.'

So she yelled to them to stop and stand still, and we went round hauling people into position. Needless to say, those who couldn't control their ponies promptly went wrong again. Some went wandering round the field and some merely cropped the grass.

'I give up,' said Clarissa. 'Why don't you send these nitwits home and have only people who can ride?'

I said I didn't feel that was fair, and being the first rally people were probably nervous and only wanted encouraging. This wasn't as noble of me as it sounds, because actually I wouldn't have had the nerve to send anybody home, which only shows how unfitted by nature I was to run a riding club.

While I was dithering worse happened, as a boy rode out of the line and said, 'I'm fed up with this. I thought we were going to have treasure hunts and things like that.' He was a boy called John Watson, a farmer's son whom I had met several times in the show ring. 'I didn't come here,' he said to Clarissa, 'to ride round and round with a pack of kids.' Unfortunately two or three others heard him and they rode out of line too. Diana Bush was just behind, and she said, 'Oh, do get back in line. After all, it's the first rally and we've got to have some sort of drill. It's no good having treasure hunts until you've got people accustomed to being called to order.'

'Order!' said John Watson with a snort, but he saw the force of Diana's remarks and added, 'Well, when you get them in order, or whatever you call it, tell me and I'll come back.'

'Oh, for the love of Mike, don't argue, John,' I said, 'or we'll never get organised,' and Ann added, 'This is what I thought it would be without a grown-up to give the commands – argue, argue, argue.'

John said he wasn't arguing, he was telling us; but after a minute he got back into line, and said, 'Well, get on with it.'

'We'd better change the drill,' said Clarissa.

'What to?' said John Watson sarcastically.

'I'll tell them to halt,' said Clarissa, and then yelled 'Halt!' at the top of her voice. Of course about half of the people hadn't the slightest idea how to halt, and those who did couldn't halt properly because of the people in front backing into them.

'Let's have a free-for-all canter round the paddock,' said Ann. 'That'll cheer everybody up.' This didn't seem a bad idea, so some of us set off and told the others to follow on, and it was rather like a chase of wild Indians, and three people came off, including Mercy Dulbottle who landed with a whack and made no attempt to get up while her bay went cantering on, trailing his reins.

'Are you hurt?' I said. 'You should get up at once if you're not, and even if you're practically dead you should never let go of the reins.'

'I've lost my hat,' said Mercy, as if that was the only thing that mattered. And she still sat on the ground.

'Suffering cats!' said Diana Bush, getting down and dragging Mercy to her feet as if she was a sack of turnips. 'It's a good thing nobody's watching us.'

'But somebody is,' said Mercy who had caught sight of her hat in the hedge. 'There's a man standing over there, beside my hat!'

'Oh!' said Diana. 'It's Major Hooley.'

Major Hooley was a retired officer of the Household Cavalry who did a lot of judging at local shows, and was the last person on earth you would wish to see you at your worst. When he saw us looking at him he walked round to the gate and came across to us.

'What's all this?' he said. 'Bedlam in the cattle market?'

I felt so low at this insulting remark that I got quite mad and said, 'We're the Greenlee Riding Club.'

'Riding club? You don't say? Who's in charge?'

'Jill,' said Ann, pointing at me, and at the same moment Clarissa Dandleby said, 'Me.'

Major Hooley glared, and said in a very chippy voice, 'If there's one thing I can't tolerate it is people not knowing who is supposed to be running a show. No organisation. Very slack indeed. Well, what are we waiting for? Get along and collect your crowd, and let me see what they can do.'

Clarissa and Ann and Diana and I rode round telling people to try and get into line. Everybody made an effort, and soon we were at it again, riding round and round in a rather gloomy sort of ring. Round and round. Round and round. It seemed to be going on for ever. Some people were riding quite well and others so badly I can't describe it. I found myself going into a daze and paying little attention to anything, and before I knew it Rapide had crowded the pony in front, which happened to be ridden by Ann's young sister Pam, who turned round and made a face at me and shouted, 'You beast, Jill! You nearly had me off.'

'You!' roared Major Hooley, pointing at me. 'Has anybody ever taught you manners?'

I felt about six and very humiliated, especially as I caught a glimpse of Clarissa with a mocking grin on her face. I hoped the Major would notice how smartly I collected Rapide, but he wasn't even looking.

My cousin Cecilia was the next to get it in the neck. She was very well mounted on a lovely pony and wasn't riding at all badly, and she had in her hand a silver-mounted hunting crop that she was terribly proud of, and every time she passed the Major she gave this crop a bit of a flourish so he couldn't fail to notice it.

'You!' he barked, stopping the whole line and striding up to Cecilia. 'Where did you get that atrocity?'

Cecilia looked as if she couldn't believe her ears. 'Do you mean my crop?' she said. 'Isn't it a beauty?'

'Burn it,' said Major Hooley. 'Do you hear what I say? Burn it. Schooling with a hunting crop! Never heard of such a thing.'

Cecilia went the colour of a tomato, and I felt almost sorry for her. She collected her pony and went jogging on, but she was biting her lips and I knew she was furious, though of course Major Hooley was perfectly right about the hunting crop.

By now all the ponies had realised the situation and were playing us up in a sickening way. Apart from a few experienced people who wouldn't stand any nonsense, nobody was attempting any sort of control. Everybody looked fed up, and a few had ridden off and gone home.

Major Hooley got us all to a halt, and after clearing his throat, remarked, 'So far as I can see, the only person who knows how to sit on a horse is the long girl on the bay hack.'

This, believe it or not, was Mercy Dulbottle. Everybody stared at her, she looked terrified, lost both her stirrups, slithered on to the bay's neck and hung there. Major Hooley said, 'Give me strength!'

He then yelled, 'Dismount!' and came up to me and said, 'Well, I suppose you think you're riders?'

'I don't think anything,' I said sulkily. 'But most of us *can* ride. It's just that we started off in a muddle and never got out of it.'

'Well, that wasn't much good, was it?' he said. 'Did somebody say you were running this show?'

'I don't know whether anybody did or not,' I said. 'In the first place it was the general idea. I don't seem to be much good.'

'Oh, don't say that,' he said. 'Just carry on, and I shan't mind giving you a bit of help occasionally.'

'That's very decent of you,' I said, 'but it won't be much good if we're all so rotten.'

'You can't expect much at first,' he said. 'I've seen worse. You've got the raw material and it's up to you to make something of it.'

I didn't much like being called Raw Material myself, and as for Clarissa Dandleby she was just about bursting, which amused me a lot.

'What you ought to do,' said Major Hooley, 'is to get a proper school marked out for next time. A good big one. Then you can fix up your jumps in the middle. Can any of you jump?'

'Quite a lot of us,' I said, 'have taken prizes for jumping.'

'Well, get them working,' he said. 'Playing around won't get you anywhere. And when you're a bit more organised I'll come again. You might make quite a decent riding club, even out of this shocking lot.'

I could see that everybody round me was writhing under all these insults, but I just said meekly, 'OK. We'll do our best.'

'Come along now,' he said. 'Let's have another shot at it. Mount, everybody, and we'll try a trot and a canter.'

This time things went a bit better, though I wasn't very happy because several people had ridden out and were standing looking on rather superciliously, and I knew there was going to be trouble later.

When we were at the opposite side of the ring from Major Hooley, Ann came up behind me at a beautiful trot and said, 'Well, what did you think of that? I feel as if I was a spaceship being hurled through the stratosphere at five thousand miles an hour.'

'In one minute from now,' I said, 'you're going to be barged into by the Neville boy who is coming up on your left side. He looks furious, and I don't feel so good-tempered myself.'

Major Hooley yelled, 'Canter on!' and we cantered. Then poor Cecilia, my unfortunate cousin, got it again, as she had quite forgotten the hunting crop episode and was still carrying it.

'I thought I told you to get rid of that thing,' said Major Hooley.

Cecilia looked round wildly, and then took him at

his word. She hurled the crop away from her as if it was on fire, and it hit John Watson's pony across the hocks and he bolted. We all came to a ragged halt, and watched John's pony careering madly round with John trying to pull him up. At last John managed to slither down and stop the pony expertly. He then walked up to Cecilia and said, 'You silly clot!'

Cecilia said, 'Don't be so disgustingly rude.'

Major Hooley said, 'I think we'll call it a day. Remember what I told you, and I'll look in on you some other time.'

He then cleared off, and as I expected everybody began arguing.

Cecilia said, 'I propose that this riding club be well and truly washed up.'

Ann said it was silly to talk like that just because everybody had got a bit demoralised by Major Hooley's efficiency, and Cecilia said, 'I beg your pardon! Efficient? The old fool's a hopeless incompetent.'

'You know that isn't true,' said Diana. 'He does know about riding, and he said we had the makings of a riding club.'

'He also said we were a shocking lot – ' I began, and Ann said, 'I think you're a feeble crowd if you can't stand a bit of criticism.'

A girl called Vera Harley said to me, 'Well, I'm not bothering to come again, and neither is Mary.'

'Oh, don't be so unsporting,' I said furiously. 'You'll be sorry when we really get things going.'

'When!' said Cecilia with a hollow laugh.

I said in disgust, 'Oh, let's go home!' and then I wished I hadn't said it, because it gave the wrong impression and I hadn't meant to sound feeble.

Clarissa said in her foghorn voice, 'Anybody can go home that wants to go home. At least we'll know where we stand then, and get rid of the drips. But there'll be another rally on Monday afternoon. Two o'clock. And it'll be a working party for building jumps. Bring wood and tools and old bedsteads and bracken, and anything you've got in the way of red and white paint and brushes. And you'd better bring some food too, as we'll probably be here till midnight, and anybody who doesn't want to work needn't bother to come.'

One or two people said good show and some of those who were hesitating said, all right, they would come. I felt very humiliated, because what Clarissa had said was what I ought to have said myself, only I had been too feeble, and it served me right that she should get the credit for saving the riding club from fading out altogether.

When I got home Mummy said brightly, 'Well, how did the riding club go? Did you have a wonderful time?'

'No,' I said. 'It was rotten.'

Mummy asked what went wrong? So I told her. She said, Well, did I expect everything to be perfect the first time? If so, I was very silly. I said she just didn't understand, and I went out to the orchard to give Black Boy some apples and tell Rapide that he'd let me down, only he looked so sad I had to give him some apples too. Then I sat down under a tree and read a library book called *The Spy with Eleven Fingers*, only I couldn't stop thinking about the riding club and wondering whether I had better let Clarissa run it after all. I had just got to the bit where the girl agent tries to get out of the country by having herself packed in a trunk and handed over to British Rail for shipment to the Channel Islands, when Mummy called from the back door that there was somebody to see me. I thought it might be Ann or Diana, but it was Mercy Dulbottle.

'I just came along,' she said kindly, 'thinking you might be feeling dim about the rally.'

'So what?' I said.

'Oh, buck up,' she said. 'We'll get things going in no time, won't we, Mrs Crewe?'

When she had gone Mummy said, 'What an awfully nice girl. I've never seen her before, who is she?'

I said, 'Mercy Dulbottle,' – without thinking that Mummy had never before had this peculiar name sprung upon her – and she just said, 'Mercy – what? Oh no!' and went into a fit of giggles, and I couldn't help starting to giggle too, and by the time we were both helpless with giggling I felt a lot better and decided that I still wanted to go on running the riding club.

5 Treasure hunt

I started looking round for stuff for making jumps. There was plenty of brushwood about, but it occurred to me that that was what other people would think, and what would happen would be that we would get enough brushwood to build ten hedges and probably no timber at all. What we wanted was stiles and gates, and if we were lucky, some blocks to build a wall.

I was cantering Black Boy along the grass verge of the lane and thinking hard when I saw something that I had often passed before but hadn't really noticed.

The thing was an old gate which had dropped off its hinges and was lying flat at the entrance to a turnip field. It was probably rotten and no good as a gate, just waiting until the farmer got round to fixing up a new one, but I could see a lot of use in that gate. I knew it was Mr Trimble's field, and after one brilliant burst of thought such as I get from time to time, I went charging up the lane to the farm.

I was lucky. Mr Trimble was in the yard.

'That gate?' he said. 'No, it's no use to me. I'm expecting the new one any day now. So you want it for your riding club? Well I'm glad it'll be useful as I never like to see anything wasted.'

I beamed at him, and he went on, 'As a matter of fact, I think there's a drop of white paint lying around somewhere, left over from when Joe painted the garden fence. There isn't much, but it might be enough to give the gate a slosh over.'

I said that would be marvellous, and I'd evidently caught him in a most helpful mood, as he said, 'Well, Joe has to go down to the station tonight with the flat cart, and he'll be passing your place so he can easily drop the things off for you.'

I said, 'It's simply wonderful of you, Mr Trimble, and how much will it be?'

He said, 'Oh, that's nothing at all. But I wonder if you'd consider giving my Stanley a few lessons? I'd pay at the usual rate of course. He's twelve and wants to learn to ride, so if you could start him I'd get him a pony.'

I thought it was a case of one good turn deserves another, so I said I'd work Stanley in if Mr Trimble cared to send him down next morning. I was very bucked up about the gate.

As soon as I got home I rang Ann up and told her. She said, 'Well, as a matter of fact, I think the jump-building's off for the moment. I mean, it's wonderful about the gate and it'll be jolly useful later on; but a lot of people have got very bored with the riding club already, and unless we do something about it they won't come any more, and we shan't have any members.'

I said, who told you that? And she said that practically everybody in Chatton was talking about it, and she didn't know where I'd been not to have heard. I said I thought this riding club was just about the worst thing that had ever happened to me. It was like one of those nightmares you read about in books where people dream they are loaded with chains.

Ann said, 'Well, I think we ought to have some fun, such as a treasure hunt, that will attract people and make them think they're going to enjoy themselves, and not just be bashed round in a ring and yelled at by Major Hooley and Clarissa Dandleby.'

I said, OK we'd have a treasure hunt, if that was what she wanted, and she said she'd start spreading the news round.

As soon as I put down the telephone I started thinking about the treasure hunt, and it seemed to me a good idea.

I went out and leaned on the orchard gate and watched the ponies doing nothing. It was very soothing. It was a lovely day and gold patches of sunlight were tumbling about in the long orchard grass. Rapide nibbled his foreleg and then tossed his head joyfully; Black Boy looked at me thoughtfully, knee-deep in daisies. I began to wonder what sort of things we should go hunting for in the treasure hunt.

Just then Mrs Crosby came to the back door and yelled, 'You're wanted on the telephone.'

I said, Oh blast, and she said that was no way to talk when it might be to say that my long lost uncle in Australia had died and left me a fortune, as had happened to her sister's son-in-law's mother; and I said, 'Fate!' – very darkly – and went to the telephone, and it was Clarissa Dandleby.

She said, 'I've got an idea. I think we should have a treasure hunt, to make the riding club think it's getting something.'

I said, 'You're too late. We're having one.'

She said, 'Oh, nice work. Well, as soon as I've got some ideas worked out I'll let you know.'

I said, 'Oh, thanks very much, Clarissa, but I've got loads of ideas.' Then I rang off and wondered whether it wouldn't have been as well to have a few of Clarissa's ideas to start with, as my own mind was a complete blank.

I drifted into the sitting-room to see if Mummy might have any bright suggestions, and there she was, typing away like mad.

'Don't speak!' she said, in a sort of squeal.

I stood pawing the ground, and after a minute she stopped typing and said, 'There! It's finished. I've been about three days trying to find the right last sentence, and just when you came in I got it.'

From this I gathered that yet another of Mummy's immortal works was ready to go to the publisher.

'What's the last sentence?' I asked, because I do honestly try to take an interest in Mummy's books though they are not my type at all.

Mummy read out rapturously, '"As the Golden Doll tumbled into little Jessica's arms, all her dreams came true."'

'Gosh, she was lucky!' I said ironically. 'Mummy, do you know anything about getting up a treasure hunt?'

'Oh, are you going to have one? That will be fun.'

'That's what you think,' I said darkly. 'I have my doubts.'

'Really, Jill,' said Mummy briskly, 'I don't know what's the matter with you lately, but whatever it is I don't like it.'

'Mostly,' I said, 'it's coping with people who get me down.'

Mummy's eyes flashed, and she said, 'I never heard such ridiculous nonsense. You'd better snap out of this dying duck attitude, and realise that nobody on earth can get you down. You get yourself down, that's the only way you get down in this life.'

This impressed me, and I said, 'Perhaps you're right. Oh, well – Mummy, could you give me some ideas for things we could hunt for in the treasure hunt? It'll be on ponies, of course. And the people are very mixed ages, from sixteen down to about eight.'

'So you'll want outdoor things?'

'That's the idea,' I said. 'I'll write them down. What

about a bird's nest? It's all right to take one now because they're all empty.'

'Yes – and a horseshoe.'

'I pity the farrier!' I said. 'They'll all be bombarding him, but it's rather good because he won't have enough for everybody to have one. What about a mushroom?'

'There won't be any mushrooms in early August.'

'Oh, yes there will. There are some in our larder now.'

'Is that fair?' said Mummy. 'I mean, shop ones?'

'I don't see why not. Everybody has got a larder at home, and if their mothers haven't bought any mushrooms they'll be unlucky. So what?'

Mummy giggled and said, 'A brown egg.'

'Great,' I said. 'What about a white feather?'

'Better not,' said Mummy. 'You'll have all the young ones chasing people's white hens to make them drop a feather. Make it more difficult. Say a red feather. That'll make them think.'

I giggled and wrote it down.

In the end the list ran:

A brown egg
A red feather
A mushroom
Ten different wild flowers
A horseshoe
A bird's nest
A white stone.

The last was very difficult because all the stones round our way are grey.

By now I was really excited about the treasure hunt, and when Ann came round she said she thought the list was very good, and we made about thirty copies on Mummy's typewriter so that everybody could have one. It took us hours to do because of the mistakes.

I kept on putting down the key that says shift, and instead of A Brown Egg I got A Brx = 58 eG38. In the end Mummy helped us out, and it was done.

The idea of the treasure hunt had roused the dying enthusiasm of many, and there was quite a crowd at the rally. Clarissa, who had to have her say, thought the mushroom was feeble, and what about a picture of a famous rider? I had to admit that this was a bright thought, so we altered all the lists with a pencil and gave them out. People said, Help! Oh, gosh! and How beastly difficult!

My cousin Cecilia said – she would! – 'I suppose you'll be staying here, Jill, to do the judging when people come back.'

I felt very dim. I hadn't thought, but of course we'd have to have a judge for people to bring their treasures to, but I didn't want it to be me because I was looking forward to the ride and had promised Black Boy a good afternoon's fun.

Just at that moment two mounted figures appeared. They were Mercy Dulbottle and, of all people, Miss Durdon in a high-necked shirt and tight tie and baggy black jodhpurs, looking like something out of the Indian Mutiny.

They rode up, and Miss Durdon said, 'I think this treasure hunt is a good idea. Mercy must ride, and if you like I'll stop here and be the judge.'

'Oh, that would be simply smashing!' I said, grinning with relief.

'Don't mention it,' said Miss Durdon. 'I'll be quite happy here, exercising Westminster Abbey,' – which was the peculiar and inappropriate name of her rangy grey hunter.

At the last minute three fat and panting figures arrived on three fat and panting ponies. They were April, May, and June Cholly-Sawcutt, who you will recall if you have read my previous books were the unteachable daughters of the famous show-jumping Captain Cholly-Sawcutt.

This made up the field, and we cantered away. Ann and I were hunting together. First we pelted off to the farrier's to make sure of our horseshoes, but practically everbody else had the same idea, and after handing out three – of which Ann and I got one between us – the pestered smith closed his door and told us to clear off. So we dashed up to Mrs Darcy's place, and luckily one of her ponies had just cast a shoe, and we got it, so we had one each. We were only just in time, as by then half a dozen other people hove in sight and Mrs Darcy shouted, 'It's no good coming here for horseshoes!'

The brown egg was easy and we got one each at Mr Trimble's farm, but then wished we'd left this particular treasure until the end, as we hadn't anywhere to put the eggs except in Ann's saddlebag where they soon came to a sticky end, and we hadn't time by then to get any more.

Then we madly collected wild flowers in Goose Lane. We soon got nine different ones but couldn't find a tenth, and in the end we had to ride to Neshbury Common where we got some sprigs of gorse which we hoped would pass as wild flowers. At any rate they were flowers, and they weren't tame.

I said, 'Let's dash home to the cottage. There are two empty sparrow's nests in the orchard, and I can collect my picture of Marion Mold at the same time. That'll kill two birds with one stone – oh, and you can have that snap of David Broome that I took at Chatton Show.'

Ann said you couldn't tell it was David Broome, and I said, 'Well it is.'

We did all that, and also managed to drink a lot of lemonade and give the ponies drinks, which was kind but wasted a lot of time.

'What about this red feather and white stone?' Ann said.

'Gosh!' I said. 'I thought those two up myself. It serves me right.'

'If we had any white paint we could get two stones and paint them white,' said Ann, 'if you think that wouldn't be cheating?'

'There's nothing against painting them,' I said. 'And I've got the white paint that Mr Trimble gave me for the gate.'

So we got the paint and sloshed it over a couple of stones, but they wouldn't dry and we didn't know what to do with them. In the end we wrapped them up in some newspaper, and most of the white came off, but we shoved them in Ann's saddlebag and hoped for the best.

'My saddlebag's full of burst eggs and white paint,' said Ann. 'And as for red feathers! What bird were you thinking of, may I ask?'

I admitted that I'd gone a bit too far with this red feather idea.

'If we had some white feathers we could paint them red, if we had some red paint,' I said; and Ann said we hadn't got either, and she already had white paint all over her jodhpurs and she didn't want to turn up looking as if she'd done a murder.

'It was a silly clue,' I said. 'But I expect everybody else will think so too, and nobody will get any red feathers.'

'Well, *we* don't stand much chance,' said Ann, 'and we've been out two hours already, so we'd better go back. The ride has been fun, at least.'

The ride *had* been fun and everybody had enjoyed it. When we got back to the paddock the place was already seething with people, and soon the last of the treasure hunters turned up. They all admitted they'd had a super time, and John Watson said, 'Whoever thought of that red feather ought to be made to eat one. I've got everything else but that, but I'm too late back to have any chance of a prize.'

Clarissa Dandleby said smugly, 'I've got a red feather. It was off a pheasant.' But when Miss Durdon, who had sportingly entered into the spirit of the thing, looked at it she decided it wasn't red, it was gold.

Believe me, or believe me not, the whole thing had already been won by June Cholly-Sawcutt who was back half an hour before anybody else and had got everything!

What happened was this. When we all rode off, June, who was only eleven, followed her two sisters who with sisterly callousness rode away and left her, although she kept calling, 'Wait for me, you beasts!'

She was an even worse rider than they were, and soon she found herself all alone. She was fed up and disappointed, so she gave up the hunt, and turned her pony round and went home, and because she was only a kid she began to cry. She was crying like anything when she rode into their yard and the girl groom, Pansy, said, 'What's the matter, June?'

June told her, and Pansy said, 'Well, that's all right. Let's have a look at your list.' She read the list, and said, 'Come on, June, get cracking. You did right to come home, we've got everything here. I've a brown egg in my hand this minute, and there's a photo of your father in the sitting-room – he's famous enough – so oodle in and get it. There's about a million different kinds of flowers in the hedge along the paddock, and while you're picking those I'll slip up and unpick the red feather out of my beret that I wear on Sundays. There's a horseshoe hanging on the stable door, and there's an empty bird's nest in the gooseberry bush by the back door, and there's a line of white marble stones that your mother brought from the seaside and put round the rosebed. So what are you waiting for?'

By now June had brightened up and her eyes were nearly popping out, so she wiped them and blew her nose and dashed round collecting all the things, and Pansy found a paper carrier bag to put them in, and she wrapped the egg in tissue paper so that it wouldn't get broken.

June rode peacefully back to the paddock and handed the paper carrier bag to the astonished Miss Durdon, who said, 'There isn't a sign of anybody else yet, and your things are all correct, so it looks as if you've won.'

She'd won all right. Most people were short of at least one item, and several people's eggs were broken – including Ann's and mine – and some others had brought all the same kind of wild flowers, such as ten buttercups.

Diana Bush had got a red feather, but she had snipped it off her mother's best hat and it was already broken at the end, and Diana was feeling very dim about what her mother would say.

April and May Cholly-Sawcutt hadn't got half the things, and April had fallen off her pony – she spent most of her life falling off her pony, and would have fallen off a tabletop – and hurt her leg, and May was plastered with lime because she had had the bright idea of dipping a stone in a handy lime pit in a builder's yard and had got both her arms in up to the elbows. So June had the satisfaction of saying sucks to her elder sisters.

'What's the prize?' said John Watson.

I went cold, because I hadn't even thought about the prize, which shows how unfitted I am by nature to run a treasure hunt or anything else, but Miss Durdon said, 'The prize is six free lessons in dressage from me.'

John Watson said, 'Gosh, I wish I'd won,' but June, who *had* won, looked completely blank, because far from needing lessons in dressage she had not yet managed to grasp the idea of sitting on a pony properly.

Miss Durdon said, 'Ring me up when you want the first lesson,' and June said, 'Oh. Um. Yes. No. I mean – ' And everybody knew she wouldn't.

Miss Durdon, who seemed to have surprisingly and completely altered her character, which had hitherto been grim and non-cooperative, then said, 'Now if you'll all come up to the Hall there'll be buns and tea for everybody.'

'Well, I'm blowed!' said Ann. 'She's read my thoughts. Three cheers for Miss Durdon!'

Everybody yelled Hip Hip Hurray at the tops of their voices, and Miss Durdon went pink and looked frightfully pleased.

So the treasure hunt finished magnificently, and the whole point of it was that the riding club was now well and truly established and everybody was keen about it, and I could see we weren't going to have any more trouble. Even Clarissa Dandleby was pleased, and started nattering about 'now we'll get down to some real work and fix those jumps', and I went home feeling on top of the world.

6 Good hard work

We next got down to the jobs of building jumps, tidying up the paddock, pulling thistles, etc., and by now we had a good idea of how many people were going to stick to the riding club and be any use. You know what it is like in anything you are doing, when it gets to a bit of work there are always some people who just ooze off, or have very convenient colds and toothache and the only afternoon the dentist can see them is the afternoon you are doing the work. I hate to sound like a hoary old cynic of ninety, but alas, what I say is true.

However, about eighteen people turned up to work, which wasn't bad. As I thought, we had far too much brush, but some people had brought wood, and my gate was a terrific success. We got two of the young ones to slosh white paint over it. One girl had been crazy enough to bring a lot of gorse. Clarissa said sarcastically, as well she might, 'What do you think we're going to do with that?' and the dimwit said, 'Make jumps,' and Clarissa said, 'If you want to make yourself into a walking pincushion I couldn't care less, but Heaven help the ponies.'

We got one lot of people clearing the ground, and another lot pegging out a sort of school, and another lot building jumps; then when we got browned off with these labours we all switched round.

Suddenly Ann said, 'Do you see what I see?'

I said, 'What?'

'Little Sunshine,' she said.

It was Major Hooley. John Watson said, 'It only wanted that!'

Major Hooley walked right over to us and said, 'Bit of good work going on here. That's what I like to see, ha-ha.'

None of us said anything, as we couldn't think of anything that wasn't either sarky or rude.

'How many jumps do you propose to have?' said Major Hooley to John, and as John had to say something he said, 'We want to have six, but unfortunately it looks as though they're all going to be hedges except for the gate that Jill brought.'

'H'm,' said Major Hooley. 'What height are you making that contrivance?'

'If it'll stand up,' said John, 'it's supposed to be three feet. We thought we'd have four at three feet and two at two-foot-six for the younger ones, because in a riding club we think the way you jump is more important than the height you jump.'

'Very sensible,' said Major Hooley. 'I believe in helping those who help themselves, so I've got a lorry coming along with some useful stuff. Ah, here it is.'

We couldn't believe our eyes when we saw the stuff that the Major had got for us. There were posts, bars, wood blocks, and even hurdles. It was like one of those dreams where you get everything you want and then wake up and remember you forgot to do your geography homework, only we didn't wake up.

Everybody flocked round the lorry and helped to unload it. It was very exciting. Then Major Hooley took charge. He gave everybody their jobs and he and the lorry driver went round helping to knock in posts and similar heavy tasks. We built a wall with the wood blocks, and arranged a bar jump with hurdles. We then made a frame for the in-and-out and filled it up with brushwood, and Major Hooley produced a pair of hedge-clippers and trimmed it; and finally my gate was properly erected and given some very professional-looking wings.

Major Hooley then sent the lorry back to his place to bring whitewash and several brushes, and when they came we started to whitewash everything. The wall, hurdles, and bars were done, and the ring marked out. It looked supersonic. I couldn't believe this good jumping course was really ours, and by now we were all dying to try it.

'All we need now,' said Clarissa, 'is a triple bar.'

'Gosh!' I said. 'Is that all? You would think of something we haven't got.'

Ann nudged me and said, 'Don't you think you'd better make a speech to thank Major Hooley?'

I hadn't any time to think, but I had to say something, so I said, 'On behalf of everybody I want to say a terrific thank you to you, Major Hooley. We think this is terrific of you, honestly we do. If it hadn't been for you we shouldn't have had a proper riding club at all.'

He looked quite pleased, and said, 'Well, I hope you'll make use of the jumps now you've got them,' and somebody said, 'I vote we all whizz home and get a snack and then come back here and do some jumping.'

We all forgot we were aching with weariness and bleeding from a thousand scratches, and we went pelting off home, and then came back for the evening. When we got back we decided that everybody should jump a round in turn. Some of the younger ones said they couldn't possibly do three-foot jumps, so we decided that they could jump the two-foot-six ones twice.

'Jill ought to have first go,' said Ann, 'because she's running this thing, anyway.'

A few mouths opened in surprise, but nobody said anything, so I started off on Rapide.

It was a lovely course, but I felt uncomfortable because it would look awful if I didn't do a clear round.

I cantered Rapide and went for the first jump, which was the two-foot-six hedge. Rapide went over like a bird. He also took the bar without any trouble, but for some unknown reason he refused at the gate and brought it down at the second attempt. He soared over the three-foot wall, but hated the sight of the in-and-out and ran round it, and then did the next two-foot-six in great style.

'I think you had about nine faults,' said Ann when I got back, and I said, 'It was a ghastly exhibition, but after all it was the first time, and I don't think Rapide is cut out to be a pathfinder. Black Boy could have done it on three legs.'

Clarissa Dandleby went next on her chestnut pony Havelock. I think she thought she was going to show the world, but Havelock didn't shine either as he even managed to knock down one of the two-foot-six brush fences, and bucked like mad all the way round. Diana Bush's pony refused the wall three times; and then John Watson went in to show us how it ought to be done and created a complete scene of destruction, laying practically everything flat on the ground. We were all laughing so much we could hardly get the jumps put up again, and John said, 'I believe there's a hoodoo on this course.'

However, the first rider after we'd re-erected the jumps did a clear round and said, 'Hoodoo, my foot. All this course wants is people who can ride.'

'I like that!' said my cousin Cecilia, who was next. 'Just you watch me.' And to my amazement and humiliation she also managed to do a clear round.

We spent the next half-hour watching the Cholly-Sawcutt girls making the whole place look like a bomb site, and by the time we got it straightened out again some of the little ones rode and did very well indeed. The funny thing was that when we had all had a turn, it was the people who were really good who did so badly. We were all inclined to giggle about this, except Val Heath who took her riding frightfully seriously since she had once won a prize at Richmond Horse Show.

'I don't know what's the matter with me,' she kept saying, and her sister Jackie said, 'It's either your legs, or you've put on weight.'

'Oh, don't be silly,' said Val as her pony gave a half-rear. 'I think all these jumps want reorganising, the distances are wrong.'

'Well, of course if you want the whole place altered specially for you – ' said Clarissa, and Cecilia said, with perfect truth, 'I should think if I could do a clear round anybody could.'

'Well, let's all have another go,' I said, and this time I managed to do a clear round, though I had an awful moment when Rapide neighed as we approached the gate and I thought he was going to run out. This time Val Heath also managed a clear round, but her sister was all over the place in spite of using her stick a lot more than she ought to have done.

'It isn't all that easy,' said Diana, and John Watson said, 'Well, you don't want it to be, do you? I think this is teaching us all a lesson, that we've got to improve our jumping, especially those of us who think we're good because we've won a few cups. I vote that instead of trying to show off and jump clear rounds we ought to concentrate more on jumping *well* – never mind whether we get over or not. For instance, I've just done a clear round but I know I had daylight between me and the saddle at the bar jump.' And Clarissa said, 'You're telling us! I could see the whole county between your legs.'

'John's quite right,' I said. 'In a riding club, we're not

competing with each other, we're working to improve our riding and to help the young ones;' to which Diana said, 'Really, Grandmamma?' and Ann said, 'One gets a bit too much of encouraging the young entry.'

'Let's give the young ones half an hour now,' said John, 'or they'll think they're not being encouraged at all.'

So we started coaching the young ones, and showing people how not to flap their legs about, and not to use their sticks except at the right time and place, and not to jump on a short tight rein or burst into tears if they got three refusals.

It was very hot and tiring, and I got the worst of it as I had a child who thought she could jump anything and was so awful that she ought to have been on a leading rein.

'Pauline, for goodness' sake!' I said. 'Let the pony do it! You haven't got to drag her up by the reins. And if you do pull her head up like that and suddenly let the reins go, of course you'll fall off. And don't say "Hup" when you don't mean "Hup". Don't say "Hup" at all, you're not up to that stage yet.'

'My pony knows what I mean,' said Pauline huffily.

'She must be a marvellous mind-reader,' I said, 'because I don't think you know yourself. Come along now, and do try to remember what I told you about your legs.'

By now we were all worn out except John Watson, who very gallantly stood in the middle and made his pupils go over and over two low jumps while he criticised and gave advice.

'What would you do?' he complained. 'When I shout for them to take off, they don't!'

'Oh, leave it, John,' I said. 'We've all had enough for today, and the ponies are overexcited. We'd better pack it up.'

Nobody really wanted to go home, but we were all tired and we felt we had had a terrific day and achieved quite a lot, so we tidied up the jumps and went home, after arranging to come again next morning.

'Well, I think the Greenlee Riding Club is now well and truly launched,' said Ann as we rode wearily but happily home through the evening sunlight. The fields were shining like gold on either side of the lane and little rabbits were popping out to sit contentedly munching their suppers.

'Yes, it's going to be a success,' I said, 'only we'll have to work hard if we're going to put on our own gymkhana.'

'Wasn't Major Hooley great?' she said. 'It's a funny thing how people start off by being the most frightful clots and then suddenly become nice when you know them better. Even Miss Durdon; and Clarissa wasn't too bad today.'

'It's the noble cause of equitation,' I said. 'It does bring out the best in people.'

I really did feel on top of the world, and went home singing a melancholy song called 'The autumn leaves must perish', as I always do when I feel happy. Mummy said I looked like a tramp, and I certainly was a mass of brushwood and whitewash from head to foot. I rubbed Rapide down and gave him his supper, and then I went and had a long and boiling hot bath during which I sang 'The autumn leaves must perish' through about seventeen times, until Mummy banged on the bathroom door and said, Must we have that dreary row? I said it would be much drearier if I sang something cheerful, as that would mean that I was In The Depths.

I then went down and ate an enormous tea, with rounds and rounds of hot buttered toast, and jam and shrimps and chocolate biscuits.

However my day was not ended, as I had hardly

finished my tea when who should appear but Stanley Trimble to ask if he could have a lesson.

He was a very nice boy, though he looked rather shaggy and had to keep pushing his hair back. I couldn't say it wasn't convenient to give him a lesson, as his father had been so decent to me about the gate, so I said I would give him half an hour on Black Boy who is a very good pony with beginners, having suffered all my own early efforts.

As we walked to the orchard Stanley said, 'I can stick on anything with four legs.'

I said that wasn't really the idea in riding, unless one's only object in life was to be a second Dick Turpin or that dreary man who took the good news from somewhere to somewhere else; and Stanley said, 'Oh, but I do want to learn to ride properly.'

I went to my tack room and got out a leading rein, and Stanley said suspiciously, 'What's that for?' as if he thought I was going to start by hanging him.

I said, 'It's to lead the pony by, until I see how you ride. I don't want you to start by losing control and galloping all over the place.'

I saddled Black Boy, and then said, 'Can you mount?' Stanley said, 'Of course,' and putting both arms across the saddle he leapt up as if he was climbing a stone wall.

I said that way might do if he was escaping from Red Indians, but not otherwise, so I explained how he should mount. I put his hand on the pommel and his foot in the stirrup and said, 'Now get up properly.'

He really did know the way, only he dropped the reins and I told him off about that. Then I made him get down and do the whole thing three or four times, after which he managed it alone quite nicely. Then I fixed on the leading rein and walked him round, and thanked my lucky stars when I found that he had naturally light hands and didn't haul and pull.

He said, 'Do you think you could take that leading rein off, it makes me feel about six,' and as he was riding quite quietly I did so. He just went on riding round and round contentedly, though really it was Black Boy who was doing it all, and would have gone on at an extended walk for ever and ever.

'Am I all right?' he said. 'Can't I canter now?'

I told him he could try, but needless to say he knew nothing about how to canter; he simply dug in his heels and grabbed Black Boy's mane, and as my pony was not used to that sort of thing he gave a startled snort and bucked Stanley off.

He picked himself up and said, 'That's the first animal who ever threw me.'

'You surprise me!' I said sarkily. 'Black Boy isn't in the habit of throwing anybody. It's your bad riding.'

He took this remark very well, and said, 'I suppose you know.'

I said, 'For goodness' sake, don't rein him in like that, it makes his neck ache. You can control him perfectly well by letting him walk out, and you've got an awful fault, Stanley. When in doubt you take your feet out of the stirrups. I never saw such a thing.'

He said, 'Well, cowboys do it in films,' and I said, if all he wanted was to be able to ride like a cowboy he was wasting my time giving him lessons.

'All right,' he said, 'I'll keep my feet in, only sometimes they slip out.' I said they couldn't possibly slip out if he kept his knees up and didn't turn his toes down, and I told him he had better learn off by heart my useful little poem:

> Hands down and head up,
> Heels down and heart up,
> Knees close to your horse's side,
> Elbows close to your own.

Stanley was impressed, and said he would like to have the poem written out and pin it to the wall over his bed, and I said that was all right so long as he had it in his head too.

'I've forgotten how it goes already,' he said. 'Is it "knees down and head up"? Or "hands down" – oh, blow!'

I gave a hollow groan and said, 'You'd better write it in letters a foot high. Now this time get it right.' I said it for him again, and then we unsaddled and went in the house.

Just at that moment Mrs Trimble arrived, and was so disappointed that the lesson was over as she had wanted to see Stanley on the pony, so in my goodness of heart, which is always letting me down, I went back and saddled Black Boy again, and Stanley got up and sat quite decently, and Mrs Trimble said he looked a perfect picture, which is hardly what I would have said as he did look distressingly shaggy, and I thought I would have to use some tact and try to get him to have his hair cut.

Stanley said, would he be able to join the riding club now?

What could I say but yes, though I told him I hoped he wouldn't set a bad example to the younger ones, and he thought a bit and then said what all beginners say the minute they find they can sit on a pony, 'When can I start jumping?'

I gave another groan and said, 'As soon as I consider you've learnt to ride.'

Mrs Trimble said, 'Oh, but Stanley can ride very nicely already. Now say thank you for the lesson, Stanley,' and Stanley said, 'Thanks very much for the lesson. When can I come and have another one?'

I was so tired when I tottered up to bed, I couldn't have been more tired if I had ridden to York and back, as most highwaymen seemed to do in the eighteenth century, but it had certainly been a very good day.

7 Our very own jumps

I had a pleasant surprise next morning, when who should turn up at the crack of dawn but Stanley Trimble again to say that he had come to help me muck out so we'd be in good time for the rally.

'What rally?' I said, wondering if I'd missed something.

He said, 'The riding club rally,' and I said I hoped he wasn't going to have his young hopes shattered but it wasn't going to be anything quite as well organised as that; and he said perhaps it was what you'd call a Working Rally, and I said that would be near enough.

He said kindly, 'You go and get yourself dressed, and I'll finish this.' He really was a decent kind of boy.

I had on my old jodhs already, so I whizzed upstairs and put on a clean yellow shirt and my new fawn tie, and when I came down Stanley was already up on Black Boy.

I said, 'You're sitting too far back' – because being his teacher I thought I'd better not let him get away with faults.

He came forward but held his reins too long.

'Look,' I said, 'your reins are too long.'

'You told me yesterday,' he said, 'not to hold them too short.'

'Yes,' I said, 'but don't lose contact with the pony's mouth. You've got to use your common sense.'

We set off, and I told Stanley not to push, and to give his aids more gently. He really was doing quite well.

When we got to the paddock we found a lot of people had already arrived, and Clarissa Dandleby, full of strength and joy, with her plaits flopping and her big specs glaring, was prancing about over the jumps in front of an admiring crowd of kids. She bucked just once too often and came off with a mighty thud. She certainly didn't know how to fall.

'Never mind,' she said. 'It takes seven falls to make a horsewoman.'

It was my private opinion that some people could have seventy and not be any nearer, but I didn't say anything, and I picked all the bits of brush and grass off Clarissa and gave her back her enormous specs which had landed at my feet.

'I thought we'd better give these kids some hot schooling,' she said, 'and then have a jumping competition for ourselves, just to put a bit of kick in the proceedings.'

'Kick will be the word, if you don't catch your pony,' said Ann, and Clarissa went loping off after Havelock, who was trailing his reins and cantering happily round and round the other ponies.

She caught him and came back, and announced, 'A book I have says that all the best riders fall off.'

'Possibly,' said Diana Bush dryly, 'but falling off doesn't mean that you're one of the best riders.'

The last thing I wanted was a full-scale argument with Clarissa, so when I saw her taking breath and opening her mouth to retort, I said quickly, 'At the risk of being unpopular, what do you say if we teach these kids something useful, like reining back or turning on the forehand?'

'They'll think that's awfully dull,' said Diana, and I said, 'Well, they don't come here just to enjoy themselves.'

'Good gracious!' said my cousin Cecilia, 'Surely everybody can rein back and turn on the forehand?'

'You'd be surprised,' I said. 'Anyway, would you like to get them round you and demonstrate?'

Cecilia went red, and said, 'Oh, I don't pretend to be a riding teacher. It's possible to do a thing well oneself and not be able to show other people how.'

I had an answer for this, but didn't use it, as I had to be rather careful with Cecilia. After all she was my elder cousin, and was sixteen and had left school.

In the end, the reining-back lesson fell to me, assisted by Ann; and we had a very warm time with the younger ones. Some of them weren't bad at all, but practising reining back isn't a thing you can do too much of, for the sake of the ponies who don't enjoy being backed into by inefficients.

June Cholly-Sawcutt announced, 'Father thinks you're doing me a lot of good.'

I couldn't help thinking bitterly that Captain Cholly-Sawcutt with all his experience might have tried to do his own daughters a bit of good himself instead of leaving it to a person like me.

However, I had my reward when April announced, 'Father says that we can have a rally at our place one day, and he'll inspect us.'

'Did he really say that?' I gasped.

'Yes, he did,' said April. 'He's awfully interested in the riding club.'

This was such good news to me that I whooped, and Clarissa who was still showing off by doing half-passes in front of several younger people, said, 'What's the excitement?'

'Oh, nothing,' I said airily. 'Nothing at all, except that Captain Cholly-Sawcutt is going to invite us to his place for a rally.'

'Just a selected few of us, I suppose,' said Clarissa.

'No,' I said firmly. 'The whole shoot, or none at all. This is a riding club, not a private do for people who think they're good.'

Cecilia who was hovering near, said, 'Well, I never! I don't have to look far in front of me for somebody who thinks she's good!'

'Look,' I said. 'There are just two things I want to say. One is that it's jolly bad form for us big ones to argue in front of the little ones; and the other is, Clarissa, that if you want to do half-passes, do them as a lesson and show the others how they're done.'

'Hear, hear,' said Ann. 'This is no place for showing off.'

Clarissa said she was perfectly willing to show anybody how to do half-passes, so we picked out a selection of pupils for her and left her to it.

Remembering last time and how bad the riding round had been, I collected a number of people and suggested that we should do a bit of walking and halting. As I feared, this made me very unpopular.

'More baby stuff!' said David Neville.

'You can't say it isn't needed,' I said. 'Last time we rode round the ring both the walking and the halting were appalling.'

He said that people could practise that at home, and I said, Yes, but they didn't, and what was the use of practising if they didn't know how to practise?

'All right,' he said generously, 'I'll help.' And he stopped the grumblers for me and got about ten people walking round.

'These are all pretty bad,' he said. 'Go on, Jill, tell them what's wrong with them.'

'For one thing, they're not walking out,' I said. 'They're just meandering. People aren't using their legs.'

'Yes, I am using my legs,' said a girl called Hilda

Marshall, scowling at me. 'One thing I do know is how to use my legs.'

'Well, use them differently,' said John Watson, coming to my rescue. 'Your pony's taking short, quick steps. If you'll loosen your reins a bit she'll take longer, slower ones.'

'If I loosen my reins I'll lose control,' said Hilda.

'No, you won't. You've got much too short a rein anyway. Your pony can't get her neck out, so she can't take a longer stride.'

'If I give her a long rein she'll bolt,' said Hilda gloomily.

'Don't be silly. If she tries to bolt, pull her up to a walk and start all over again. That's elementary.'

'Oh, can't we canter and jump?' said one or two who were walking correctly and getting tired of it.

'No, you can't,' said John. 'You can't possibly jump properly until you've mastered simple schooling, and if you don't jump properly you'll never win at gymkhanas. When *I* consider you've finished schooling at the walk you can begin schooling at the canter, and not before.'

One or two said that they had already won jumping competitions, and John said that was probably more by good luck than good riding. Just when I felt the whole thing was getting out of hand, who should appear but Major Hooley, and for once I was quite glad to see him.

He stood and watched us for a bit without speaking, and everybody tried to do as they'd been told.

'That's much better,' he said. 'Now prepare to halt. Halt!'

The halt was very bad indeed, and I felt that Major Hooley would have been justified in saying something scathing, but he showed remarkable patience and merely said, 'Will somebody kindly tell me what you are supposed to do when told to prepare to halt?'

Everybody looked blank and there was a deathly hush. This went on so long that I had to say something, and I said, 'Tighten your fingers and close your legs?'

'That's quite right,' said Major Hooley. 'Why put it in the form of a question when you know it's right? Then what?'

'Well, I put my shoulders back and feel the reins until the horse begins to halt,' said John.

'Right again,' said Major Hooley. 'Now all you've got to do is to get those simple instructions rammed into the heads of other people, and then put them into practice. Go to it.'

John and I went to it until we were very hot. By then the halting had improved a bit. Major Hooley suggested that we should do a bit about correcting legs and hands, and we had a round or two without stirrups.

'It's no good me doing everything right if the pony won't do anything right,' complained Ann's young sister Pam. 'He only obeys me when he feels like it.'

'We'll have to have some lessons on improving ponies,' I said, 'but at the moment I feel too hot, and anyway the ponies must be fed up.'

'Yes, we'll call the instruction off for now,' said Major Hooley kindly. 'I must say, you seem to have a more cooperative lot of people than the first time I came.'

'They've been weeded out,' I said. 'Some of the no-goods didn't come again after the first rally, and we're better off without them. This lot are reasonably keen.'

'You and young Watson here seem to be doing all the hard work,' said Major Hooley. 'What are those other people doing at the jumps? Amusing themselves?'

'I think they're doing a competition,' I mumbled.

'Let's go over and have a look.'

The jumping competition seemed to be between Val and Jackie Heath, Diana, Clarissa, Cecilia, and David Neville. A lot of people were standing round watching, including Mercy Dulbottle who said sadly, 'I can't jump and I don't suppose I ever shall.'

'You won't if you don't try,' I said.

'I wouldn't dare, except after dark,' said Mercy. 'Aren't these people marvellous?'

'They've all won lots of jumping competitions,' I said, 'but do get it out of your head, Mercy, that other people are marvellous. Nobody's marvellous in riding. Anybody can make the most frightful mistakes.'

'I wish I could practise a bit by myself,' said Mercy, dolefully, 'when nobody else was here.'

'If you'll come round to the cottage some evening I might help you,' I said, being noble again without intending to. 'Now what have we got here?'

What we had got was Val Heath, preparing to jump a round.

'We've made all the jumps higher,' she said. 'It's too silly doing two-foot-six and three-foot jumps when we practically never do anything but four-foot ones at home.'

'All right, go on,' said Major Hooley without commenting.

Val cantered a circle and then jumped a clear round. It was a very neat and pretty performance.

Major Hooley said, 'Next one, please.'

The next one was Diana, who looked at me as much as to say that this jump-raising wasn't her idea at all. Her pony was good but she managed him badly, and he showed his resentment by a first refusal at nearly every jump. At the second time of asking he went over nicely, but obviously by his own skill and not by reason of Diana's aids.

'That's not jumping,' said Major Hooley. 'That's sitting on a pony while he jumps.'

'I know,' said Diana frankly. 'The jumps were too high and I oughtn't even to have tried them.'

'It's a pity the fences are so narrow,' said Clarissa preparing for her own round. 'Havelock is used to hunting and he likes his fences wide, or at least with good wings, not these silly little makeshifts.'

Round she went, and Havelock tipped pretty well everything with his forelegs.

'There,' said Clarissa. 'See what I mean?'

'Only too well,' said John Watson meaningly.

Clarissa flared up and said that Havelock jumped five-foot jumps regularly, only these were enough to put any good pony off.

'Well, if they're so narrow and so awful, isn't it a pity you made them so high?' said John.

Nobody did well over the raised jumps. Cecilia's horse knocked the stile for six, brought down the brush fence and ran out. The Neville boy did a fairly good round but his style was awful.

'There you have it,' said Major Hooley. 'If you'd been content to jump the lower jumps to perfection you'd all have looked less foolish. As it was, you had to press, and as a result your timing was lost, or you pushed hard, or your legs weren't ready, or your ponies were either in front of the bit or behind it. And as a demonstration of jumping, I don't think this was a very good example to the less experienced riders, do you?'

'No, it wasn't,' said Val Heath. 'It was a bad show. And I'm all for putting the jumps down again.'

Nobody could say anything to this, as Val was easily the best jumper of any and had done the only decent round. Clarissa began to natter on about her hunter being too good for narrow fences and anything less than five-foot jumps, but to my surprise my cousin Cecilia suddenly showed traces of sanity by remarking, 'I think it would have been better if we hadn't put the jumps up. I'd much rather do a three-foot jump well than a four-foot one badly. After all, style is what counts.'

This, of course, started an argument with the Neville boy, on the lines of 'Pooh, style! Just like a girl. Good riding is all that counts,' and Cecilia saying, 'Well, good riding is style, so don't try and be tough.'

Major Hooley then suggested that we should give the younger ones a chance on a few low jumps without stirrups, to make them use their legs properly; so though we were nearly staggering with exhaustion and heat by now we nobly did this.

Then he went away, and Ann said, 'What a slave-driver!'

'I think it's a jolly good thing,' I said, 'that we've got a grown-up to take an interest and give a few orders. I couldn't have coped without him, and Clarissa would have taken charge, and it would have been a muddle. I think it's decent of the old boy.'

We then declared the rally over, and everybody began to go home. I hoped the Cholly-Sawcutt girls would remember to remind their illustrious father that he had promised us a rally.

Ann and I rode our tired ponies home, and stopped on the way at a lemonade stall where we each had about a gallon, which set us back two pounds.

While we were drinking this highly coloured but cooling brew who should come along but Mercy Dulbottle.

'Oh, Jill,' she said, 'do you think I could come home with you now and have a jumping lesson, like you promised? Aunt Henrietta has gone to town and it's so boring to go home by myself.'

The last thing that appealed to me was the idea of putting Mercy over a bar on the ground and giving her a few elementary ideas of timing, but seeing she had got us the field I couldn't very well say no, especially as I had been the one to tell Ann she had got to be nice to Mercy. So I said, 'OK, you can come along if you like.'

We went to the cottage. Mummy was out, but had left a stack of sandwiches. Mercy and I hurled ourselves on this repast. Then while Black Boy and Rapide stood idly watching us, swishing their tails under the cool orchard trees, I dragged myself and Mercy into the hot sun and put a bar down on two bricks, about six inches high.

'See what you can do with that,' I said.

Mercy said, 'I'm nervous.'

'Help!' I said.

Looking like a grasshopper with rheumatism, Mercy walked her pony over the bar and said, 'How's that?'

'Jump him,' I said. 'Don't walk him.'

'I don't know how.'

'Perhaps he does,' I said sarkily. 'Give him a chance.'

Mercy brought her pony round to the jump again, and this time it seemed to occur to his dim brain that it *was* a jump he was facing. He got terribly excited, his head went up and his quarters went sideways.

'Oh, oh, oh, oh, oh!' yelled Mercy. 'Oh, help!'

The pony rushed at the small jump as though it were a hurdle and leapt over it with at least a foot to spare. Then away he loped round the field and Mercy clung on with everything she'd got. She made no attempt to pull him up, and at last he quietened down and brought her back to me at a smug trot. I was quite glad to see her all in one piece, as I didn't want to be the cause of her death.

'I jumped it!' she said, panting. 'Jill, I jumped it!'

'You're quite hopeless,' I said.

She looked dashed, and said, 'I don't see why you

should say that. I want to get good enough to ride in competitions.'

I said, 'Well, they say that anybody can do anything.'

'But I really did jump it,' said Mercy. 'When I felt myself flying over I nearly passed out.'

'So did I,' I said grimly. 'If you want to have another try you can, and this time you'll make an effort to do it properly.'

'What, jump it all over again?' said Mercy, as though she had just done a steeplechase course.

'Don't be silly,' I said. 'The jump is so low that you should hardly notice it. In fact I'm going to make it a bit higher.' I raised the bar by a couple of extra bricks. 'Now! Keep calm, don't press, and leave it to the pony.'

'But that's what I did before, and he jumped a mile into the air and then simply flew round the field.'

'That was because you had no control over him. Not one scrap. Grip him with your knees, and keep your balance, and go *with* him. Let him feel he's being ridden, but for goodness sake don't hang on to the reins to keep your balance or you'll jag his mouth and then he'll refuse to jump at all. Keep your legs firm, and lean slightly forward.'

'Oh, what an awful lot to remember,' Mercy moaned.

'You've got to go on until you don't have to remember it, it becomes second nature.'

'I'll try,' said Mercy. 'When do I say "Hup"?'

'You don't say it at all,' I said patiently. 'Not for a one-foot bar.'

Mercy got over, and not too badly. She was the most earnest person I had ever taught. She was so earnest that she reduced me to a shred, and she did that little jump again and again, and was so pleased with herself it might have been a five-foot hurdle.

I told her to go home and make herself a low jump, and practise over it without stirrups and her arms folded. She looked at me as if I'd suggested she should stand on her head in the saddle.

I was afraid I was going to have her on my hands for the rest of the night, but at last Mummy came home and called me in. I disentangled myself from Mercy's thanks, and mopped my streaming brow.

8 A pony for Stanley

Stanley Trimble was beginning to jump quite nicely. He seemed to have a natural talent for it, and a week later Mr Trimble asked me if I would like to go with them to buy a pony for Stanley.

I was very pleased at this idea, because next best to buying a pony for myself there is nothing I would rather do than buy a pony for somebody else.

We got the local *Exchange and Mart* and spread it out on the Trimbles's kitchen table, while Mrs Trimble took a tray of hot jam tarts out of the oven and passed them round.

'You know a lot more about this sort of thing than I do,' said Mr Trimble to me, which was flattering but probably incorrect.

We all leaned over the table and breathed heavily on the paper.

'Here it is,' said Stanley. 'Horses, etc., for sale. What does etc. mean? Giraffes, and things? I'd rather have a horse than an etc.'

'This one sounds all right,' said Mr Trimble, pointing. "Bay pony, show-jumper, 14.2, three years, spirited, one owner, sure winner."'

'Too good to be true,' I said briskly. 'What about this . . . "grey pony, 14.2, suitable ride for child."'

'Oh gosh!' said Stanley in disgust. 'I don't want a suitable ride for a child. I'd rather have "chestnut mare, 15 hands, very sound, useful hack, has hunted."'

'I'm never very taken with "has hunted",' I said. 'It

usually means the animal is over twenty years old. And you can't ride anything over 14.2, Stanley. I know what I'm talking about.'

'Yes, Jill knows what she's talking about,' said Mr Trimble valiantly. 'You leave it to Jill, Stanley. She knows all about buying ponies.'

This made me feel a bit cold with responsibility, and reminded me of the occasion which you may remember reading about in one of my previous books, when I had gone out to buy myself a show-jumper and returned with a fifteen-year-old hack, because I liked the look of her, and a poor wretched little pony that a man in a cart had been knocking about.

'I still like the "suitable for a child",' I said, 'and that doesn't mean it's a kid's pony, Stanley. It probably means it's suitable for show-riding for anybody in the under-sixteen classes. Do you think we might go and see it, Mr Trimble?'

We wrote down the address, and in the afternoon we set off in the Trimbles's car. Stanley was very excited as if the pony was as good as bought, while I had my doubts, which made me feel I must be getting old; aged people being noted for their lack of enthusiasm even about horses.

When we got to the house Stanley cried, 'That must be him!' and we saw a grey pony in a small paddock. I felt slightly gloomy, because I realised that in one particular at least the advertisement had lied. The pony was certainly not 14.2, and I thought 12.2 was nearer the mark, which would be no use to Stanley. We knocked at the door, which was opened by a woman in a red beret, a cotton frock, a diamond brooch and Wellingtons.

She said, 'Oh, have you come about the pony? It'll break my little boy's heart to let him go.'

I thought, Well why sell him, then?

I said, 'Could we see him, please?'

She said, 'Is that the little boy he's intended for?' and Stanley went absolutely scarlet with rage at being called a little boy, and I could see that so far as he was concerned the deal was off already.

We went along to the paddock, and the woman, whose name was Mrs Webster, said, 'Well, there he is. He'd do with a good clean up, but he only gets dirty again, so why bother?'

This peculiar reason for not grooming ponies struck me with such force that I could only gasp. Meanwhile Mr Trimble was looking the pony over and said, 'He's got a sensible head and nice clean legs, but isn't he a bit undersized?'

'You said in the advertisement 14.2,' I said to Mrs Webster, 'but he only looks about 12.2 to me.'

She looked very apologetic, and said, 'Well, perhaps he is. I didn't really know, so I just guessed.'

I felt as if every remark of Mrs Webster's was taking my breath still further and further away; and it really was the climax when Mr Trimble asked why she was selling the pony if her little boy would be so upset about it, and she replied that he had got tired of riding and wanted a multi-speed sports bike instead of the pony, and though he really would break his heart when the pony went away he would be consoled by the fact that the money he got for the pony would pay for the bike. I thought he must be a soulless child.

Stanley said, 'I think he's too small for me, don't you, Jill?' and I said, 'Oh yes, he wouldn't be any good for you, Stanley.'

Mrs Webster looked awfully depressed, and said the pony was very cheap, only three hundred pounds, and perhaps we knew of some other child who was wanting to buy one.

I said, I supposed he was schooled for the show ring,

and could he jump? And she said, she didn't understand much about schooling, and he could jump a *bit*, and her child had ridden him in several gymkhanas but had never won anything, and they had always kept him more as a pet.

Mr Trimble said, 'He's a nice pony,' and I said, yes, but apparently unschooled and therefore dear at three hundred pounds. Mrs Webster looked as if she was going to cry, and said perhaps she might take two hundred and fifty, though that wouldn't buy the multi-speed sports bike.

Mr Trimble looked so sympathetic that for one awful moment I thought he was going to buy the pony just to stop Mrs Webster from crying, but I managed to catch his eye in time and said, 'It's a pity the pony isn't going to be any use to us, but thank you for showing him to us, Mrs Webster.'

Mr Trimble looked relieved, and five minutes later we were out of the gate.

'Fancy anybody wanting a bike instead of a pony,' said Stanley, and I said, 'He must be pretty revolting.'

Stanley said, 'What do we do now? It looks as if I'm going to get a pony,' and I said, 'Oh, don't be so hopeless,' and Mr Trimble said, 'What about slipping over to Rychester? It's market day and they always have some horses for sale.'

I said, if there was one thing that upset me it was going to a horse sale because I always wanted to buy them all, and lay awake for hours at night wondering what soulless people had bought the ones I'd fancied; and Mr Trimble said, why should the people who'd bought the horses be any more soulless than me?

I said, 'You've got something there, Mr Trimble, but it doesn't alter my feelings,' and then he horrified me by saying that horses were only livestock after all, which made me wish I hadn't come, or hadn't had anything to do with the Trimbles. I don't think he was really as bad as this sordid remark would lead one to think.

'Well, what about Rychester?' he said.

I had a bright idea.

'Couldn't we go round and see Mrs Darcy?' I said. 'She might know of a pony.'

So we went round to the riding school, and Mrs Darcy said at once, 'There's a lovely pony for sale at Fortune Farm, if it hasn't gone already. Shall I give them a ring?'

'What's it like?' said Stanley. 'Actually I want a grey.'

'It's a chestnut,' said Mrs Darcy. 'Very quiet.'

'Oh dash!' said Stanley. 'I want a grey, and I don't want a quiet pony.'

'You'll have what you're given,' said Mr Trimble, which I thought was quite a constructive remark though a bit hard on Stanley.

Mrs Darcy rang up Fortune Farm, and came back and said, 'If you go round now they'll show it to you.'

Mr Trimble hummed and hawed a bit, and then said that the one thing he couldn't do was go round to Fortune Farm, as he and Mr Bedwell who farmed Fortune Farm hadn't been on speaking terms for years, owing to some hoo-ha about the drainage scheme.

I said, 'Shall Stanley and I go?' and Mr Trimble hummed and hawed some more, and said he'd rather have a look at Rychester Market first, and if all else failed there was always the Fortune Farm pony to fall back on. I thought this was a dim way of going on, but Stanley said, 'Good! Perhaps I'll get a grey after all.'

So we got back into the car and drove to Rychester, to the squalid, tram-shed place where they sell the horses.

I knew under my skin that this wasn't a good idea and that something would happen to me, and sure enough there was a dream of a bay mare, 15 hands, and the minute I saw her I forgot everything else in the world except how much I wanted her. Her hogged mane and tail were black, and she had lovely clean legs, a long flexible neck, high withers, and large soft sensible eyes. She looked at me and I patted her neck.

A little bow-legged man who was standing by said, 'Now that's a nice job for you, lady. Lovely bit of horseflesh. I've seen her jump and she's a treat.'

'I know,' I said miserably. 'I can't buy her, I haven't any money, and I've got two ponies already, and I wish I hadn't come.'

Mr Trimble came up and said, 'That's not much use for Stanley.'

'She'd be of use to anybody,' I said wretchedly, 'but of course she's outside the pony class. I knew it would be like this. I wish we'd gone to Fortune Farm.'

'Come on,' he said, 'let's look at the ponies. There are one or two up here.'

I tore myself away from the mare and didn't even look back at her. We went over and inspected the ponies, but I didn't have my mind on the job at all. I was planning some way I could save some rich old man's life and be given two thousand pounds reward, and buy the mare, but things like that only happen in books.

'I like this one,' said Stanley, pointing to a wicked-looking animal with mean eyes and a long back.

'Don't be silly,' I said crossly. 'You ought to know a bad pony from a good one at a glance.'

'But he looks spirited.'

'He'd murder you,' I said.

The only other possibility was a rather nice little roan, at least he was described in the catalogue as roan but he was quite pinkish.

'Do you think he's a bit thickset?' asked Mr Trimble.

'No,' I said. 'He's only over-fed. Perhaps they'd let me try him round the yard before the sale starts.'

A horsy man came up, and as he knew Mr Trimble he said I might try the roan pony. He went quite nicely and had been schooled, but I had the instinctive feeling that he wasn't going to make a jumper. I didn't want Stanley to be disappointed.

The horsy man said, 'They'll sell him privately if you'd like to do a deal now.'

Mr Trimble asked how much, and the horsy man said the owner was asking four hundred pounds.

'Too much,' said Mr Trimble. 'Three hundred's my price.'

'They'll get more than that in the sale.'

'I'm not giving more than three hundred.'

'I don't think I want it,' said Stanley. 'I want a grey.'

'We'll stay for the sale,' said Mr Trimble, 'and if we can get this one for three hundred pounds, this is the one we're having, and I don't want to hear any more about a grey.'

Stanley sulked, and I wished we weren't going to stay for the sale as I couldn't bear the thought of seeing that mare sold.

However, I was doomed to suffer. The mare went for one and a half thousand pounds, and my only comfort was that the woman who bought her didn't actually look unscrupulous and hard-hearted, but rather a decent person.

The roan pony fetched three hundred and fifty pounds, so we didn't get it, and the black wicked one went for two hundred and fifty, and Stanley burst into tears, and Mr Trimble told him not to be a stupid little cry-baby, and I didn't know which I hated most, Mr Trimble or Stanley.

However, we still hadn't bought a pony, and I was

feeling very low; but Mr Trimble then showed a spark of humanity by suggesting that we went to a café, and after two chocolate ice cream sodas Stanley and I both brightened up.

'We'll end up at Fortune Farm after all,' I said.

Stanley said indignantly, 'But I don't want a quiet pony. It sounds beastly and only fit for pulling bath chairs.'

'Don't be silly,' I said. 'Quiet doesn't mean what you think it means. It doesn't mean the pony's a slug, it means it's amenable to schooling.'

I was so pleased with this phrase 'amenable to schooling' which of course I had got out of a book, that I began to smile in a smug, superior way, and Stanley looked impressed.

'Mrs Darcy wouldn't recommend it if it wasn't a really good pony,' I said.

'Three hundred pounds is my price,' said Mr Trimble.

I had a feeling we were going to finish up without any pony at all.

When we got to Fortune Farm we saw the pony in a field being ridden round by a girl whose legs were too long for it.

'Oh, it's sold!' said Stanley. 'She's bought it.'

'More likely she's the owner and has grown out of it,' I said.

'You go and ask, Jill,' said Mr Trimble. 'I don't like the Bedwells.'

So I went up to the girl on the pony and said, 'Is this the pony that Mrs Darcy said was for sale?'

'Yes,' she said. 'Do you want to buy him?'

'Not for myself,' I said. 'For this boy.'

She said, 'Would he like to try him?'

I said I'd try the pony myself, so I rode him round a bit and he was quite a nice ride, and had been well schooled.

I asked if he could jump, and the girl said she had won prizes with him when she was smaller. She put up a bar for me at two-foot-six and I jumped the pony over. For myself I thought he was a bit stodgy, but quite a useful animal for Stanley Trimble to start on.

I asked if he had a vet's certificate, and she said there was one in the house dated the previous week, and she'd get it for me to see. I asked how much she wanted for him, and she said two hundred and eighty pounds, so I said, 'Just a minute,' and went back and consulted Mr Trimble who was slinking in the hedge, out of sight.

Mr Trimble said, 'He sounds OK. Buy him, and let's put an end to this nonsense.'

I went back to the field and found Stanley already riding the pony round.

'Do you like him?' I said, and Stanley said he wasn't too bad, though he had wanted a grey. I cheered him up by saying that he could use this pony until he had improved himself and then get a grey, and so the deal was done. I got the two hundred and eighty pounds from Mr Trimble and paid for the pony, and the girl gave us a halter made of dirty knotted rope, and came with us to the lane.

'Well, that's that,' said Mr Trimble, and was I thankful!

'I'll have the extra twenty pounds, Father,' said Stanley. 'Towards some new tack.'

The girl, who must have thought Mr Trimble slightly mad to be slinking in the hedge all the time, said, 'The pony's name is Stardust.'

Stanley said, 'I don't like that name. I'm going to call him Peter.'

I said that ponies didn't like to have their names altered, but the girl said that Stardust had never answered to Stardust anyway, so it didn't matter and he might as well be Peter.

9 An invitation

When I got home, April Cholly-Sawcutt was there having tea with Mummy. She looked rather important, and said she had brought an invitation from her father to the riding club to have a rally at their place the following Friday.

We had just a week to get ready. I could hardly wait to get April out of the cottage before I started ringing everybody up to call a practice for the next day. Everybody was rather awed at the prospect of going to Captain Cholly-Sawcutt's place. Miss Durdon herself came along with Mercy, and announced that as President of the riding club she would be going to the rally too. Several of us looked rather stunned at this, as we were not aware that Miss Durdon was President of the riding club; or anybody else for that matter, as we had never really considered who we wanted as President, but we couldn't say a thing. Even Clarissa Dandleby was dumb, which was the eighth wonder of the world.

Before you could say knife Miss Durdon then began acting as President of the riding club. We found ourselves lined up while she drilled us with crisp orders. After a bit, Clarissa couldn't stand it any longer. She went red in the face and mumbled, 'We don't do it like that.'

'Were you speaking?' said Miss Durdon. 'If so, speak up. You won't find any mumbling in the show ring.'

Clarissa said, 'I only said, we don't do it like that.'

'You'll do it as I tell you,' said Miss Durdon. 'Don't be a silly little girl.' Clarissa was so taken back that she nearly fell on her pony's neck and we all started giggling.

In one sense it was a bit useless, as Miss Durdon's schooling belonged to about the period of the Indian Mutiny when you sat well back, nearly on your pony's rump, stuck your legs out in a cavalry-boot kind of way, and held your hands under your chin; but on the other hand she had lots of authority, and she had everybody in such a state of awe that they obeyed her without a giggle. Nobody whispered, nobody got out of line, even the ponies seemed to know they had met their match.

'Well that's very creditable,' said Miss Durdon at last. 'Very creditable indeed. But to see the way you children sit nowadays, my dear father would have swooned. However, I suppose there are fashions in riding. If you all obey me as nicely when we get to Captain Cholly-Sawcutt's, we shan't disgrace ourselves.'

'Help!' said Ann to me in dismay. 'She doesn't mean she's going to give the orders?'

That was just what Miss Durdon did mean, only fortunately for us when Friday came she had a bad cold and couldn't turn out at all. She sent us a lot of instructions by Mercy, none of which we bothered about.

I knew all the people who hadn't been to the Fairbridge training stables would gasp when they saw that wonderful place. It was a horsy person's dream of bliss. Long rows of loose boxes, perfect horses, a big gravelled yard, green paddocks, and a marvellous jumping field set out with the sort of jumps you find at a first-class Show.

There were twenty-six of us, and when I had got everybody lined up for inspection we didn't look bad at all; nor did the lining up take so long as I feared, as the more experienced people helped to shove the others into position and hoped this wasn't being noticed. Fortunately it was a very hot afternoon and the ponies didn't feel like being nappy. I ran an anxious eye along the line. Everybody looked amazingly clean and tidy. Everybody's boots were polished, everybody's tie was straight, and only three people hadn't bothered to iron their shirts. These, strange as it may seem, were April, May and June Cholly-Sawcutt.

'Right,' I said. 'Just freeze yourselves for about five minutes while we're being inspected.'

Captain Cholly-Sawcutt came out of the house with quite a party of friends. He laughed, and said, 'Let me introduce the Greenlee Riding Club,' and one of the men said, 'A very nice turn-out too,' the effect of which was rather spoiled when Ann's young sister Pam for some reason leaned over to scratch her ankle, lost her balance, and swung on her pony's neck. This upset two other people who backed raggedly out of line.

'Never mind,' said Captain Cholly-Sawcutt kindly. 'It happens in the best circles.'

The other man asked, 'Which are your girls, Fred?' and Captain Cholly-Sawcutt said quite casually, 'The ones in dirty shirts. Need you ask?' I thought it was a wonderful way to pass it off, rather than die of humiliation.

Captain Cholly-Sawcutt then ordered the whole line to walk forward, which we did quite successfully; and then to rein back, which we also did fairly successfully as we had been practising hard. We then walked a circle, trotted and cantered. I tried to avert my eyes from Mercy Dulbottle who with a smile from ear to ear was proceeding round at her only pace, a cross between a lollop and a hop. However, at least nine people were riding so beautifully that I hoped Captain Cholly-Sawcutt's fascinated eyes would not leave them to rest upon more sordid sights. In front of me, Stanley Trimble on the new pony, Peter, was sitting up straight as I had taught him, though he looked as if he had pokers pushed down his back and legs. I muttered, 'Knees up!' with a vicious hiss, and he brought them up so quickly he nearly hit his chin.

Captain Cholly-Sawcutt said, 'Halt. Line up again.'

I had cunningly made arrangements for this to happen, every good person being responsible for a duddish kind of person. As soon as the order was given the good ones collared their 'duds' and fairly rammed them into line, so the whole operation only took about two minutes, except that my dud was Mercy, and she kept saying, 'What are you *doing*, Jill?' in a sort of anguished squeak. I could have murdered her.

'Just a few questions,' said Captain Cholly-Sawcutt. 'First one who knows the answer shout it out. What's the first thing you do when you bring your pony out of the stable for schooling?'

Before the rest of us had time to think, Clarissa said smugly, 'I ride him round and let him relax and loosen up before I begin schooling.'

'Quite right. Next question. You wish to give your pony an order, what do you do?'

'Prepare him, and then apply the aids gently,' said Clarissa, all in one breath before anybody else had time to open their mouth.

Captain Cholly-Sawcutt looked a bit dazed, but said, 'Correct. You, the boy third from the left, you are sitting slightly too far back. Where is the proper place to sit?'

David gave a sort of stutter, and Clarissa chipped in, 'In the lowest part of the saddle as near as possible to the pommel.'

'Er – quite,' said Captain Cholly-Sawcutt, looking

nervously at Clarissa. 'I think that'll do for the questions,' he went on, probably afraid that in a minute Clarissa would be asking *him* a few questions that he couldn't answer.

'Show-off!' muttered Val Heath, glaring at Clarissa, who said, 'Well, somebody had to answer and the rest of you were as dumb as coots.'

By now we were all rather excited, and I was afraid if the inspection went on much longer there would be chaos among the younger ones. To my relief Captain Cholly-Sawcutt said, 'You've done quite well and you're a promising lot. I think we've had enough hard work. You've come here to enjoy yourselves, so just say what you'd like to do. The place is yours for the afternoon.'

Of course nobody cared to speak first, and then April Cholly-Sawcutt said the first sensible thing I ever remember her saying. She said, 'I think some people would like to do some jumping and some people would like to do some competitions.'

This was exactly what we did want.

John Watson said to me, 'Do you think he'd let us try his jumps?'

'They're terribly high,' I said. 'I'd love to try them if he'd put them down a bit.'

'So would I. I'll ask him.'

Captain Cholly-Sawcutt said, 'Of course. With pleasure,' and sent a man to lower the jumps to suit us. They were the most beautiful white-painted jumps, just like a show-ring course, and about half of us had the time of our lives going round them. You know how it is in a jumping competition, you often wish you could have the chance to do one of the jumps again and do it properly. Well, we could do any of these jumps again, and make them higher or lower to suit ourselves. It was the most superb place for practising.

Meanwhile one of the grooms was arranging some competitions for the younger ones, and they had put up the poles for a bending race by the time we had reluctantly decided that our ponies were too tired for any more jumping.

'I wish I had thought to bring a second pony,' said Val Heath. 'I could have gone on for ever on that lovely course.'

'So could I,' I said, thinking of Black Boy at home in the orchard.

'Look at those poles,' said John Watson. 'They're far too close together. No pony could get round them.'

'It isn't my fault,' said the groom. 'I put them the right distance apart but Miss May altered them all.'

'I like them close together,' said May Cholly-Sawcutt, 'because my pony is shaped like a worm and he wiggles in and out.'

'Good lord!' said John.

May then gave an exhibition of how her pony wiggled in and out of the poles which were too close together, and she certainly could do it, but nobody else could have done, so John insisted on putting the poles as they ought to be, and May said, 'Now I shan't win the beastly race and it'll be your fault.'

John said, 'As it's your father's party I suppose you're the hostess and the hostess isn't supposed to win,' and May said, 'I think that's beastly unfair,' which shows what a hopeless sort of person she was.

Mercy Dulbottle said she didn't see why she shouldn't have a try at the bending, it looked easy enough, and Pam Derry said, 'It isn't easy at all, you've got to gallop like mad, and if you miss one out you're disqualified and if you knock one down you're disqualified too.'

'All right,' I said, 'if you know so much about it, you go first, Pam.'

I picked out another girl about Pam's age and set them

off. Pam's pony leapt forward and simply raced down the posts, and was halfway home before the other girl had reached the turn. Pam won by several lengths.

'I could do this standing on my head,' she said.

I started off the next two, and when they got back Pam said, 'Gosh, don't they dawdle! It isn't any fun if people don't gallop. Why don't they whack the ponies round? It's like a slow-motion film.'

'If you don't shut up,' said Ann to her younger sister, 'you can jolly well go home. I'll tell Mummy tonight you're a menace.'

Pam piped down a bit, especially as two or three people did very good races, but when they came to ride off the heats she won again and again, and in the final she again came in by lengths.

'I wish she hadn't won,' said Ann. 'She's too cocky by miles, and now she'll get the idea she's a star rider.'

'She'll soon get it knocked out of her,' I said, 'if she enters for any open competitions.'

'Oh, look at Mercy!' said Ann.

Mercy, who had parted from her pony about a quarter of an hour before while going round the second pole, was still sitting on the ground.

'Are you hurt?' I said.

'I don't know,' said Mercy. 'I feel as if my backbone's coming through the top of my head.'

'Well, it isn't,' said Ann. 'Do get up, Mercy. You've been told before, you must get up immediately after a fall, or make an effort anyway. Don't be so feeble.'

Mercy got on her feet with a lot of 'oohing', and said, 'Where's my horse?'

'That's for you to say,' I said. 'You oughtn't to have let the reins go.'

'Oh, look, it's over there,' said Mercy. 'It's lying down. If the horse can lie down I don't see why I shouldn't.'

'Oh, leave her alone,' said Ann. 'She's nuts.'

Captain Cholly-Sawcutt then came up and said, how would everybody like to go in for a grand egg-and-spoon race? He would go in for it himself, and also everybody on the premises. We all thought it would be fun.

So everybody turned out and the stable people rode bareback, and out came Mrs Cholly-Sawcutt and Pansy and the vet who happened to be there, and all kinds of people, though some of them couldn't ride for nuts and I don't think any of them tried very hard because they obviously wanted members of the riding club to win.

We rode off the heats in fours. Mrs Cholly-Sawcutt provided four teaspoons and the eggs were knobbly potatoes.

I won my heat, mainly because I was lucky enough to get the least knobbly of the potatoes. Captain Cholly-Sawcutt who was in my heat dropped his potato four times, but he was only fooling about and making people laugh.

Eventually I got into the semifinal but that was the end of me. I dropped my potato, and when I dismounted to pick it up Rapide thought it was part of a game and began to dance about.

By then the heat had already been won by David Neville who was a natural at this kind of thing, and had never once dropped his potato. He easily won the final too, and wasn't even out of breath.

Captain Cholly-Sawcutt gave him a riding stick for a prize, and said he would take it away again if David used it too much or in an improper way.

Then we all went into the big empty barn, and there was a long table spread with lemonade, buns, and cakes, which disappeared like magic.

John Watson said, 'I say! We've got to do a special vote of thanks to Captain Cholly-Sawcutt for all this. I mean, it really is something for a member of the British Show-Jumping team to invite a potty little riding club like us to a "do" like this.'

'Well, you know why he does it,' said Ann. 'It's for Jill's sake, because she's taken such a lot of trouble with his revolting, unsportsmanlike, and ham-handed daughters.'

'Oh, I say!' said John. 'April's quite pretty.'

'I didn't say she wasn't,' said Ann. 'I said she couldn't ride.'

'About this speech, anyway,' began John.

My cousin Cecilia then chipped in, and said, 'If there's to be a speech I'm going to do it. I'm the eldest.'

'All right,' said John. 'Nobody particularly wants to do it; but if you do it, you'd better be good!'

Cecilia said he needn't worry, she was an expert at speeches; and so in fact she proved to be, because not only was she very flowery in her language but she went on for ages until everybody thought she was never going to stop. We were all fidgeting about, and Captain Cholly-Sawcutt who was getting thanked was as red as a beetroot. In the end, Clarissa Dandleby, who was standing next to Cecilia, gave her a kick on the ankle and said gruffly, 'Shut up,' and strangely enough Cecilia shut up. At least Captain Cholly-Sawcutt couldn't say he hadn't been thanked, as Cecilia had thanked him nineteen times all in different words, I know because I counted.

When it was all over and we got outside, he said to me, 'I believe you're running this riding club, aren't you, Jill?'

I said that I had actually started it, but I couldn't say who was running it. In fact a lot of different people seemed to be doing so.

'What's your aim and object?' he asked.

'Well, we do want to improve our riding, and we

thought it would be a good thing to bring on the younger ones a bit, and let them mix with us in events. It makes things rather friendly. And then we thought we'd run a little gymkhana in about a month's time, and anybody can enter for that, but we hope the riding club members will carry off all the prizes.'

He laughed, and said, 'I suppose you'll have to beg the prizes from somewhere. You can put me down for three.'

'Oh, that is good of you!' I said.

'Not a bit. I daresay my wife will give you one. Let me know when you get your schedule ready. In a month, did you say? That'll be after Chatton Show, I suppose?'

'Yes, the week after. A lot of us will be riding at the show.'

'Any difficulties at the riding club?' he said. 'Anything you need to help you?'

'I think what we really need,' I said, 'is a bit of expert instruction for the older ones. We seem to spend a lot of our time teaching the younger ones, but nobody ever teaches us. Except of course Major Hooley, but he gets rather irritated and I don't think he brings out the best in us.'

'If you would like to call a rally,' said Captain Cholly-Sawcutt, 'I'll ask a friend of mine to come round and give you an hour. He's very good. Would you like that?'

'Oh, would we!' I cried. 'I think it's marvellous of you.'

So a few days later we met at the field and a Mr Storm appeared. Miss Durdon wasn't too welcoming to him at first, because she rather resented the idea of any stranger giving us instruction in her field under her very nose, but when they began to talk she found out that Mr Storm had actually known her father in India, and after that he could do nothing wrong. I kept wishing they would stop talking and get on with the rally. Miss Durdon kept saying, 'Did you know old So-and-so? I always said he'd die with his riding boots on,' and Mr Storm said, 'Do you remember Mrs Thingummy? She hunted till she was ninety-four.'

However, when Mr Storm did get down to work on us he proved to be very good indeed. Of course, we had to be willing to be told our faults, even in front of the others, but what I say is, if you can't bear to be told where you're wrong you had better sell your pony and buy a sewing-machine or something equally dreary. Mr Storm was dressed in corduroys and a hacking jacket, and from the minute I saw him handle one or two restless ponies in a nonchalant way, and magically get everybody into perfect order while not seeming to take any trouble at all, I knew he was a flawlessly horsy person.

Miss Durdon kept butting in, with Indian bits about pig-sticking and Yoga.

'I wish the tatty old witch would dry up,' said John Watson. 'This old bird knows what he's talking about, if she'd give him a chance.'

'Oh, do be quiet, John,' I said. 'You've got the most awfully penetrating whisper I ever heard in my life. He'll hear you calling him an old bird, and she'll hear what you say about her, and before we know where we are we shan't have a field or an instructor or even a riding club.'

'Don't be silly,' said John. 'They won't hear, they're miles away, inspecting the way the ponies are groomed. By the way, yours could do with a dust over, couldn't he?'

I was mad at his superior tone, and pointed out that the worst of black horses was the way they showed the dust, and that Black Boy had looked like patent leather when I left home; and John said it was the same with black cars, though he still liked them best.

By now, Mr Storm was telling everybody to dismount and take off their saddles. He then went over every pony in turn, as carefully as a judge in the showing class. I was thankful for all the grooming I had done that morning, but one or two people got it in the neck, including Clarissa.

'How long did you spend in grooming your horse this morning?' said Mr Storm to her.

Clarissa gasped, and said, 'None at all. Our groom sees to all that.'

'Well, in this case,' said Mr Storm, 'he has seen to nothing. I don't blame him. If the rider doesn't care, why should the groom? However many Arab steeds I had, each with its own groom, I should still take off my saddle before I rode out, and inspect my horse's ears, and see that his hoofs were oiled.' Then seeing that Clarissa's eyes were boiling over behind her specs, he went on, 'On the other hand, I must congratulate you on your own appearance. You look extremely neat, and your jodhpurs and boots are spotless, and your coat well brushed. Your hair is tidy, too, in that beautiful plait. Not like – ' and his eyes swivelled round to my cousin Cecilia who was wearing her long hair loose on her shoulders. I hadn't noticed Cecilia's get-up before, or – cousin or no cousin, elder or not elder – I would certainly have torn her off a strip for coming to a rally in that sort of get-up.

'No, no, decidedly wrong,' said Mr Storm, fixing Cecilia with his glassy eye. 'Push it into your hat, girl.'

Cecilia looked annoyed, and John Watson began to giggle.

Mr Storm told Mercy Dulbottle that her girth was loose enough to go round two horses and stood by while she fumbled about, tightening it, and Miss Durdon danced with impatience and said, 'Really, Mercy, really!' which didn't help things at all. When it came to my turn I got off lightly, though he said my crash cap was a bit to one side and he preferred a plain tie. He certainly was frightfully particular.

He then made us ride round a circle, and I could tell he was concentrating on the people who considered themselves good riders. He had some fault to find with everybody, and I for one was glad of this, because you do get careless when you think you are good. He corrected nearly everybody's seat, and told me that I was apt to come forward in front of my hands. Other people, he said, were too far back, or held the reins too short, or were not sufficiently relaxed and looked stiff at the trot.

Then he went on about legs, legs, legs, and here John Watson got the axe, because I had noticed myself that instead of keeping his knees close to his pony's sides and pressing them, he opened them wide and clumped them in suddenly, which was not only ugly but prevented the pony from going quietly into a trot or canter. John's movements were jerky, but I must say after he was told he improved a great deal.

'You!' said Mr Storm to Val Heath, who was probably the best rider of any of us. 'You have a perfect pony who understands you so well that she has let you become thoroughly lazy. You are doing no work at all. You are sitting on your pony and thinking how effective you look, because you know she will obey your lightest touch and that all this is child's play. What I want you to do is dismount and change ponies with somebody – anybody, that girl next to you – yes . . . That's better. Now you have got a pony who is not so good as your own and doesn't know you. Now you will *have* to work, and I shall be able to see if you can really ride.'

Val didn't look pleased for a minute, but being a sensible person she soon realised that Mr Storm was right. She got up on the grey pony, which had a startled eye, a slightly coffin-shaped head, and a barrel body. For a minute she was at a loss, and then she showed she was a real horsewoman by the way she gently but firmly applied the aids and got the pony going at a nice controlled pace, correcting each fault as it occurred.

'Bravo, bravo!' said Mr Storm. 'That is riding. The pony has never been so well ridden before, and he appreciates it. His rightful owner can learn a lesson from this too. It wouldn't be a bad idea if you all changed ponies occasionally.'

The girl who owned the pony, her name was the peculiar one of Posy Meadows, looked as happy as a tomtit riding Val's pony, and beamed all over as she watched Val riding hers and getting such a lot out of him that Posy hadn't been able to get.

'Dear, dear, dear!' said Mr Storm, looking at Ann Derry. 'You have a shocking fault, and you don't know it, it is just a bad habit you have got into. You look down to see if your pony is on the right leg. That is frightful. You know perfectly well when your pony is on the right leg, and yet your silly little head has to go down to make sure. You do know, don't you?'

'Yes,' said Ann. 'It's just a crazy habit I've got into. I must have been doing it for ages without realising it. I won't do it again.'

'I hope you won't, or the next thing that will happen will be that you'll become the sort of person who looks back at jumps in the show ring. Nothing can be worse than that. Do you ever look back at jumps?'

Ann went red, and said that she couldn't remember, but she probably did, and Diana Bush nobly said, 'Directly I've done a jump I have the most beastly feeling that something is sawing my head round to look back. I have to fight it.'

Mr Storm then picked on David Neville, and said, 'Here you have a case of a rider and a pony who are at variance with one another. They don't think they are, but I can see it. All the time there is a struggle going on. The pony is trying to escape from the rider's legs and from his own bit. It is a case of strength against strength, and that is no good at all. The rider must be more gentle and relaxed, then the pony will be the same. What's your name?'

'David,' said David.

'Well, David, I can only tell you, you must feel your reins and you must keep your legs closed, and you must never, never push. However much you want to push, don't push. You'll find your riding much easier. That's better already. And now, everybody, we're going to trot and canter, change legs smoothly, halt slowly, and rein back. Please concentrate. This has got to be very good.'

It was a very strenuous afternoon, but we all had to admit that Mr Storm had done us a lot of good.

'A few afternoons with him, and I should melt away altogether,' said Val Heath. 'Gosh, how he made me work on that dud pony of Posy's.'

'It's the best thing that ever happened to you,' said her sister. 'If you can't ride any sort of pony you're not a real rider at all. Next time we have a rally I'm going to borrow a dud from one of the kids and see what I can do with it.'

I remembered to go and thank Mr Storm, who was going back to tea with Miss Durdon to talk about the Taj Mahal and paper chases in the Punjab, and he said there was no need to thank him, it had been a pleasure to do something for the cause of equitation and he hoped we would all work hard and have jolly good luck in any competitions we entered for, and that he himself would be judging at Chatton Show and would look forward to meeting some of us there. I hadn't realised he was so high up in the horsy world, and I thought we were terrifically fortunate to have had such a man to instruct us, but it just shows that the highest are usually the most humble and willing to help others.

'He was really a decent old lemon,' said John Watson as we clattered out into the lane, 'though if I do meet him in the show ring I shall feel he has an unfair advantage in knowing which of my faults to look out for.'

'Don't worry,' said Diana. 'He'll have forgotten us all by then; I hope so, anyway. I think he'll be quite a tough judge, but what's the good of having a riding club unless it makes us improve enough to face tough judges? I'm all for it.'

'Phew, haven't we worked the last few days?' said Ann. 'Couldn't we have some fun next time instead of all this hard labour?'

So we decided we would have an afternoon of games and races, which would be fun for the ponies as well as for us.

10   Planning a gymkhana

The games–and–races afternoon was more of a success for the younger ones than for us experienced ones, as we felt it was our duty to give the young entry a good time and make them think they were getting something out of the riding club. Quite a lot of fond parents came along to watch, and to swoon with rapture at the sight of their tots on ponies shying potatoes at a bucket and missing every time.

A number of people from school came to watch too, and said they had heard we were getting up a gymkhana, and would anybody be allowed to enter or was it just for our members?

I said we wanted as many people as possible to enter, whether they belonged to the riding club or not, though of course we hoped that our own members would carry off most of the prizes.

'Isn't it time we did something definite about this gymkhana?' said John Watson. 'When's the thing going to be, anyway?'

'The Saturday before we go back to school,' I said. 'That's the first Saturday in September.'

'All right. That's one thing arranged. What about judges and schedules and rosettes and prizes and seats for the people who have so little sense as to come and watch us ride? Gosh, this thing's going to cost money, isn't it?'

'It won't have to,' I said. 'We must go round and ask everybody we know to give things.'

'My father would be a judge,' said Val Heath, 'and you needn't be afraid of favouritism, he'll be equally tough with everybody. And I think Mrs Darcy would be a judge if you asked her, Jill.'

'Good show,' I said. 'That's the judges fixed. What about rosettes?'

'Easy,' said Ann. 'If we all put in about twenty-five pence we can buy yards of ribbon at Woolworth's and wheedle our mothers into making them up when they go out to tea with each other. And I'm sure Stanley Trimble's father would provide the ropes for the ring; and they'd lend us the seats from the Parish Hall for nothing, if somebody would take a lorry to fetch them.'

'Stanley Trimble's father!' yelled about six people in chorus.

'It's all going to be quite simple,' said David Neville.

'Not so simple as all that,' I said, 'because the reputation of the riding club is at stake, and if the gymkhana is a flop we shall feel terribly small and all these weeks of practising will be wasted.'

'Oh dear, need we have a gymkhana at all?' said Mercy Dulbottle, and we all squashed her flat by screaming, 'Of course we must have a gymkhana! What's the good of the riding club if we can't put on a gymkhana?'

'The most important thing,' said Diana Bush, 'is the schedule. What sort of events are we going to have?'

'Perhaps I could have a word here,' said Clarissa very loudly. 'I vote we draw the line at kiddish events, definitely.'

'Don't be silly,' I said. 'Half the members of the riding club are under fourteen.'

'Well, that crowd hardly count at all,' said Clarissa. 'They're only learners, and they ought to be jolly glad to stand by and watch the rest of us. If you make this gymkhana a kiddish thing nobody worthwhile will bother to come, and what's more, *I'm* not going to waste my time on it.'

'All right, Clever – stop away,' said John Watson. 'The under-fourteens have got as much right to have their events as we older ones have. Also, considering the help we've had from Captain Cholly-Sawcutt and people like Stanley Trimble's father, and considering that we're going to expect the kids' mothers to work their fingers to the bone making rosettes, the least we can do is to see that *their* kids have a fair chance of competing and winning something.'

'Hear, hear!' I said.

'I'm not thinking so much about the under-fourteens, as the under-tens,' said Ann. 'If my sister Pam doesn't get a look-in at some event my mother won't be pleased, and I'm counting on her to give us an awful lot of lemonade for the day.'

'Right,' said John Watson. 'Event for the under-tens, in return for a lot of lemonade from Mrs Derry.'

'Of course if you're going on like that,' said Clarissa, very snootily, 'the whole thing is going to be a farce.'

'Oh, go and boil your head,' said John. 'You old fusspot! You'll get your senior jumping all right, but Ann's talking sense. We want people who really matter in the riding world to come to our gymkhana and give our riding club a boost, and what will they think if they see the big ones prancing about all the time and grabbing all the fun? They'll think a great deal more of us if they see we're not being greedy but giving a fair innings to the young entry.'

'Good for you, John,' said Val Heath. 'Well, here and now I vote we have a showing class *and* a game for the under-tens; they won't take long, because there won't be many entries. Also showing and jumping and a game or competition for the under-fourteens, and then jumping for us older ones, and an open competition which the under-fourteens can join in as well. I think that gives the juniors a jolly good innings, and really the best treatment of any section in the club.'

'It's ridiculous,' said Clarissa, 'it only gives us seniors one event worth calling an event, and that's the jumping. Surely we can have dressage, or handy hunter, or something?'

'It'll be too boring for the spectators,' said Diana. 'This gymkhana isn't a pony show, it's supposed to amuse us and the public. I'm quite content with the jumping and an open competition.'

'If there's time,' said John Watson, 'we might have bareback trotting and cantering for the seniors. That's interesting to watch and very good for us too.'

'Good idea,' I said. 'Have you got some paper, John? Stick it down.'

'I vote we make John the gymkhana secretary,' said Ann.

'Right-oh,' I said, and John said, 'Well, speaking with the utmost modesty, I don't think anybody else would be as good.'

He then produced a notebook and a pencil and said, 'Let's stick down what we've got. We'll start at two, or one thirty would be better. Let's put one thirty, showing class, ten and under. Then a game, ten and under. What game?'

'Oh, something frightfully simple, like standing on one leg at the gallop,' said Clarissa sarkily.

'If you don't shut up,' said John, 'you'll be needing an ambulance in about five minutes. The obvious game for the under-tens is Musical Chairs. The parents adore it.'

'The ones that don't win,' said Clarissa, 'will scream, cry, fight, hit their ponies, and run to Mummy.'

'Will somebody murder that woman for me?' said John, and to my surprise my cousin Cecilia said, 'Oh shut up, Clarissa. Don't be so feeble.'

'Next,' said John, 'we'll have the showing class for fourteen-and-under, followed by – cheers! – tea.'

'Tea he says!' I said scathingly. 'Where's the tea coming from?'

'Fond parents,' said John. 'Don't tell me we can't grind some sort of a tea out of people's mothers? They'll want tea themselves, so the least they can do is to provide the cakes and things, and some tea and milk, and we'll have to find somebody who'll lend us a marquee for nothing, and – '

'You don't want much!' said Diana.

'I hadn't even finished,' said John with dignity. 'They can give the tea, and the marquee, and also make the tea and serve it. They'll love to, if asked nicely. I'll bet my mother will make dozens of cakes and help to serve the tea too. Now where are we up to? I know, junior jumping.'

'You've missed out the junior game,' I said.

'Oh blow, so I have. What game, do you think?'

'Bending?'

'Potatoes in buckets?'

'Handkerchiefs on poles?'

'Hadn't we better ask the juniors what they want?' I said. 'If we try to wish a game on to them they'll think they're being swizzled, and make a riot.'

'OK. I'll just put down junior game, and we'll shove it in before tea. Then some of us hardy types can spend the tea interval helping to put up the jumps and get the course ready. After tea, junior and senior jumping. That'll take ages and we can wind up with a grand finale, a good competition.'

'Gretna Green!' said Val Heath. 'It's terrific fun to watch and to do, and it brings in all ages. The seniors can be the bridegrooms and the juniors the brides. It's good fun.'

'Never heard of it,' said Clarissa, in a voice which suggested all that sort of thing was beneath her. She then added, trying not to sound curious, 'What do you do?'

Val explained that the seniors had to mount, race to a given point where the brides were waiting, dismount, hoist the bride up behind the saddle, remount, and race back again. Clarissa said the main point in that seemed to be to pick a bride who weighed about two stone; and Val said, you didn't pick them, you drew them out of a hat; and John Watson said the under-fourteens in the riding club were the fattest lot of girls he'd ever seen in his life, and wasn't there some sort of race that didn't involve slave labour?

Clarissa said, 'Let's have a hurdle race. You just go on jumping the hurdles till you knock one over, then you drop out;' and I said, 'Thank you, I'd rather not take my pony home buckled up with exhaustion,' and Clarissa said, What made me think I'd jump all that many hurdles?

Ann said, 'Let's vote on it. Hands up for the fat brides.'

Everybody wanted the Gretna Green race except Clarissa and Cecilia, so it was carried.

'That's OK,' I said. 'Next thing is to get it all copied out and the schedules printed, John. The sooner we get the schedules out the better, and then we can start on the entries.'

'How much are we charging for each entry?' asked Diana.

'Well, seeing it's our own riding club we can't charge much,' I said. 'I should think fifty pence each entry for our own members, and one pound for outsiders. That ought to make some money to pay for the printing and the ribbon from Woolworth's. And they must pay when they make their entries, to give us some cash to be going on with.'

'Shark!' said Clarissa.

'Shark yourself,' I said, which was far from clever, only I was getting too bored with Clarissa to bother to think up any bright retorts.

'That's all, then,' said Diana. 'Stick it down, John, and let's see how it looks.'

John produced the following schedule:

GREENLEE RIDING CLUB GYMKHANA

at the paddock, Bent Lane
Saturday, September 9th, at 1.30 sharp

Class 1	Showing Class	Ten and under
Class 2	Musical Chairs	Ten and under
Class 3	Showing Class	Fourteen and under
Class 4	Game	Fourteen and under

INTERVAL FOR TEA

Class 5	Jumping	Junior
Class 6	Jumping	Senior
Class 7	Gretna Green Race	Open
Class 8	If time. Exhibition of open bareback riding, non-competitive.	

'I hope it doesn't look too kiddish,' said Clarissa.

'You've got kiddish on the brain,' said David Neville. 'It's probably because you're kiddish yourself that you're so afraid of *looking* kiddish. I think the schedule looks utterly gamoosh.'

'Utterly – what?' I said.

'Gamoosh. Quite the latest word. I'm surprised you haven't heard *that* before,' said David.

'I bet he made it up,' said Clarissa. 'It's the silliest word I ever heard.'

'What about numbers?' said Ann.

'Numbers of what?' said John.

'Just numbers, you idiot. For the competitors.'

'Oh, those. Help! It just shows what a lot there is to think about. We're sure to forget *something*. Numbers, of course. We can make those ourselves.'

'What out of?'

'Sheets of cardboard, of course, and Indian ink.'

'And what's all that going to cost?'

'Oh, help! More expense!' I groaned. 'We shall simply have to have some funds.'

'OK,' said John calmly. 'Uncle John arranges everything, and without fuss. We'll have a White Elephant sale.'

'Only we haven't got any white elephants to sell.'

'Funny, aren't you? White elephants are just things you don't want. You bring them along here, and somebody else wants them and buys them. *Compris*?'

'Great,' said David. 'I've a perfectly revolting tie that my aunt sent me for my birthday. I'll sell it to anybody for thirty pence.'

'And who do you think would buy your revolting tie? Be your age. They've got to be saleable things. Let's go and tell all the kids to ask their mothers for things to sell, and tell all their mothers to come to the sale, and we'll have it here, on the field, tomorrow afternoon.'

I had my doubts about this sale, as those of you who have read my previous books will remember that once Ann and I ran a sale and it was by no means a success. However, this one arranged by John was all right, and you should have seen what turned up!

There were books and cushions and evening shoes, and cardigans and blouses, and vases and milk jugs and photo frames, and dandy brushes that were only a bit worn, and in fact lots of stable equipment brought by the Cholly-Sawcutt girls that was so good we practically fought each other to buy it; and ties that weren't in the least revolting, only people's fathers didn't want them any more, and ashtrays, and garden plants, and tools and toys.

It was a magnificent sale, only John Watson strutted about with such an alone-I-did-it smirk on his face that we all wanted to murder him.

We raised eighty-five pounds, which was such a good start that we all knew we were going to have a smashing gymkhana, worthy of support by the equitation experts of the district.

The next thing was to go round asking people to give us prizes, which we felt was a bit thick on top of everything else, but the response was marvellous. We got string gloves, ties of a horsy nature, ties of a less horsy nature, two tie-pins with foxes' heads on them, stable brushes and rubbers, two large tins of saddle soap, six teaspoons in a velvet case, a lovely pair of stirrups – from Captain Cholly-Sawcutt, and I thought whatever else I didn't win I wanted to win those – and a small silver cup which was the *pièce de résistance*, presented by Miss Durdon for the senior jumping class.

'The stirrups had better be the first prize for the junior jumping,' said David Neville, who was fourteen.

A lot of us felt a bit dashed at this idea, which put the seniors out of the running. I wasn't the only one who wanted those stirrups, by a long shot. In the end we decided we'd have them for the first prize in the Gretna Green race, which gave both seniors and juniors a chance.

'That's not much good,' said Clarissa. 'Do the winning pair get one stirrup each?'

'Blow!' said Ann. 'It only wanted that.'

'I think the only fair thing,' said David, 'is to make them the first prize for the junior jumping. We ought to give a decent prize for that.'

We agreed that that was the fairest thing to do with the stirrups, and all the juniors at once began talking about what they'd do when they won them.

'They'll probably be won by some awful type who isn't even a member of the riding club,' said David.

We allocated the rest of the prizes, and then Miss Durdon announced that she would like to give a special riding prize for an event of her own invention.

'It will probably be for the one who has made the most progress,' she said, 'and the judges will decide. I shall be one myself.'

We all felt a bit overcome at this idea, as we already had for judges Mrs Darcy and Val Heath's father, which for a small gymkhana was quite enough, but after what Miss Durdon had done for us we had to let her be on the panel if she wanted to, and she obviously did.

11 Across country

It was absolutely tropical weather, and when I got home after making all those arrangements, I said I was worn to a shred.

Mummy said rather acidly, so was she – from hearing about nothing but horses from morning till night, and did it never occur to me that there were other worthwhile things in the world that I might and could do?

I said I quite agreed that there were other worthwhile things in the world, and for the people who cared about doing those other worthwhile things it was very nice that there were those things to do, but Mummy had said herself that it was better to do one thing properly than a lot of things in a mediocre manner, and therefore she ought to be glad that I was doing properly the thing that I considered most worthwhile instead of wasting time on doing a bit of this and a bit of that.

Mummy said, 'Really, Jill, you are the most hopeless person to argue with; you think you know all the answers, and what about the world of art, about which you haven't a clue?'

I said I was quite ready and willing to take an interest in the world of art, and Mummy produced a picture of a rather brownish nature which she had bought at a sale, and told me to hang it in my room and look at it often, which I did, though I must admit it never looked to me like anything but a woman in a dressing gown leaning on a pile of plates.

By now John Watson had bought the cardboard and

Indian ink, and he and one or two others came round to the cottage in the evening and we worked like mad, making the numbers.

I knew Mummy was dying to mention several ways in which we might be better employed, but she didn't say anything, and after about an hour of toil we looked up to see her appearing with a tray of orangeade, iced buns and chocolate biscuits, which made me want to hug her there and then.

'Gosh!' said John Watson. 'Isn't your mother super? Mine would probably have made some searing remark about, couldn't four healthy teenagers find something more useful to do on a fine summer evening?'

I didn't say anything, but I thought, it just shows.

The numbers looked marvellous, and not at all smeary, and we made holes and threaded the strings through. Then we had the first thrill of realising that this was our own gymkhana, when we could choose our own number, the one we liked best or thought was lucky for us. I chose fifteen because it is a number I always like the look of, and John chose seven which is supposed to be the luckiest number in the world, and Ann chose twenty-one, and Mercy Dulbottle, who, strange as it may seem, was the fourth member of our party, shut her eyes and drew a number and it was eleven, and she said it would do as well as any other as she hadn't the slightest chance of winning anything in any case.

John said that was the wrong attitude altogether, and it was known as a defeatist approach to life, and people with such an attitude shouldn't be in a riding club at all or enter for a gymkhana; and I said, 'Shut up, John,' because for one horrified moment I thought Mercy was going to weep. But she came round and said she hadn't meant it like that at all, and she knew that, thanks to Miss Durdon, she had a beautiful pony, and Miss Durdon herself had said that if Mercy would pull herself together and remember that she wasn't a human grasshopper but had hands and feet like any other rider, and would keep her head up and look as if she was enjoying herself, she might even get a few marks in the open horse-and-rider class.

At that moment there was a knock on the door. It was Stanley Trimble who had ridden over from the farm on his new pony, Peter, which I had helped him to buy. Stanley was now riding very well indeed, and I never saw so much improvement in anybody. This was partly because he was frightfully keen, and partly because he was the kind of person who never forgets a single thing he is told, so I never had to tell him twice.

Stanley said that the juniors had had a meeting, and had decided that for their competition they would like an obstacle race.

'Carry me out!' said Ann. 'You must enjoy getting hot.'

'We thought it would be fun,' said Stanley, 'and take a long time. I hate those games where it is all over in about two minutes. We're going to have a pile of coats and caps and shoes at one end of the course, and you have to sort out your own and put them on, and you have to crawl through a drainpipe and call your pony to you at the other end, and then you have to eat a dry bun, and blindfold yourself and ride in and out of some bottles and if you touch one you have to go back to the beginning.'

'And by the time you've all gone back to the beginning about ten times,' said Ann, 'that competition will have gone on for an hour and we'll all be bored stiff with watching you.'

'Oh, let the kids have their own fun their own way,' said John. 'Personally I can't think of anything worse, but they'll think they're getting something.'

'I hope we *are* getting something,' said Stanley cheekily, 'and I hope you're going to allocate some decent prizes for the junior events and not keep them all for yourselves, you big ones.'

'Well, what do you want?' said John, and Stanley said that he would like the first prize for the junior competition to be the box of stable equipment that Mrs Darcy had given.

'I suppose we'd better let them have it,' I said, 'though those lovely brushes and clippers would have been nice for the senior jumping.'

Meanwhile in spite of all the preparations for the gymkhana we had to keep up the ordinary activities of the riding club, so we planned a cross-country ride for the following Tuesday.

'And that's the last big event we'll be able to have,' I said, 'because the Saturday after that is Chatton Show and we'll all have to practise.'

Clarissa and Cecilia made rather a fuss when they discovered that the cross-country ride was to be just a ride, and did not involve water jumping and stone fences, but we managed to squash them by weight of numbers, and John pointed out that the younger ones had as much right to the fun as we had, and that people who wanted fancy prancing should enter for show events elsewhere.

'You needn't come if you don't want to,' I said, but Clarissa and Cecilia were too afraid of missing something not to come.

'That's settled then,' said John. 'Nothing like taking a firm line.'

'You'll be sorry,' said Clarissa darkly, 'if you take a pack of kids on a cross-country ride. However it's your funeral. I'm not in the least responsible.'

The day of the ride was lovely. Blue sky, rolling white clouds, and enough breeze to make it exhilarating.

Ann came to call for me, and we rode slowly to the field where we were going to meet the rest, so as not to lather the ponies. When we arrived, there were Clarissa and Cecilia mounted and looking very trim.

'Hello, Jill,' said my cousin. 'Not got your riding hat on? Bad example to the young ones. I was taught that you should always wear a hard hat.'

We started to round up the field, and found there were twenty-two of us, of whom eight were juniors; and then I realised what Clarissa had meant, because most of the mothers of the eight juniors had turned up too, and were making a great fuss about how far were we going, and was it dangerous, and Hilda mustn't attempt to jump any water, and we simply must not go on any road at all because Richard's pony couldn't bear the sight of even the family car.

'Why did they come at all?' I muttered angrily, and Clarissa overheard me and said, 'I told you so!'

John very patiently explained to all the mothers that we were going to ride across Neshbury Common, and through the pine woods, and along the edge of the Downs and back through the lanes, and it was all perfectly simple and straightforward, and anybody could drop out at any minute and go home if they wanted to; whereupon some of the mothers said they would go in the car and meet us halfway.

'You see?' said Clarissa, rolling her boiled gooseberry eyes at John. 'We haven't to go on the road, and we haven't to cross any water, or ride at any pace above a trot, and we're to be met halfway with smelling salts and bandages. What is this – a pram parade?'

Of course it wasn't really as bad as that. The juniors were all as keen as mustard, once they got out of their fond mothers' clutches, and we all went cantering across Neshbury Common in the sunshine.

'When we get to the main road, everybody halt,' I

called back. 'We've got to cross it to get to the woods. Pass the message back.'

John and Clarissa galloped on ahead to get to the road first and make sure that everybody *did* halt, and it was just as well, because you could see the cars simply sizzling along the tarmac.

Everybody came to a very ragged halt. Two ponies reared, one girl fell off, and Alec Manston's pony turned and bolted.

Alec yelled, 'Shan't be coming back. My pony won't cross the road, anyway. See you later.' And that was the last we saw of Alec that day.

John stepped into the road and held up his hand to the traffic, like a traffic cop. Several lorries and cars stopped, I suppose from sheer curiosity to see what was coming, and the riding club began to cross. Some of the cautious ones dismounted and led their ponies, and some of us just rode, trying to look nonchalant, which wasn't easy as one lorry driver was yelling, 'Tallyho, tallyho!' all the time, and a would-be funny man in a car shouted out, 'Which way to the Derby?'

'I think all people who don't ride and haven't any manners ought to be massacred,' said Diana, who was next to me, but I couldn't help giggling, it was so funny really.

Our one idea was to get the juniors across safely, and of course at the last minute Pam Derry's pony had to rear and stand on end, and a woman in a car began to shriek her head off, and Ann said to her sister, 'You little drip!' and Pam glared and got control of Buttons, and it was all over. We were on the other side.

'My gosh, what a good thing the fond mammas didn't see that bit!' I said.

We rode along a rough, winding track, skirting the woods, and as we passed a group of cottages some men who were doing their gardens straightened up to wave at us. Then we came to the top of the hill, and there was a magnificent view ahead of us. It made you feel you could ride on for ever.

'There are some lovely steep banks about here,' said John. 'Couldn't we stop a minute and try some Italian cavalry stunts? Now, you kids, you're not to do this.'

He then shortened his stirrups, sat forward, and proceeded to slither down the bank. It looked rather exciting and showy, so we all tried it, only I don't suppose we looked a bit like Italian cavalry; and when the juniors began to shriek, 'Oh, you mean things! Why can't we do it?' we thought we had better stop and get on with the ride, rather than face the fond mammas with a lot of unconscious Bods.

Diana then suggested that we should go out of our way a bit, because there was a ruined castle about two miles away where she had once been taken for a picnic, and it was great fun and we could pretend to be a troop of horse clattering over the drawbridge, except that there wasn't a drawbridge nowadays because the moat wasn't a moat but just a grassy ditch.

We thought this was a good idea and we set off in an organised string, with Diana leading as she was supposed to know the way; only we lost a bit of time because one of the juniors' ponies went lame with a stone in his hoof, and we had to get down and give the aforesaid junior a lesson on how to get the stone out without hurting the pony, which I must say Clarissa did very deftly and quickly. I daresay I could have done it as deftly and quickly myself, only I didn't get the chance, and honour where honour is due.

We found the castle and clattered in through the massive arch. All that was left was a ring of broken walls round a turfy ward. The ponies liked it, and began to crop.

'Wouldn't this make a smashing place for circus

practice?' said somebody. 'Let's ride them round like Liberty horses.'

So we did that, and one or two of the boys tried circus tricks, like jumping off and on again at the canter, and the kids were most impressed. But the ponies had soon had enough of this, so we left them cropping happily in the peaceful enclosure and began to explore the ruins.

We found a staircase leading up to what had been a room. There was still part of a fireplace there, and a big window embrasure with a stone seat all round.

'Oh, isn't it romantic?' said my cousin Cecilia. 'I can just picture the beautiful ladies in flowing martingales – '

'Farthingales, you dope,' said Clarissa.

'I mean those chiffon things they held their hats on with,' said Cecilia indignantly.

'Simples,' I said scornfully.

'Wimples, you drip,' said Clarissa. 'Simples are what they gave the knights when they had colic.'

'I think you're all perfectly sordid,' said Cecilia. 'I wonder what happened to the people who lived in this room?'

'Murdered, I should think,' said John. 'They made a speciality of it in those days. I say, wouldn't it be smashing to stay here and camp? We could make some sort of barrier across the gate to keep the ponies in, and we could build a fire in this hearth and cook sausages. Then we could pull some of the stones out and find buried treasure of ye olden tymes.'

'More like some mouldy old buried bones,' said David.

'Oh gosh!' yelled Ann. 'Have you looked at your watches? We're about an hour late, and all those parents will be waiting at the end of the woods and thinking we're dead.'

'To horse! To horse!' I yelled, and we all stampeded

towards the ponies. It was fun. We all leapt into the saddles and went charging out of the main gate with such a din as you never heard, and just outside there was a very sedate picnic party who must have arrived after we went in.

They were practically terrified to death, thinking the Middle Ages had come to life again or something, so of course some of us had to go back and apologise.

'We're frightfully sorry if we scared you,' I said. 'We didn't know anybody would be there. There was nobody about when we went in.'

The picnickers were quite ancient, about fifty years old I should think, but in spite of that they were quite intelligent and grasped the situation at once, and one of the men said, 'I'm only too glad to see a crowd of young people engaged in such a healthy pastime as riding their ponies to visit a ruined castle. It takes me back to my childhood. Do you happen to be a riding club?'

I said that was exactly what we were, and Ann with great presence of mind said, 'Would you like to come to our gymkhana? It's on Saturday week.'

They all said they'd like nothing better than to come, and wouldn't fail to be there, so we told them where it was and rode off after the others.

'Nothing like improving the shining hour,' said Ann.

I said, 'The shining what?' and she said, 'Well, it's Shakespeare, or something. It means killing two birds with one stone.'

By the time we caught the others up we were all terribly hot, and we proceeded to the woods at a walk that was practically a dawdle. We lolloped along the narrow track in single file, and gradually the shade of the pines closed in on us, and the ponies loved the feel of the soft turf under their feet, and there was a kind of mysterious feeling that is also adventurous; you know what it is like riding through pine woods.

We went a bit out of our way again so that we could splash through a shallow pond, because everybody knows how lovely it is to ride through water, but of course a kid called Hilda Marshall had to skid and slither off her pony slap into what was only about six inches of water. It is surprising how wet you can get in six inches of water. Hilda looked as if she had been in the Atlantic for a week.

'There!' said Diana. 'Look at her. . . And it was *her* mother who said we hadn't to jump any water.'

'I haven't been jumping any water,' said Hilda.

'Your mother will think you've been jumping the Thames,' said John.

Hilda half began to cry, and then stopped and said, 'Oh look! Some of the others are jumping gorse bushes!'

'Stop them!' I said to John. 'I don't care if they go home full of prickles, but *not* the ponies.'

'Whoops!' cried John, and raced after the others, flicking his riding stick at them and rounding them up.

'OOh!' yelled Hilda. 'Come quick, Gooseberry is sinking.'

'You dope!' I said. 'Why didn't you lead him out at once?'

There was poor Gooseberry, his eyes wild with fright, trying to heave himself the wrong way. John and I got hold of his head on either side, and began to work him back, and what with Gooseberry twisting and plunging and the slime popping and squelching we soon had as much water on us as Hilda, who merely stood on the bank and said, 'Oh dear, can't you get him out?'

With a final heave out came the pony, and John and I fairly got christened with a shower of muddy water. Then we all sat down on the bank to have a rest.

'Now you can get some grass, Hilda,' said John, 'and jolly well clean up your own disgusting pony.'

Hilda got a wisp of grass and transferred some of the green slime from Gooseberry to her own jodhpurs, and said, 'Blow! That's all I'm going to do. We're frightfully late. Mummy will be having a fit.'

So we collected the rest of the crowd and got back to the woods. It wasn't much cooler among the close-growing pines, and there were more flies than you would have imagined could exist in the whole of England.

I suppose I was riding along in a sort of trance. Anyway, I never even saw the branch that hit me. Suddenly everything began to whirl round, I let out one yell, and after that I don't remember anything much except a lot of confusion.

Somehow I wasn't riding through the pinewoods any more. I thought I was dreaming. I decided it was time I woke up. So I did, and I was in bed at home.

I said, 'Golly, what's the time?'

Mummy, who was standing by the window, said, 'So you're awake at last? There's not much the matter with you, only you knocked yourself right out. You should really look where you're going, and always wear a riding hat.'

I blinked, and said, 'Did I really take a toss? How did I get home?'

'Somebody's mother very kindly brought you in a car.'

'What day is it?' I said.

'Oh, it's still the same day,' said Mummy laughing. 'It happened about two hours ago. The doctor's coming to look at you again, and I expect he'll keep you in bed for a few days.'

Honestly, I felt as if I'd been sentenced to six months in the salt mines.

'But I can't!' I yelled. 'It's Chatton Show on Saturday, and I'm going to ride Mrs Darcy's Messmate in the Grade C jumping, and I want to do about three days' hard practice.'

Mummy shrugged her shoulders and said, 'I'm afraid it's just too bad,' and I lay there fretting and fuming. Was there ever such awful luck? The year before I was out of the Chatton Show because I sprained my wrist, and now once more Doom had overtaken me.

'I'm perfectly all right,' I grumbled. 'I'm going to get up.'

'Not till the doctor has seen you,' said Mummy in a voice that sounded like iron chains clanking together. 'By the way, there are about nine of your friends waiting outside to hear how you are. I'll tell them you're becoming quite yourself again.'

'Tell them I'm going mad,' I said gloomily. 'I shall, if I can't ride on Saturday.'

The doctor came about an hour later. I was sitting up eating an enormous supper of crab sandwiches, ice cream, chocolate cake and coffee. He tapped my back and head all over, and as there were no hideous grinding noises of broken bones he said, 'No harm done. Just a few days nice rest, young lady, and you'll be as good as new.'

I said miserably, 'A few more days nice rest and there'll be plenty of harm done, because I'll be biting people and smashing up the furniture,' and he said, 'What's the trouble?' and I told him about Chatton Show and the Grade C jumping.

'Tch! Tch!' he said. 'You horsy people! You're not made like ordinary human beings. I remember a woman I used to attend a few years ago. Dislocated collarbone and concussion on the Wednesday, and on the Saturday she was riding in a point-to-point and seemed all the better for it.'

'That's wonderful,' I said. 'That's all I wanted.'

'Oh dear,' he said. 'I shouldn't have said that. Whatever will your mother think? I'd better tell her you're to stay in bed a week, with your door locked.'

'Be a sport!' I said, grinning at him. 'I know I'll be OK, if I can only get up. I'm frightfully tough, honestly I am.'

He said, 'Let me see, when's the show? Saturday? And it's Tuesday now. You can get up on Thursday, and no riding before Friday, do you hear?'

'Friday? Oh, please make it Thursday,' I implored. 'I must have two days' practice.'

'*Friday*,' he repeated firmly. 'And one more squeak out of you and I'll lock your door myself and give your mother the key.'

Wednesday felt much like being in prison, and every moment seemed an hour; but in the afternoon Mrs Darcy came round and we talked about the show.

'You'll be quite all right,' she said. 'You can take it easy, because it will be Messmate's first big competition and I don't expect much from him. It's just the experience. He's a nice ride, and very sensible. Come round tomorrow, and even if you can't ride you can watch me put him round the practice jumps and get an idea how he goes.'

This brightened life for me considerably. The next morning, if Mummy had any ideas of me enjoying some more nice rest and breakfast in bed she was disappointed because I was up and dressed in shirt and jodhs before she was downstairs. I did this in case she stopped me.

By nine o'clock I was round at Mrs Darcy's, and found her lunging a pony.

She said, 'Back on your feet again? Good for you. Feeling a bit rocky?'

As a matter of fact I was, but I didn't want to admit it. She asked how many events I was entered for at Chatton

Show, and I said six. She said, what about cutting everything but the Grade C jumping, and I gave a yell of dismay and said, 'Oh help, it's not as bad as that!' I was particularly keen on the under-sixteen jumping and I didn't want to disappoint Rapide in this, so in the end we decided that I would do the two jumping competitions and cut out the other events. Fate seemed to have a down on me as regards Chatton Show so I thought I'd better be cautious, especially as I hadn't done the Grade C jumping before, but Messmate was a nice friendly bay gelding who knew me well and was very cooperative. Not a horse with a great deal of imagination or initiative, but most willing and quick to respond and a light, neat jumper.

I spent most of Friday morning round Mrs Darcy's jumps, and in the afternoon she let me bring Rapide and practise him too. By then I felt as if my legs were bending under me and I had quite a headache, but of course I kept quiet about these trifles.

12 Me – and Grade C

When I got home Ann was there. 'I say!' she said. 'You did take a toss. We all thought you'd get into the papers, but you didn't. Mummy was so unnerved by your accident that she went out and bought me three more riding hats, and in future I think she'll expect me to wear them one on top of the other. Have you got a huge bump?'

I told her that my bump had been practically as big as a tennis ball, but it was now fading away.

'I never heard what happened at the end of the ride,' I said, and she said that nothing much else had happened, the parents had all been waiting at the end of the woods, but what with me and my toss everything else had paled into insignificance.

Unfortunately we got a poor day for Chatton Show, one of those days when you don't know what the weather is going to do. By noon it had settled down to a messy drizzle. It meant wet macs and wet ponies, and we spent most of the waiting time eating Mars bars and trying to keep ourselves and our ponies reasonably tidy.

The grass of course was sopping wet and the takeoffs were greasy. In the under-sixteen jumping I was lucky enough to ride second, before the takeoffs were reduced to actual mud. Rapide was in very good form. As soon as I felt him increase speed of his own accord for the first jump, I knew he was going to have a decent round. This was important to me, as it was my first year in the senior event. I hadn't hoped to be in the first three, but at the same time didn't want to disgrace myself. To my delight I got off with four faults, which considering the state of the ground was little short of miraculous, only Rapide had always liked soft going.

As we rode out of the ring Rapide half turned his head to me and I saw he was giving me his smug smile which meant, 'There you are! You didn't think I'd be so good, did you?'

Nobody did a clear round. Two boys tied with two faults each and jumped off for first and second, and to my amazement I was placed third. I have never been so thrilled as I was to receive the yellow rosette.

In the other events our riding club members showed up well. John Watson won a senior showing class, Alec Manston a best pony class, David Neville won the junior jumping and another of our members was second, Val and Jackie Heath won the teams competition, and several other people got prizes in the competitions.

I must say when it was time for the Grade C jumping I had chunks of qualms. Cold shivers ran up and down my spine when we were called into the collecting ring.

'Go on with you!' said Mrs Darcy, slapping Messmate's slightly wet flank. 'Keep calm, Jill, this is nothing at all. I only want Messmate to get the show ring experience, and he's so sensible he won't play you up or run out or anything. He'll just go on jumping.'

'I don't want to let you down,' I mumbled.

'Don't be an idiot,' she laughed. 'Go on. You're riding seventh.'

I watched a young farmer called Knowles ride to the start at the far end of the ring. The first jump was a brush fence, then there was a stile, a wall, an in-and-out, a gate and a triple bar.

The rain had stopped by now and there was a drying wind. They had put down a lot of sawdust at the takeoffs, and Billy Knowles's horse loathed the sight of it. He refused at each of the first three jumps, and finally knocked the gate over and ran out of the ring. This wasn't a very encouraging sight for me. The next three competitors also had a bad time, and I thought, three refusals at the first jump is probably what I'll get, and that'll be the end of me.

Then a woman called Standish did a clear round.

'Help!' I said. 'She must be exceptional with the grass in this state.'

'It's what I expected,' said Mrs Darcy. 'She's particularly good, with years of experience, but she never enters a horse that she isn't sure of. It's silly, really. I mean, Grade C jumping is meant to bring on and encourage horses, and even if you've got a bit of a dud you ought to give him a chance by riding in a decent event. Messmate is far from a dud. He's going to enjoy himself and so are you.'

By the time my number was called I was thinking of something else, and had to be called twice. I could see the judge glowering at me and thought, well this isn't too good a start! However, to my delight Messmate took charge, and before I knew where I was we were cantering away to the first jump, and over he popped, so easily that I hardly noticed it.

I never knew such a horse for enjoying himself. By the time we were in and out of the in-and-out I began to enjoy myself too, and though we came to grief at the triple bar and collected six faults. I felt very pleased with the round as a whole.

'Jolly good,' said Mrs Darcy. 'You were both a bit overexcited by the time you got to that last jump, that was all that was the matter with you.'

Ann rode up and said, 'Gosh! I nearly thought you were going to do a clear round. The first five jumps were supersonic; Messmate had inches to spare. He's going to make a great jumper, Mrs Darcy.'

'Yes,' she said, 'he's surprised even me. I'll be riding him in the open jumping some day. And Jill handled him really well.'

'Fluke!' I said modestly. We all petted and flattered Messmate, and waited for the rest of the competitors to finish.

'You've got a chance,' Ann said. 'Apart from Mrs Standish nobody has got less than six faults.'

'You spoke too soon,' Mrs Darcy said, as a storm of clapping broke out. 'There goes Meg Wilson with only four faults.'

I was so sure by now that I was out of it that I didn't pay much attention, and before I knew it they were calling in the winners.

'Twenty-nine, eleven, and nineteen,' said Ann, and then shrieked, 'Nineteen! That's you, Jill.'

'What about it?' I said.

'They've called you in, you dope.'

I rode in, feeling like a dream, and found that another competitor had also got six faults and we had to ride it off over three jumps. He got a clear three, and I got two faults at the wall. It was entirely my own fault and not Messmate's, and I was furious with myself, because it is a failing of mine that if anything depends on a certain jump that's the one I muff. However, I was reserve, and got a certificate, and everybody was thrilled about it, particularly Mrs Darcy.

I said, 'I could kick myself. I had to go and put on pressure at the wall, and if I'd left it to the horse he'd have been over like a bird.'

Ann said, 'You've done jolly well, so now you can come and watch me make a mess of the bending race.'

'Don't be silly,' I said, 'you'll win it hands down. It's an art, the way you do a bending race, there's nobody in the county to touch you at it.'

Ann won her heat quite easily, and also the semifinals.

By the time the final came up the four ponies who were racing were all hot and excited, and there was some plunging and bucking. The judge, who was one of those impatient types, got annoyed and kept yelling No! Ann's pony thought he said Go, and off she went, only to be called back, while the judge was purple. However the four of them finally got off at a tremendous gallop and went down the line of poles like lightning, so fast in fact that at the turn one of them went straight on and was seen no more. Ann took the turn with an expertness which it was a joy to watch, and though the other girl was a neck ahead Ann caught up and there was an apparently dead heat finish.

'They're going to have some fun sorting that one out,' said John Watson who was watching with me. 'It's a real photo finish, and I doubt if they'll make them ride it off again.'

However they did, and in the midst of thunderous cheers Ann remained as cool as a cucumber and won by a head.

When she joined us she said, 'Honestly, I don't remember a thing about that race. I never rode so fast in my life. It was like being swept away by a whirlwind. Wasn't George marvellous?' she added, leading her pony away to rub him down.

Then we all went to watch the open jumping, which I need not describe as you have all seen open jumping so many times you know exactly what it is like. When you see such wonderful riding it makes you feel that you know nothing and are less than the dust.

I went home with two rosettes, a certificate, fifteen pounds, and a clothes brush with a leather back, which was so much more than I'd expected that I felt quite light-headed.

In the evening Mrs Darcy came round with a box of chocolates for me.

'Oh no,' I said. 'You shouldn't. It was enough of a treat to be able to ride Messmate in the competition.'

'Go on,' she said. 'You've earned it. You got more out of Messmate than anybody else could have done. By the way,' she went on, 'I hear good opinions on all sides about this riding club of yours. I think it's been a really good thing for the neighbourhood.'

I said I didn't know about that, and I had even had moments when I thought the riding club nothing but a menace, but certainly everybody had improved since they joined.

'The work you've put in is a credit to you,' she said.

'Oh gosh, no!' I said. 'Not me. Some of the others have worked as hard or harder. John and Diana and Val have given up loads of their time, and even so the whole thing would have been a flop if it hadn't been for Captain Cholly-Sawcutt and Mr Storm and Miss Durdon and Major Hooley taking an interest.'

Mrs Darcy said that was the beauty of riding, experts being so willing to help the young ones, and if they weren't willing they had no right to call themselves riders at all, and I said, How true.

Just then about five people from the riding club turned up, and we all had coffee and discussed the show, and said how good it was that our members had done so well because it would make people think that our gymkhana was going to be worth attending.

'And I jolly well hope it will be!' I added.

When Monday came we were all so up to the eyes in preparations for our own gymkhana the following Saturday that we had forgotten Chatton Show. The field became a scene of furious activity as everybody practised for their events. There was Miss Durdon looking very intense and simply bursting with energy as she schooled Mercy, for she was determined that Mercy should win *something*. In the end we had to stick in an extra class, just to please Miss Durdon. This was an open class and consisted of riding round the perimeter of the ring at a collected walk, and it was of course designed especially for Mercy to shine. Actually we couldn't think of anything duller to do, or deadlier to watch, but we had to give in to Miss Durdon. Unfortunately only eight people, including Mercy, entered for it, and the others were small juniors which was going to make poor Mercy look more like a grasshopper than ever.

'Look,' said Diana, 'we can't leave the poor dope like that. Let's be noble and enter for it. Come on, Jill – you and I and John will enter, that'll make it look better, and what about you, Clarissa? You're big. It won't kill you.'

'OK,' said Clarissa who was in an obliging mood. 'Cecilia can come in too. We'll all lollop round, and Mercy is sure to win, and we'll call it the Creeping Race.'

So we put it down on the schedule directly before tea, because we guessed by then that nobody would stop to watch it and we would get it over painlessly.

We were very pleased that the entries for all the events were pouring in, and everybody in the village seemed to be coming to watch. We were charging twenty-five pence for entrance, half-price for under-fourteen, and forty-five pence for teas and cakes, so we looked like making a lot of money after expenses were paid, and this we were of course going to give to animal charities.

I started having frightful dreams at night. One was that on the day the gymkhana field was all covered with snow; another was that Black Boy turned into a giraffe as I was riding him into the ring, another was that nobody came to the gymkhana and John Watson said we would have to eat fifty cakes each to get rid of them. I thought these dreams were rather unique, but when I told the others they said that they themselves had much more spectacular and appalling ones before which my own paled; in fact Diana Bush had dreamed that when we started to ride everything went into slow motion and got slower and slower until it stopped and there we all were glued to the ground, and John Watson said he had dreamed that Captain Cholly-Sawcutt turned into a black panther and ate all the ponies, only I didn't believe that one. I was sure he had made it up.

Then of course we were convinced it was going to pour with rain on the day. But it didn't. It was a very fair sort of day, not too hot, with some sun and some cloud and a nice breeze blowing from the north-west.

But I'm going too far ahead.

On the Thursday Clarissa Dandleby said, 'It's time we got these kids together and gave them a briefing about turning out decent on Saturday. We don't want any pink shirts and orange ties, and they might not even be *clean.*'

'That would be *lamentable!*' said Diana, copying Clarissa's voice.

Clarissa was mad, and said very snootily, 'Just for that you can lecture them yourself. I couldn't care less what they look like. I shall enjoy myself on Saturday and feel *no* responsibility at all.'

'Oh, don't be such a wet drip,' said John. 'I'll get the kids together and brief them. I think the best thing to do is to tell them that anybody who turns up on Saturday looking grubby, or with a dirty pony, just won't be allowed to ride.'

'I say! That's a bit drastic,' I said. 'It would quite likely be May Cholly-Sawcutt. You know what she is.'

'All the better,' said John. 'I'm sure it's what her father would wish.'

So we got everybody together and John laid down the law about clean people, clean clothes, and clean ponies and tack.

'And no pink shirts with orange ties,' finished Diana.

'Who on earth would come in a pink shirt with an orange tie?' said one of the juniors.

'I don't know,' said Diana innocently. 'It was Clarissa's idea.'

Clarissa glared, and it was all rather funny, because a rumour went round that Clarissa had intended to ride in a pink shirt with an orange tie and had been suppressed at the last minute, and practically everybody in the village got hold of this story, which took a lot of living down, as Clarissa found out later.

The night before the gymkhana we went up to Miss Durdon's, by invitation, to check over and allocate the prizes. She was as keen as mustard, and had added a few prizes off her own bat, which was very kind of her. In fact, we began to realise that we owed a lot to Miss Durdon and it was a good job we had let her be President of the Riding Club. So I thought it was up to me to express this in rather shaky words, which I did, and the others clapped. Miss Durdon snorted with pleasure, and in came Mercy pushing the trolley with coffee and chocolate eclairs, which was just the finishing touch.

'We've just been telling Miss Durdon that we think that everything she's done is pretty terrific,' said John.

'Oh dear, I do hope I'm going to win something tomorrow,' said Mercy despondently, 'but I'm quite sure I shan't and I shall be so humiliated.'

'Bosh!' said John. 'That's not the right attitude at all, is it, Miss Durdon? You ought to visualise yourself sailing over everything and carrying home all the prizes. That's called psychology.'

'I jolly well hope Mercy isn't going to be as psychological as all that,' said Ann. 'Some of the rest of us might like a few prizes.' Whereupon Miss Durdon told us a long and rambling story about how she had once won an open jumping competition in India just by visualising herself soaring over everything, and I began to wonder if there was anything in it, and if so, what a good thing everybody didn't try it.

'What about going down to the field to see what's happening there?' said John. So we all went down – including Miss Durdon and Mercy – and there was Mr Trimble and two or three other men, putting up the ropes for the ring and the forms for the spectators to sit on, and the tea marquee, and the smaller tent for the judges.

Mr Trimble said it was surprising to him how much interest our riding club gymkhana had aroused in the surrounding countryside, and everybody for miles around was going to be there, from what he'd heard.

I said, well in that case the few seats we'd got were going to be nothing at all; and he said, mark his words, they'd be standing ten deep.

Ann said she thought that was wildly exaggerated, as with all the superior horsy events that were being held everywhere in August, why should people bother about a potty little affair like ours that didn't mean much to anybody but us? And Mr Trimble said very darkly, 'You'll see.'

13 The big day

I have always been told you ought to get to bed early the night before a gymkhana, but it didn't happen to me this time, because somebody, I don't remember who, said at the last minute, 'Shouldn't we have some notices stuck about the roads saying *This way to the gymkhana*? The field isn't too easy to find.'

This threw us all into a flap. John said, 'People can ask, can't they?' and Ann said, 'They won't bother. If they can't find it they'll go home.'

We had some cardboard and Indian ink left over, so in the end we started doing some rather sploshy notices, *This way to the gymkhana*, and although it was practically dark by then we went out on bikes and nailed these up to trees at the corners of the lanes that led to the gymkhana field. Ann said, 'It's probably illegal, and the farmers will pull them down tomorrow morning and sue us for something-or-other;' however by then we were too tired to care, and the farmers didn't pull the notices down so perhaps it was worthwhile.

I got home at eleven p.m. and Mummy was waiting for me brandishing an axe, so to speak. She said she had been waiting for me for two hours, and she never heard of such a thing, and it was time I stopped all this riding club nonsense if this was what it led to, and so on. I said I was frightfully sorry, and explained about the notices at the last minute, and she calmed down, but the atmosphere wasn't sympathetic. I was starving too, so I went in the kitchen and ate everything that was lying about and made a jug of cocoa, and it was nearly midnight when I finally went upstairs and set my alarm clock for six a.m.

It seemed as if I had hardly got into bed before that alarm went off. I couldn't believe it was six o'clock, but it was. I felt very bleary-eyed and wobbly-kneed, and the chilly dawn didn't appeal to me at all. My spirits were at their lowest ebb – as it says in books – and I was sure the gymkhana was going to be a flop.

I put on a sweater and my jeans and looked out of the window. The eastern sky was brightening and there was a kind of shining mist over everything; the air smelt good. It was going to be a fine day, and whatever kind of a fool I made of myself it didn't matter, the gymkhana was going to be all right.

I flew downstairs and made a cup of tea and rushed out to the stable. I fed the ponies and left them with their feeds and buckets of water while I dashed round collecting the grooming tools and the soapflakes for their tails. Soon excitement seized me and I began to whistle. I worked like mad, and after about two hours the grooming was all finished and the ponies looked lovely. Black Boy looked like polished ebony, and Rapide gleamed in the sunlight and his tail was like an advertisement for somebody's shampoo.

I heard Mummy calling that breakfast was ready, and my heart went down with a honk of shame, because I really had intended to take her up a cup of tea but I just hadn't noticed how the time was going. Now I shouldn't get any credit at all for my good intentions. I went in and had porridge and bacon and egg, and I said I would make my own sandwiches to take with me for lunch. Although the gymkhana didn't begin till half past one, we were all going to be at the field early in the morning for last minute arrangements and to see that everything was OK.

I put on my jodhpurs that were just back from the cleaners, and a clean brown shirt, fawn tie, and black velvet cap. I polished my boots madly and hoped everybody else was doing the same. I pushed the polish and the rags into my saddlebag in case any of the younger ones hadn't bothered. In any case, we should all want a rub up before we rode. I knew I should forget something, and it turned out to be a clean handkerchief, but Mummy ran after me with one.

'Do get down early,' I said to her. 'I'll try and keep you a seat in a good place by putting my saddlebag on it, but you know what people are if there's a crowd.'

I wasn't by any means the first at the field. I suppose everybody else was excited too and wanted to be at the scene of action. Mr Trimble was still working away, making everything trim.

'Gosh, do you suppose he's been here all night?' said Ann. 'It nearly looks like it. After all he's done, I can't help hoping that Stanley wins a prize of some sort.'

As the members of the riding club appeared we checked them off to see they were clean and dressed properly, and that their ponies were OK. Then we tethered all the ponies in a row under the trees at the far side of the field. The whole set-up looked quite professional, and I was delighted; the ring and the seats, the tea tent and the judges' tent, and away at one side the beautiful freshly painted jumps.

'I've got the final list of entries,' said John Watson, coming up. 'Lots of people I never heard of.'

'Help!' said Val Heath, reading over his shoulder. 'Half those people do nothing but go round riding in all the gymkhanas, and winning everything. We'll be lucky if we stand a chance at all.'

'Never mind,' said Diana ironically. 'We'll get a nice ride.'

Just then Clarissa and my cousin Cecilia appeared.

They looked terrific. Both were attired as though to ride with the Queen, in black coats, cream cord breeches, and brilliantly polished boots that made your eyes ache to look at them. They both had powder and lipstick on and looked hard and experienced and about twenty-one.

'Crumbs!' said John. 'Are you women looking for the Royal enclosure?'

'I say, Cecilia!' I said. 'You look just like a film star. Even if none of us wins anything you'll give tone to the party.'

'If I were you,' said Ann, 'I'd get those saddles off and the ponies parked under the trees or they'll be in a worse sweat than ever when it's time to ride.'

They cantered away, and John said, 'We ought to have those two at the gate to lure people in. They'd certainly make it look like a supersonic gymkhana.'

At last we were satisfied that everything was ready, and while we were gobbling up our sandwiches a lot of spectators began to arrive and find seats, and the non-riding club entries began to pour in, all looking frightfully superior and riding the most competent-looking ponies I ever saw.

'Oh, why did we start this?' I said to Ann. 'Shan't we look small if nobody in the riding club wins anything? It could easily happen.'

Ann just shrugged her shoulders and said, 'Kismet, it is the will of Allah.'

At last everything was ready, the seats were packed and people were standing up all round. The judges were in their tent, and had been joined by Miss Durdon who was a self-appointed judge, but nobody could very well tell her not to be. The first class, the under-tens showing class, was ready to go into the ring, surrounded by anxious mothers and cool-looking nannies telling them how sweet they looked. Then they rode in, led by a very fat little boy on a Shetland. Behind him was Pam Derry.

'Oh, for goodness' sake, look at Pam,' said Ann crossly. 'She's gazing round and grinning at everybody she knows. She's got simply no ring technique at all, and I told her fifty times to look straight between her pony's ears and remember where she is. She'll be disqualified in a minute and I'll die of shame.'

There were several very dressed-up children holding their ponies on much too tight a rein, and one or two small ones who just sat on their ponies in a dazed sort of way and couldn't be said to be riding at all. The one I liked best, hoping I wasn't prejudiced, was a child called Paul Carris who belonged to the riding club. He was only eight and just about our youngest member, and he really rode very nicely, letting his pony walk out and then collecting him as he had been taught. When told to trot he was one of the few who did so. Some of them merely went on walking, some turned round and tried to go the other way, throwing the rest into wild confusion, one child burst into tears and fled to its nannie, and others' ponies began to crop grass. The judges looked a bit nonplussed, and Mrs Darcy said loudly, 'Walk! Walk!'

Nobody took much notice, so I suppose the judges thought the best thing was to start calling in.

Paul Carris was called in first, then a rather haughty-looking little girl I didn't know, who did everything correctly in a very dollish way, and third was Pam Derry who had at last come to her senses and showed a bit of control over her pony. The rest found their own places, except for those who had already given up and gone out of the ring.

The judges examined the ponies, and Pam behaved very smartly, so that the judges went into a huddle and you could tell they were considering whether to put her in second place; however they didn't, and simply doled out the rosettes, red for Paul, blue for the doll-girl, and yellow for Pam.

I was so thrilled at this good beginning, with two prizes for the riding club already, that I shrieked out Hurrah, and Clarissa who was passing said 'What manners!'

Ann said gloomily, 'We'll never hear the end of this from Pam, and quite honestly she was only the best of a bad bunch.'

'Never mind,' I said. 'It's two rosettes for the riding club and we mightn't have got any.'

The next event was the under-tens musical chairs – or sacks – and this was fun to watch. Most of the children behaved quite well, until seven or eight were left in and then they got overexcited and began to snatch sacks away from people who had claimed them. One girl rushed out weeping and the judges sent a boy off the field. Finally there were four very tough-looking small boys left in, none of them members of the riding club, and they fought out the finish rather murderously. Several mothers who were standing near me began to say it wasn't fair, and I thought it was a good thing when that particular event was over.

The under-fourteen showing class came next, and I was very anxious about this because half the entries were riding club members, and I felt it was important that we should make a good show here.

'I say, it'll look grim if we don't win anything here,' said John Watson coming up to me. 'It'll look as if we hadn't taught them anything. There's a lot of opposition,' he went on, as the class began to ride into the ring. 'That kid at the front, I don't know who she is, but she looks pretty good.'

She was a very pale, neat girl on a blood pony, and she rode with terrifying technique and efficiency and looked as if she spent her whole life doing this kind of thing at gymkhanas. Behind her came Hilda Marshall, one of our members, forgetting everything she had been taught, sitting too far back and sticking her legs out, and I gave a faint moan. David Neville came next, looking cool but a bit too self-conscious; and then a very smart boy on a pony that was much too big for him. He gave his pony one or two whacks as he rode and some mammas who were standing near said, 'That's a marvellous little rider, just look at him.'

'Our members look much too stiff,' said Ann. 'I hope the judges won't think we taught them to ride like that.'

'Oh, they don't look too bad,' said John, 'they'll relax in a minute. Look at this bunch meandering round – I'm glad they're not our members.'

It was a very big class, with thirty-five entries, but you could see that about twenty of them weren't much good. Among these were some of our own members who through nerves or carelessness weren't doing themselves justice.

'Oh, look at June Cholly-Sawcutt!' said Diana. 'She's crowding the pony in front – she's passing – why will she do these awful things? She'll be disqualified in a minute.'

'Yes, but May is riding quite nicely for once,' I said. 'And she's gone into her canter just like I told her! Good for May!'

The canter was quite a test and weeded out the riders. One or two came off, one pony ran out, and the very smart boy was told off for using his stick. I counted five people on the wrong leg, and one hanging on to his pony's mane.

When the judge began to call in I was so anxious I shut my eyes.

'Tell me,' I said to Ann. 'I can't bear it.'

'You'll pass right out when I tell you,' said Ann. 'May Cholly-Sawcutt is in second place. The first and third are strangers. David Neville is fourth and Stanley Trimble fifth.'

I opened my eyes, and she was telling the truth.

I held my breath when May was told to lead her pony out, but she did it correctly. The test was the usual figure of eight. As if by magic May remembered to do it slowly and to change legs properly. David Neville's pony was a bit nappy and he didn't collect well. Stanley Trimble looked stiff and was frightfully pale, but his pony Peter behaved like an old hand. They all dismounted and took off their saddles while the judges examined the ponies.

'Oh, I hope May's is clean!' I breathed. But it must have been, because the judges made no alteration in the order except to change David and Stanley, so that Stanley was fourth and got the white rosette. While the prizewinners were cantering round the ring we all clapped and cheered like mad. I was better pleased than if I'd won a prize myself. May Cholly-Sawcutt simply lost her head and galloped madly, waving her rosette above her head and yelling, 'I've got a prize, I've got a prize. Daddy! Daddy, look at me, I've got a prize!'

Yes, Captain Cholly-Sawcutt himself was there, and believe me he was nearly weeping. If you can imagine a member of the British Show-Jumping team being all of a dither at a kids' gymkhana, this was it. He came up to me and said in a dazed sort of way, 'My daughter's got a prize. A second prize in a showing class. My hopeless, ham-handed daughter! I've never been so excited in my life. And look how badly she's behaving now, she'll cover me with shame.'

'She was jolly good,' I said. 'I knew one of the girls would do well some day.'

'I'll buy her as many ices as she wants,' he said. 'She can have fifteen if she wants them. I don't care if she bursts now. This is the greatest day of my life, including the day we won the European Championship.'

The next minute my hand was seized and wrung until I yelled. It was Mr Trimble. He was so choking with pride over Stanley's reserve that he couldn't speak at all. It was rather funny, all these proud fathers, but it did speak well for the riding club.

The next event was the under-fourteen obstacle race which was run off in heats. It was the hottest thing I ever saw in my life. The juniors had organised it themselves and had put in everything they could think of. They had to ride to a pile of clothes and shoes and sort out their own and put them on, they had to crawl through drainpipes, ride sitting backwards in the saddle, eat a dry bun, whistle a tune, and finish up by riding blindfold without knocking down bottles. It went on for ages, but the juniors didn't seem to care though most of them looked as if they were going to burst into flames. The whole thing was won by Stanley Trimble – Mr Trimble was by now roaring his head off with excitement – second was a stranger, and third a girl called Poppy French, who didn't belong to the riding club.

The next thing was Miss Durdon's special prize, the parade round the ring at a collected walk, to give Mercy a chance to win something. Only twelve people had bothered to enter for this, and they were all members of the riding club. It was the one that Clarissa had called the Creeping Race, and she and Cecilia, John, Diana and I were all in it, so as not to make it too tame and hurt Miss Durdon's feelings. Mercy's pony was so beautiful that the judges didn't look any further. He arched his neck and his lovely tail blew in the breeze. Mercy was neat and well turned out, and she sat up straight and kept her hands down, and the collected walk was just her cup of tea. She won it, of course, but after it was over she came up to me and began to weep.

She said, 'It was beastly. It looked as if I was showing off, just to get a prize. I wish I hadn't entered for it.'

'Don't be silly, Mercy,' I said. 'You were much the best and you deserved the prize.'

'Do you really think I did?' she said, brightening up.

'Yes, you did. You earned it. You don't think judges like Mrs Darcy and Mr Heath would have let you have it just to please Miss Durdon if you didn't deserve it?'

That satisfied her, and we were all quite pleased she had got a prize, because she was an awfully decent sort really and very well-meaning, if dim.

By now, of course, all the spectators were thinking of nothing but refreshments, and flocking to the tea tent where Mrs Watson was presiding over a long table simply piled up with home-made cakes and buns and biscuits. We all followed, and it was a thoroughly happy jam. People kept coming and telling me they thought the gymkhana was a jolly good show; Captain Cholly-Sawcutt was still rambling on about May being second in the showing class (which naturally he couldn't get over; neither could anybody else) and May was there actually wearing her rosette *in her hair*. Clarissa Dandleby was glaring at her and muttering, What frightfully bad form, but May couldn't care less. Stanley Trimble's father and mother were holding a kind of reception in one corner, with Stanley very and embarrassed blushing between them, and looking at John Watson as if to say, Do come and rescue me; but John just grinned and walked away to where the ices were being sold.

Ann and I worked our way at last to the counter and bought cakes, lemonade, and ice cream; then we fought our way out and sat under the trees near the ponies.

'It's jolly good,' I said. 'Better than I hoped. The

riding club has already got two prizes in the under-ten showing class, two in the under-fourteen, as well as Stanley's obstacle race and Mercy's creeping race prize. I'm awfully glad Paul Carris won the under-tens, he's such a nice kid.'

Ann began to giggle, and said that there was something funny about Stanley Trimble and May Cholly-Sawcutt and Mercy Dulbottle being the ones to cover the riding club with glory in the early events, the very last people you'd have thought of, and she hoped it wasn't an omen.

I said, 'An omen of what?' And Ann said, 'It would look frightful if nothing went as we expected the whole afternoon and we made a flop in the major events like the jumping.'

'You would think of that,' I said. 'Don't put me off.'

'You've simply got to win the senior jumping, Jill,' she said, and I said, 'Don't be silly. How could I when there'll be at least nine other people much better than me?'

Ann said she hoped that if I didn't win it John Watson would, and she could bear even Clarissa to win it rather than somebody who didn't belong to the riding club.

14   The last parade

The jumps were all put up, and the junior entry was riding into the ring to inspect them, twenty-seven entries in all, fifteen of them members of the riding club.

We were standing by the rails looking at them with anxious critical eyes.

'Our main hopes,' said John, 'are David Neville and Alec Manston. I don't think the rest of our bunch stand much chance against outside opposition. There are some kids there who've won jumping competitions for miles around.'

'It all depends on David's timing,' I said. 'Some days he times quite brilliantly and other days he's hopeless, and the worst of it is that on the days when he knows he isn't timing well he won't leave it to his pony, but presses. He isn't awfully reliable.'

'I've just given him a good briefing,' said John, 'but I thought he was a bit too cocksure. Alec looks steady enough, but I'm afraid he's nervous. He hasn't had an awful lot of show experience, and though he jumps very well at practice it's a different thing in the ring with masses of people watching you.'

As Alec led his pony round the jump which was nearest to us he smiled at us and we said, 'Good luck, Alec!' John said, 'Let her go, boy, and don't tighten up.'

The first competitor into the ring was a farmer's daughter called Betty Prince who seemed to spend her whole life riding at pony shows. Wherever you went you saw Betty and her pony Blue Ticket. Blue Ticket had been an expensive pony and was a born jumper, and though Betty was rather an uninspired type of rider she had the sense to do everything correctly and leave the rest to her pony. Also, she never seemed to have any nerves.

Betty jumped a clear round without any apparent difficulty and rode out amid clapping.

'Well, that sets the standard!' said John with a whistle.

The next competitor was a stranger to us, a boy on a grey pony that was too big for him. He took the first three jumps much too fast, crashed the fourth, and ran out. Then came a small girl called Lassie Perritt, who went round so slowly that we thought every minute she would be disqualified. I suppose she just got round in the allotted time, but she had fourteen faults.

The next three riders we were interested in, because they were our own members, but alas, they didn't do very well, getting six to eight faults each. Then came a very competent and experienced boy who was just on the verge of being out of the junior class and had won a lot of prizes. He got a clear round.

'David and Alec have got to be awfully good!' groaned John. 'Oh, here comes David.'

It appeared to be one of David's good days; he took the first two jumps beautifully.

'Legs! Legs!' breathed John as David flashed by us. 'Oh, he's too fast – too fast – he's going to lose his head – there you are!'

David had just collected four faults at the wall.

This seemed to sober him down, and he pulled himself together and finished the course without any more faults.

'He *was* a fool,' said John bitterly. 'He needn't have crashed the wall.'

The next two competitors both had refusals; then there were several indifferent rounds. Alec, who was one of our hopes, proved to be simply awful. It was painful to watch him when we knew he could have jumped the course with his eyes shut if he'd only kept his head. He was horribly nervous and of course that made his pony nervous too. He got fourteen faults and rode off with his head down.

'There's still Hilda Marshall of ours,' said Ann cheerfully. 'You never know.'

'Hilda Marshall!' said John ironically. However to our surprise Hilda rode in as cool as a cucumber on Pretty Pete, her neat pigtails hardly swinging, and popped round the course as she had never popped round it during practices. She only collected two faults.

'Gosh!' I said. 'She might even be third. Wonders never cease.'

'She could easily be third,' said Ann excitedly. 'All the funny people are winning everything today.'

However, there was another clear round by an outsider, and then somebody else besides Hilda got two faults.

The three clear round people jumped it off, and Betty Prince won. That settled the first, second, and third. Hilda and the other girl who had got two faults then jumped it off for fourth place, but Hilda's luck didn't hold and the other girl was much more experienced. Hilda got six faults over the three selected jumps and the other girl only two.

'So that's the junior jumping!' I said. 'Not one of our members in the first four. Isn't it murder!'

We all said, 'Bad luck, jolly well tried,' to Hilda as she came off. The jumps were raised for the seniors.

'Isn't it grim?' I said to Ann. 'I've got the needle much worse than I ever had it at Chatton Show.'

'Oh, don't let's think about those wretched juniors,'

said Ann. 'It was just bad luck on the riding club, because both David and Alec could have done clear rounds if they'd been more careful. Let's ride as if we couldn't care less.'

'I'd love to be in the first three myself,' I said, 'but honestly, in my present frame of mind I don't care who wins so long as it's a member of the riding club.'

'Well, we've got a terrific chance,' said Ann. 'I mean, look at John – and Val – and Diana – and even Clarissa, quite apart from you and me. There's only really Helen Batterby and Judy Trowt and Peter Wishart to beat, and they've all been beaten by our crowd before. Come on. Up the Riding Club!'

I suddenly felt frightfully cheerful and contented. It was pretty hopeful that at least *one* of us would be in the first three.

I rode Rapide round the jumps and he looked confident and felt very steady. He was always a very reassuring pony to ride, because he showed me clearly what he was feeling and I could understand him.

Clarissa Dandleby rode first. Some people hated riding first, but Clarissa said she didn't care. She held her pony back so tightly that his canter between the jumps wasn't much more than a collected walk, and jumped from what was practically a standstill in a very correct and uninspired way. I could see the judges frowning, but Clarissa only got two faults and rode out in a very businesslike way.

The next competitor, not one of us, got three refusals at the first fence; then Judy Trowt rode and had awfully bad luck as her pony shied at something in the crowd, reared and put her down. The next few competitors got about four or six faults each. My cousin Cecilia was warned by the judge for whacking her pony and this annoyed her so much that she let herself be put off, and got eight faults.

John Watson did a beautiful clear round; so did Val Heath. I felt I didn't care now, as it was fairly certain that unless there were an awful lot more clear rounds we should have one or more of our members in the first three.

Ann was unlucky and got six faults. Peter Wishart – one of those I feared – got a clear round. Diana Bush, one of our best, for some unknown reason got three refusals at the last jump, the triple bar, and went out looking very disappointed. Helen Batterby, who told us before she started that she had a strained leg and was disobeying the doctor and her parents in coming at all, had to retire at the third jump.

As I rode into the ring I summed up the situation. There were already three clear rounds, John Watson, Val Heath, and Peter Wishart. There might still be another or two from non-riding club members. A lot depended on me still. As I gathered Rapide for the first jump the light but firm pressure of my hands told him that this round was frightfully important, and a slight quiver of his satiny shoulder told me that he understood.

He took the brush fence so neatly that I hardly realised we were over, and without checking went competently over the next three. I helped him with the next one, the wall, for I knew it was his least-liked jump, and he obeyed beautifully. I had an instant of heart failure at the gate, for I thought he had taken off a fraction too soon, but it was all right. Now for the triple bar. He was cooler than I, as if to say, it's OK this time.

Over we went, and I had never been so thrilled in my life as when I was riding out and patting Rapide while the spectators clapped our clear round.

'Jolly good!' said Ann. 'Oh, terrifically good!' John Watson and Val also thumped me on the back, and we three stood waiting to see if there would be any more clear rounds. If not, it meant that the riding club would get three of the four prizes. But there *were* two more clear rounds, one of them by a very smart boy on a blood pony, and the other by – of all people on earth – April Cholly-Sawcutt!

We just couldn't believe it. Nobody could. We were stunned. April came out of the ring shrieking at the top of her voice that she had never jumped a clear round before in her life and she had simply kept her eyes shut all the time. Her father was standing there looking very pale and saying, 'Hold me up, somebody. It isn't true.' And the rest of us were thumping April on the back until she yelled for mercy.

'Six clear rounds!' said John. 'Six to jump off, four of ours and two outsiders. April, you were terrific. Now you've got to shut your eyes, go into a trance, and do it again.'

'I can't, I can't,' wailed April. 'I shall crash every-thing, like I always do.'

'If you get into the last four,' said her father, 'I'll buy you the finest racing bike in Rychester, I swear I will.' I had never seen him so excited, in spite of his own great international successes. I knew it had been his life's greatest trial that his daughters were such utterly dud riders, and now to have two of them shine like stars on one day was too much joy.

At last the judges announced, 'The six competitors who jumped clear rounds will now jump again. First, number twenty-three.'

This was Peter Wishart. The three selected jumps were the wall, the gate, and the triple. Peter's pony took the wall and the gate in a rather too dashing way, and then steadied for the triple.

'Oh, I hope he brings it down!' breathed Ann, and John said, 'Don't be so beastly unsporting,' though I'm sure he felt the same as Ann.

The triple had been widened, and it was unlucky for Peter that he was riding first, for he took off too far away, jumped short, and brought down the farthest bar. The crowd groaned, and we were all sporting enough to call out, 'Bad luck!' instead of 'Hurrah!' Peter had four faults.

'You next, John,' I breathed, as his number was called. I knew in my heart that John was going to be all right because his pony looked so confident and was obviously dying to do the jumps again. To see her whisk over the wall and the gate was lovely, and she came up to the triple as if it was the easiest thing in the world. John went over like a bird, and the crowd clapped and cheered like mad.

Val rode next and got two faults by hitting the gate with her pony's forelegs. Then the smart boy, whose name was Barry Noble, went in and had awfully bad luck because his pony was overheated and refused to jump at all.

'It's really his own fault,' said John. 'I noticed that he was too lazy to unsaddle and rest his pony while he was waiting and now he has to pay for it.'

Next it was April's turn. None of us could bear to look. We expected nearly anything to happen. If April had stood on her head in the saddle I don't think anybody would have been surprised. But it certainly was her day. I saw her take the first jump with her eyes tightly shut. At the wall she got two faults, looked back, and yelled 'Murder!' at the top of her voice. Then off she went for the triple like a steam engine and we all covered our ears not to hear the crash.

There was no crash, only the sweet landing of hoofs on turf, and the next minute there was April riding off, grinning all over her face.

'Only two faults,' she said. 'You thought I couldn't do it. Shucks to you!'

I will not go into details, but will only say that I did the three jumps with no faults. So there were John and I with no faults and Val and April with two each. The judge asked us what we would like to do.

We went into a huddle together, and then announced that we thought the ponies had had enough, and we had agreed to divide the first prize between John and me and the third between Val and April. John and I each got a red rosette and Val and April a yellow one. It was beyond our wildest dreams that the riding club should have won all four places in the senior jumping, and when we rode round the ring with our rosettes the cheering could be heard for miles away, led by Captain Cholly-Sawcutt. April was in tears by now, she was so thrilled, and she finished up by falling off her pony and sitting on the ground with her legs stuck out in front of her, roaring her head off.

Even Clarissa came up to me and said very decently, 'Congratulations, Jill. Nobody can say now that the riding club isn't the tops. And I heard Captain Cholly-Sawcutt telling your mother that anything less than a horsy career for you would be a crime.'

I was so pleased I said, 'Oh thanks, Clarissa. And it was jolly hard luck that you didn't get a clear round, because you deserved to.'

By now the jumps were being cleared away, and it was the Gretna Green Race. The seniors' names were put into one tin and the juniors into another. We all prayed we should get a nice lightweight 'bride', but of course I had to go and draw Stanley Trimble who was as big as I was! Ann was worse off still as she drew a very solid little girl called Meg North, who looked as if it would take a crane to get her off the ground. Peter Wishart was the luckiest as he drew Pam Derry who was very small and light, and Clarissa said, 'Just my luck! I did hope I'd win *something*, and this was my last chance, and I've got June Cholly-Sawcutt who weighs a ton.'

We all mounted and went thundering down the course at a mad gallop to where the 'brides' were waiting. Peter Wishart was miles ahead, it looked as if he only had to sweep little Pam up and be home long before anybody else.

As I struggled to heave Stanley up behind me on Black Boy I saw Ann and Meg North flat on the ground, and just beyond them was Peter looking wildly at Pam. He had swung down impatiently and lost his reins, and his pony, thinking this was part of the game, had cantered away. I hadn't time to see what happened next, Stanley was up behind me and I was trying to convince Black Boy that he enjoyed the double load.

To my surprise I saw Clarissa, cool and unbothered, with fat little June already clasping her waist and the pony behaving beautifully. They were off, and about a dozen of us pounding after. One or two of the 'brides' were practically upside down and clutching on fiercely. Val Heath was in the lead but she didn't keep it for long; Peter Wishart had recaptured his pony, whisked Pam up, and was off in hot pursuit.

But now it looked as if Clarissa was in front. A crowd of us crossed the winning line in a bunch, and as we pulled up the 'brides' flew off in all directions.

Clarissa, in spite of the weight, had won, and Peter Wishart in a furious gallop had come in second. Amid clapping the rosettes were given out.

I thumped Clarissa on the back and said, 'You were terrific, and I hope you get a jolly good prize for that effort.'

With surprising modesty she said that she had under-rated June, who instead of being a dead loss had kicked Havelock in the right spot at the right moment and so shot home.

We thought everything was now over and that the ponies and we ourselves would have time to cool down before the prizes were given, but Cecilia came up and said, 'What do you think? This will slay you. Miss Durdon says that all the members of the riding club have to tidy up quickly and do a grand march past.'

'Oh no!' I gasped.

'That's what she says.'

Hurriedly we rubbed the ponies down and tried to make ourselves look presentable, which wasn't easy. I tidied Ann's hair and she tidied mine, as we hadn't a mirror, and we straightened each other's ties, and that was about all we could do.

Miss Durdon, resplendent in hunting kit, was waiting. She had even got a rose in her buttonhole. We all lined up behind her, the younger ones in front and we big ones at the back, and slowly rode round the ring, blushing madly when people cheered. I caught the eye of Major Hooley who was muttering something about, 'Legs! Legs!' Then he turned to the man next to him and talked very earnestly. Doubtless telling what a time he had had with us.

It suddenly occurred to me that people had something to clap about. The riding club was riding very well indeed, with straight backs, hands down, knees up, and cool but conscious pride on their faces. They looked good. They looked wonderful. They really were something to shout about and I felt frightfully happy.

Behind Miss Durdon we went twice round the ring. Then she dismissed the parade and disappeared into the judges' tent, only to emerge about five minutes later to present the prizes. She was completely transformed, having somehow managed to get out of her riding clothes and into a very fashionable rigout of pink, with beads and a floppy hat, and gloves.

The numerous and smashing prizes took every eye. John Watson and I had to share the silver cup for the senior jumping, so we decided to have it for six months each in turn, and he very sportingly insisted that I should have it first which gave me the privilege of carrying it off the field. The silver stirrups we had so much admired went to Betty Prince, who wasn't in the riding club, but she deserved them.

Stanley Trimble won Mrs Darcy's box of stable equipment and nearly forgot himself so far as to whoop for joy, but managed to turn it into a cough. All the other winners got useful things like ties and brushes and boxes of chocolates, and Mercy got a martingale as Miss Durdon's special prize and didn't know what it was for! She stood looking at it in a helpless kind of way, and said to John Watson, 'Which end of the pony does it go on?'

The three Cholly-Sawcutt girls all got prizes, which nearly rendered their father unconscious. One felt it was the sort of thing that could never happen again in the history of the world. June got a box of chocolates for being the winning 'bride', and within one minute had the lid off and was passing them round the judges! This wasn't conventional, but everybody was rather pleased and thought it quite a gesture for June.

Then Major Hooley worked his way to the front and made a speech which I couldn't hear, and somebody called for three cheers for the judges. After that Miss Durdon called for three cheers for everybody who had worked so hard to make the gymkhana a success, and we realised it was all over.

Major Hooley came up to me and solemnly shook hands, saying, 'I didn't think you people had it in you but I was mistaken. I congratulate you on what you've achieved.' Which I thought was very nice of him.

Some of us stayed behind to help to clear up.

'I must say, I think this gymkhana has been the most fun of anything I've been to this summer,' said Ann.

'I think the riding club has been the best fun of anything I've ever done,' said David Neville.

'I seem to have learnt a lot from it,' said Val Heath.

Stanley Trimble said he really didn't see how the seniors could have learnt anything as they had been teaching the juniors all the time.

'I expect what we've learnt is how to teach,' I said. 'That's a good thing.'

'And how not to be cocksure about ourselves,' said John Watson.

'And how to share things with the younger ones and not think we were the tops all the time,' said Ann.

'Well, that's the whole point of a riding club,' I said. 'We shan't know till tomorrow how much money the gymkhana has made, but it must be a lot, and we hadn't a great many expenses so the animal charities will do well.'

'At least,' said John Watson, 'our parents won't be able to say, "It'll be a good thing when you go back to school, you never find anything useful to do in the holidays."'

'On the contrary,' said Clarissa, 'they ought to give us a pat on the back.'

We finished clearing away and the rays of the sinking sun turned the grass to gold while long shadows of trees crept over the lane.

'So the sordid shadows of school fall on the riding club,' I said poetically. 'But it was awfully good while it lasted.'

Challenges for Jill

Ruby Ferguson

Hodder
Children's
Books

a division of Hodder Headline plc

Contents

1 Just the job!

'Cast your gorgeous orbs on that,' exclaimed my friend Ann Derry, slapping a folded newspaper down in front of me and pointing to a small ad which she had outlined in red pencil. 'Isn't it the tops? Just what we want.'

With my long and disillusioning experience I did not at once burst into cheers. I had come to take a poor view of what other people thought was the tops.

I don't know if you have noticed, but other people's idea of bliss is seldom yours. I once went to stay with my cousin Cecilia (a square if ever there was one) and after whipping up my excitement about a smashing day out, I discovered that her idea of heaven was walking round an art gallery looking at some pictures of women made out of cubes with two eyes on the same side, followed by China tea and toast at a gruesome café called Ye Olde Cathedral Tea Shoppe.

I am not one to bear every wrong with patience, as the hymn says, so I complained loudly, and Cecilia said, 'Well, what *do* you like?'

I said, 'What about packing up a picnic hamper and inducing your mother to run us in the car to the nearest beach, and then do a spot of rock climbing?' and she said, 'That suits me.'

Once again I was to be disillusioned.

Cecilia's idea of a picnic was a glossy hamper full of gleaming cups and plates and knives and spoons, and glass dishes to fill with dainty sandwiches, etc.

It took us over an hour to make the dainty sandwiches and pack the dainty cakes for this outfit, and all the time we were eating Cecilia kept on fussing and counting the knives in case one got lost in the sand, and by then I had lost interest in rock climbing, and we packed the wretched hamper up and lugged it home and spent half the evening washing it up ready for the next time. I took jolly good care that so far as I was concerned there wasn't going to be any next time. So it just shows.

So when Ann came bouncing in full of girlish enthusiasm to make the remark with which this story begins, I merely said coldly, 'Well, what is it, anyway?'

'It's a job,' she said. 'Smashing. Just what you and I are looking for to fill in the next six months.'

I must at this stage explain that Ann and I were at this time in the awful state of being neither one thing nor the other. We had passed (or scraped through) our GCSEs and left school, and we weren't ready to go and train for any serious job or profession. Actually we weren't quite sure what we wanted to do. When we told our parents this they went on like mad about 'any girl who isn't an absolute clot knows what she wants to do at sixteen', but to our surprise our headmistress backed us up and said that it was

because we were so versatile and lively-minded that
we couldn't decide between all the fascinating careers
in which we were bound eventually to shine.

However, there were still about six months to fill
in. If left to ourselves we could have filled them in very
nicely, helping in various stables and riding other people's show-jumpers, but that idea was coldly received.
No, we had got to do something useful for later life,
and what could be more useful to a girl than domestic
science? There happened to be a domestic science
school in Ryechester and we could go every day.

'Think,' said Mummy, 'of the future. A girl can't
learn too young how to run a home.'

Ann and I weren't excited because, between you
and me, we'd much rather have had the prospect of
running a stable than a home.

Ann said, 'What do we do at this place, for
instance?'

'Paper ceilings,' I said. 'Very tricky.'

'And cooking, I suppose?'

'Oh gosh, yes,' I said. 'They chain you to a cooker
till your eyebrows fall off into the soup.'

'Well, it isn't my cup of tea,' said Ann, 'and I can't
think it's yours, Jill. Tell you what, let's get ourselves
a job where we're at least self-supporting, and then
nobody can grumble.'

'Find one,' I said cynically. 'Just you find one!'

And now it seems she'd found one.

I read the ad. It said, 'Excellent job for two young
girls knowledgeable with horses. Live in. Apply Little
Chimneys Farm, Blowmore, Hants.'

'There you are,' said Ann. 'Made to measure. Live

in. We'd be self-supporting and have the time of our lives messing about with other people's horses, and it wouldn't cost us a dime.'

'What about my own ponies?' I said.

'Take them with us. I'd ride one and you the other. You'd get them supported too, and no food bills.'

I said I'd think about it.

'I don't know what's the matter with you, Jill Crewe,' Ann said. 'But I'll tell you one thing. There'll be about a million girls knowledgeable about horses after this job, and unless we clinch it here and now we'll have lost the chance of a lifetime.'

'Oh, don't talk like my cousin Cecilia,' I said. 'OK, we'd better go and tell the parents.'

Our mothers said what might be expected. That if it was really a good job they wouldn't stand in our way of being self-reliant, etc., etc., but they'd have to know an awful lot about our employer in case he turned out to be another Squeers.

I rushed up to Mrs Darcy's, and said, 'Look, you know practically everybody horsy within a hundred miles. Do you know anything about this Little Chimneys Farm?'

As it happened, she did. It was kept by somebody called Captain Sound, and he was perfectly respectable.

Having heard this our mothers told us we could apply, so we sat down to write the letter. We did it about ten times, and finally composed this:

Dear Sir,
    We were very interested in your advertisement

and would like to apply for your job. We are two girls very experienced with the horse in sickness, health, and everything else. We have both had a lifetime of show riding and looking after our own ponies, and we have also taught riding and practically run a riding school single-handed. We are both very intelligent and fond of hard work as long as it is with horses. What we are looking for is a living-in job where we can be self-supporting until we can decide what sort of careers to take up. The following people will give us first-class references –

We then wrote down the names of everybody we could think of, such as Mrs Darcy, Captain Cholly-Sawcutt, and the local Master of Foxhounds.

'It sounds terrific,' I said. 'That ought to jolly well fetch them. I bet all those other millions of girls won't have anything like our qualifications.'

We posted the letter and waited breathlessly. A few days later Captain Sound replied. He asked us if we would like to come over for an interview, but suggested that as we were both so jolly good an interview might not be necessary as he was satisfied we'd do, so if we were prepared to come and start work that would be OK by him.

Ann and I were for starting then and there, but at this stage Ann's mother put a spoke in the wheel by asking how much wages we were going to get. Ann said that not having sordid minds, and caring for nothing but the noble cause of equitation, we had not thought of such a thing, and Ann's mother said, rubbish, and that was just like us, absolutely no more idea than babies, and Ann must ring up Captain Sound immediately and find out.

So very reluctantly Ann did, hoping Captain Sound would not think we had miserly natures, but he took it quite calmly and said he had thought of forty pounds.

Ann said that suited us, and in spite of her mother grumbling and saying that it was ridiculous to let him think that we had no business instincts, we got our way, packed Black Boy and Rapide into a horse box, threw a few horsy garments into our suitcases, and set out for Little Chimneys Farm.

2 Welcome to Little Chimneys

'What do you think the farm is going to look like?' asked Ann.

As usual sticking my neck out, I said, 'Oh, I should think frightfully Children-of-the-New-Forest-ish, an ancient stone house with mullion windows and window seats and pewter plates all over the shop, and one of those wells that make an awful row when you pull the bucket up.'

'As long as *we* don't have to pull the bucket up –!' said Ann.

Well, of course, I was dead wrong. There wasn't anything farmy-looking at all about Little Chimneys Farm, in fact it was a large tinny bungalow, with bits of extra rooms like huts stuck on all over the place, and it was wedged in between two fir copses on the main road. We couldn't mistake it because there was a large board nailed to a tree at the road end of a cinder track, with the name on.

'Crumbs!' said Ann.

At that moment Mrs Sound came running down the cinder path to greet us. She couldn't have been more welcoming if we had been her long-lost nieces, and we certainly felt we were wanted. She was obviously slightly wacky and was wearing blue slacks, a pink jumper, and four rows of pearl beads.

'Which is Ann and which is Jill?' she asked. We told her, but from then on she never got it right, in fact half the time she was calling us Amy and Judy.

'Well, come in,' she said. 'We didn't expect you quite so soon and my husband hasn't got home yet, so you don't have to start on the ponies right away, do you?'

Actually we didn't feel like starting on the ponies right away, as we were hungry and had hopes of a cup of cocoa or something similarly cheering, so without further discussion we followed Mrs Sound into the house.

It was the most comic house, a living-room with bits of rooms, sheds, huts, cupboards, and what-have-yous, stuck on at unexpected angles. For instance, to get to our bedroom Ann and I had to go through a store hut full of bags of chicken food.

'This is yours,' said Mrs Sound. 'Such a dear little room.'

I felt like saying, 'Where's the floor?' because you couldn't see any, it was so taken up with furniture. There was a large double bed, a colossal wardrobe that I'm sure fifteen people could have kept their clothes in, a chest of drawers with two of the drawers permanently stuck out because they wouldn't go in, two chairs, and a bookcase, the sort that has glass doors and shelves going up and up to the ceiling with no books on them.

Ann and I just stood there stunned, and Mrs Sound

must have thought we were dumb with admiration because she said, 'So glad you like it.'

'Is the bathroom anywhere near?' I asked when I found my voice.

Mrs Sound said, oh yes, it was just back through the chicken food store and across the living-room, and through the door next to the window, and up three steps, and the second door you came to, very handy.

Ann began to giggle, and turned it into a frightful fit of coughing.

Mrs Sound said, was there anything she could get her, and I felt like saying, 'Yes, a cup of cocoa,' but daren't, and Mrs Sound said, 'Well, it's only a quarter to twelve and we don't have lunch till one, so that gives you time to get unpacked. You'll find lots of room for your things. I *do* like to have lots of room for my things.'

There was certainly lots of room for our things, in fact when our joint collection of garments was stowed away in the enormous wardrobe and drawers it was barely noticeable; but what we needed was room for people. One of us had to sit on the bed all the time, while the other one did a steeplechase over the rest of the furniture. We were now more or less hysterical with laughing as well as hungry, so we wandered back to the living-room where there was nobody to be seen; however, there was a lot of clattering going on in the distance, which proved to be two huts away where Mrs Sound was gaily cooking lunch and reading *Pride and Prejudice* at the same time, which was propped up against the gas cooker.

She looked exactly like the duchess in *Alice in Wonderland* making the soup, especially as she kept on grabbing two little tins without looking at them and shaking them over whatever she was cooking.

At last she looked round and said, 'I say, would you two girls mind frightfully laying the table? I've got to go on stirring this ragout, and I've just got to the bit where Mr Collins proposes to Elizabeth so I can't leave it.'

We said we'd lay the table with pleasure if she'd tell us where the things were, and she said vaguely, 'Well, I never quite know myself, but everything's in the drawers in the living-room, if you just keep looking until you find it.'

So after going through practically every drawer in the place we eventually got the table laid, though we couldn't imagine why Mrs Sound didn't make some attempt at least to keep the knives, forks, and spoons in the same drawer; and went back to the kitchen to find our hostess fishing *Pride and Prejudice* out of the ragout into which it had just fallen.

At last a car drove up. It was Captain Sound. He was a very smart-looking man and immaculately dressed, and he shook hands with us as if we were about twenty-one and said, 'Welcome to Little Chimneys.'

We said, 'Hello.'

'If I may say so,' said Captain Sound, 'you look very workmanlike. I like to see girls who work in a riding stable *dressed* like girls who work in a riding stable and not like art students.'

Ann and I didn't know what to say, as we always

did wear jodhs and shirts and pullovers, and weren't sure what art students wore anyway, so we didn't say anything but merely smiled intelligently.

One thing I was glad to know was that we were going to work in a riding stable, because up to then we hadn't been quite sure.

'Do you want to come out and see the ponies now?' said Captain Sound, 'or do you want to have lunch first?'

Ann and I looked at one another. All the time we seemed to be getting sidetracked away from food, and by now we felt like famished explorers, so Ann muttered something about lunch being ready and perhaps Mrs Sound wouldn't want it to be kept waiting, which I thought was pretty cunning of her.

'Good, good!' said Captain Sound. 'Then let us to the feast. Sit down, sit down.'

He sat down at the top of the table and waved us to either side, and in came Mrs Sound with the ragout.

There was plenty of it, but, as we feared, it tasted slightly of *Pride and Prejudice* and very much of salt and pepper.

'Potatoes?' said Captain Sound. 'Who's hiding the potatoes?'

'Oh dear,' said Mrs Sound, 'I forgot to do any.'

'Never mind,' said our employer, 'perhaps you remembered to do a nice pudding?'

Mrs Sound looked quite pathetically at Ann and me, and said, 'Now how can I have possibly forgotten to do a pudding, but I'm afraid I did. But there's some cake in the tin.'

'No, there isn't,' said the Captain. 'We ate it last

night, don't you remember? When you forgot to buy a tin of spaghetti for supper.'

'Of course!' said Mrs Sound, brightening up. 'Well, we'll just have to have a nice cup of coffee. There isn't any milk, but who wants milk!'

Ann and I daren't look at each other for fear of exploding.

At this moment there was an interruption, as the horse van arrived with my two ponies.

'What's this? What's this?' said Captain Sound.

'Actually, it's my own two ponies,' I explained. 'I thought it would be all right to have them here, as they'll provide transport for Ann and me, and I don't mind them being used in the riding school under my supervision.'

'Oh, that's all right,' said Captain Sound. 'They can go in with the others. You'll find them very useful when you have to do a bit of rodeo work.'

'Rodeo work!' I said, with my eyes popping out.

'Oh, you know. Rounding up the other ponies, and so on.'

In all my lifetime of experience I had never worked in a riding school where you had to use two ponies to round up the others. This sounded more like a circus than a riding school; however, one has to get used to other methods so I didn't comment.

'Excuse us, please,' I said, and Ann and I went out and helped the man to lead Black Boy and Rapide out of the van and down the ramp.

They both looked a bit peeved and surprised, as they had only ridden in a horse van two or three times in their lives, and then it was to emerge in a nice, grassy park at a show. Now they were standing in the road outside Little Chimneys Farm and staring round as if they wondered where on earth they had got to.

Captain Sound came out and joined us.

'If I may say so, a very nice pair of ponies,' he remarked. 'Which one belongs to which?'

'Actually they're both mine,' I said. 'I've had them ever since I was a kid. Ann's mother has just sold her pony because he was too small for Ann.'

(I may add that Ann's mother is the kind of person who sells ponies as soon as she considers they are grown out of, just as if they were old shoes, and I cannot approve of this. Neither can Ann, but she doesn't get any say.)

'I should think they're very well schooled,' said Captain Sound.

'I should jolly well hope so!' I said. 'I've been working on them for years and they've both won heaps of prizes.'

'They weren't up to much when Jill got them,' said Ann, 'so she gets the credit for making them so good.'

'Splendid, splendid!' said Captain Sound. 'I can see these two ponies are going to be a great asset to us, as well as Jill's schooling ability. Let's fasten them here to the railings for the time being and go and have a look at the rest of the gang.'

Feeling rather full of ragout and of nothing else, Ann and I followed him. If we were expecting to see a row of neat stables we were disappointed, as there seemed to be nothing behind the house but hens and henhouses. He led us round these, and at the back was a large field, and we gave a gasp.

The field was full of ponies. Wild ponies. New Forest ponies. There were nine of them, trotting about gaily and all turning their heads in our direction.

'Golly!' said Ann. 'They're *wild* ponies.'

We must both have looked a bit stunned, because Captain Sound said hastily, 'Not so wild. Just nice, raw material. You can make anything of these.'

'B-B-B-But – ' I stammered.

'Oh, I've put in a lot of work on them,' he said. 'They're all used to the halter. Nice friendly little things, they are.'

'I bet they are,' I said, 'but what about being broken to the saddle?'

'Oh come,' he said, 'that'll be nothing to experts like us three. We must get to work. I can see us having high jinks with this crowd.'

'Too right. So can I,' muttered Ann to me, as Captain Sound produced a bag of apples from his pocket and began breaking them up for the ponies who came crowding round the gate, looking slyly at us with their pretty, mischievous faces.

'Have you had them on a lungeing rope?' I asked doubtfully.

'Why, of course. At least, most of them. They're really at the stage of getting saddles on their backs and we'll soon manage that.'

It struck me that Captain Sound was something of an optimist, and I understood his reference to a rodeo, only I didn't fancy the idea of my own ponies being used to round up nine sets of dear little flying hooves.

'I should think it's going to be a long time before they'll be any good for riding school work,' said Ann.

'Oh, not a bit. They're very intelligent.'

'They've got to be more than intelligent, they've got to be jolly reliable and steady,' I pointed out, 'before you can put small kids on them.'

'Ah now, my dear young lady, we mustn't make difficulties,' said Captain Sound. 'As I said before, we're all experts, aren't we? And I'm quite sure that two fine horsewomen like yourself and Ann aren't going to be beaten by a bunch of fresh little ponies.'

Put like that he had us in what might be called a cleft stick. We couldn't let ourselves down by admitting failure.

'We'll do what we can, of course,' I said.

'Splendid, splendid. Now I suggest that this afternoon we put a lungeing rope on each of them in turn, and pick out the most adaptable, and those can try a bit of road work. You two can each ride one of Jill's ponies and lead a couple of these.'

'I hope the roads are quiet,' said Ann.

'Oh, perfectly quiet, just lots of nice lanes.'

'Meanwhile,' I said, 'where do I park my ponies? I can't leave them tied to the railings for long or they'll get restive.'

'I suppose they're used to being out at grass?' said Captain Sound.

'During the summer, yes,' I said, as it was quite obvious to me then that there weren't any stables at Little Chimneys Farm, and winter was coming on.

'Well, pop them in here with the others. They'll get

used to each other that way and the trained ponies will do the untrained ones good.'

I could feel my eyes opening as big as saucers at this peculiar idea, and for the first time I began to wonder just how much Captain Sound really knew about ponies.

'That's impossible,' I said, trying not to sound rude. 'The wild pones will kick mine. They might even gang up and attack them.'

'In that case,' said Captain Sound, 'there's another little field at the side of the house. Yours can go in there.'

'Thanks very much,' I said. 'I think I'll go and get them settled. They'll be a bit nappy after the journey and needing some peace and quiet. Come on, Ann.'

3   The comic set-up

'Well, what do you make of this set-up?' I said to Ann as we walked round the house.

'It's comic,' she said. 'I think Captain and Mrs Sound are both slightly mad, but they seem kind and it may be fun. Actually, I've always wanted to break in a New Forest pony.'

'Oh, me too,' I said. 'But I hope he doesn't think we can get them to riding school standard in about three weeks. It'll take ages before you can put a small child on any of them.'

'Between you and me,' said Ann, 'I don't think he knows an awful lot about horses.'

'That's what I'm thinking,' I said. 'Therefore he's relying on us for everything. Crumbs! When he talked about a riding school I had visions of – well, a riding school! But this is jolly well starting from scratch. Raw material! Gosh!'

'And there aren't any stables,' said Ann, 'which means he intends to keep them permanently out at grass, which won't help with their training, and they'll never be clipped all the winter. It'll be a funny riding school with unclipped ponies.'

'Don't worry,' I said. 'It'll be next summer after a hard winter's work before this outfit can invite customers.'

'Coo!' said Ann. 'I wonder if we'll last that long?'

'Oh, never say die,' I said. 'Only I do hope Mrs Sound doesn't forget the spaghetti again tonight. I'm still hungry.'

We collected my ponies and turned them into the small field, which wasn't bad and had shady trees along one side, though the whole field was on a slope and Ann said she hoped that Black Boy and Rapide wouldn't develop one leg shorter than the other through walking sideways.

'Sorry, boys!' I said cheerfully as I patted their cheeks and let them nuzzle my hand. 'You'll have to make do with this. At least the grass looks lush.'

We went back to find Captain Sound, and there he was lungeing a small grey pony.

'This one's coming on nicely,' he said light-heartedly. 'And I think those other three are ready for some road work. How about it, girls? Would you care to trot them out and see how they behave?'

I stared at him.

'But they're not shod!' I said.

He looked taken back. Then he looked down at the ponies' feet as if he expected them suddenly to grow shoes, or wondered why they had not been born with them on.

'Oh, of course,' he said. 'I ought to have taken them to the farrier this morning. I wonder if you'd lead them along there now. It's only about half a mile.'

We said we'd better do it at once, so we took the three ponies by their halters and set off.

'Well, this is comic,' said Ann. 'I'm beginning to wonder if he even knew that ponies had to be shod.

He seems very loose in the brain, when it comes to horses.'

'And Mrs Sound seems very loose in the brain when it comes to housekeeping,' I added. 'If there's a shop near the farrier's we'd better buy some chocolate in case she does forget the supper.'

They were charming ponies, small-boned and pretty, with the most lovely mischievous eyes, and they didn't behave badly at all on the way except for a bit of titupping. They probably recognised that they were in the hands of experience.

When we got to the farrier's he took one look and said, 'Blimey, what's this little lot?'

I didn't care for his attitude and replied coldly, 'I want to have these ponies shod, please. And send the account to Captain Sound.'

'Huh!' he said. 'I'll send the account to Mister Captain Sound if you like, and if it isn't settled in a week I'll be coming round to know why. I heard he'd bought a herd of New Forest ponies for about two hundred quid, but I didn't believe it till now. Thinks he's going to start a riding school and make a fortune. How mad can a chap get?'

'I see you're not busy,' I said. 'We'll wait.'

'Oh, you will, will you? And who may you be?'

'We're professionals,' said Ann. 'We train ponies and run riding schools and teach riding. We've been doing it for years, and we know what we're talking about, and we're not to be trifled with.'

The farrier said Ha-ha in a hollow sort of voice and added, 'Blimey, what sort of an animal do you call that one? The Thing from Outer Space?'

The one he was pointing at was certainly a very peculiar colour, a kind of mauvey roan if you can imagine it, and very long in the back, but I suddenly felt a great affection for this animal welling up in my noble breast, and replied heatedly, 'Actually that's my favourite, and it's called Happy Dawn.'

'Blow me down!' said the farrier. 'Well, come along, let's get cracking.'

I must admit he had quite a picnic shoeing those ponies, as you can imagine. They did everything but tie themselves in knots and Ann and I hung on until we were breathless. He must have been a pretty good farrier because eventually they were done and we were picking bits of the floor out of our hair.

I said to Ann, 'I'll see that the rest are much more under control before we bring them along here. Captain Sound knows nothing, and I'll not take his word for anything in future.'

The ponies didn't like their new shoes and behaved like temperamental Russian ballerinas all the way home. We were so occupied that we didn't have time to think about buying chocolate.

When we got back Captain Sound said, 'Oh, you have been a long time.'

Ann said, 'If you know how long it takes to shoe a docile horse you can just multiply it by ten for these. I'm afraid they're not as ready for the road as you think, and they hate their shoes. Is there anywhere we can put them until they get used to being shod? They might start lashing out, and injure the others.'

'We could tether them in the yard for the night,' he said.

'I don't think that's an awfully good idea,' I said. 'It might make them very upset. If you have any kind of stable or outhouse I could put my own ponies in, and these could go in the little field.'

'Well, there's a very big pigsty,' he said, 'if your ponies wouldn't mind.'

He took us and showed us, and it really was an enormous pigsty. It made me wonder how many and what sort of pigs had originally been kept there, but I said, 'This will do nicely for my ponies, if you can give us some water and brooms to clean it out, and some straw.'

Apparently there were some brooms Somewhere and some straw Somewhere. It took us about half an hour to find out where Somewhere was. We then got to work, and although the bucket leaked we finally had the place cleaned up.

'I must say, you are workers,' said Captain Sound. 'Now come along in and have your supper.'

No words could have been sweeter music to our ears, especially as nobody had suggested tea, and it was now about seven o'clock. We fetched my ponies in and settled them down, and turned the three newly shod ones into the small field. Then we went into the house, and washed and put on clean cotton dresses.

Eagerly we filtered into the living-room, but there was no sign of supper, the table wasn't even laid.

Captain Sound said, 'It won't be a minute.'

'OK,' we said.

Then Mrs Sound appeared from the kitchen with *Pride and Prejudice* in her hand.

'Oh dear,' she said. 'It's never supper time?'

'Can we help?' said Ann.

'Well, I don't see how you can,' said Mrs Sound, 'because actually there doesn't seem to be anything – I mean, we could have eggs, couldn't we? If Amy and Judy like eggs.'

'Ann and I could make omelettes,' I suggested. Anything to get the food situation moving.

'Oh, how kind of you,' said Mrs Sound. 'I do hope the Calor gas hasn't run out as I forgot to tell them to send another cylinder.'

We hoped so too! Fortunately it lasted while I made the omelettes and Ann knocked up a sponge pudding, but while the pudding was cooking the gas conked out. Fortunately there was plenty of bread, and we found a half pound of butter that Mrs Sound didn't know was there. We then gobbled up this meagre repast, and I muttered to Ann, 'Us for the village shop tomorrow, and lay in a private hoard and a tin-opener.'

Next morning we asked if there was a saddler's in the village and there was, so we suggested we might buy some cleaning tack and Captain Sound agreed it was a good idea and gave us twenty pounds.

The shop wasn't really a saddler's but a corn chandler's selling cattle food, poultry food, and farming odds and ends, but they kept brushes, saddle soap, and stable rubbers, so we bought what we needed, and then made a beeline for the grocer's. There we laid in tins of biscuits, chocolate bars, and fruit which could be eaten in bed on Mrs Sound's more forgetful days, and made a big hole in our spending money.

As we ambled back, Ann on Black Boy and me on Rapide, Ann said, 'I say, we ought to write to our fond mammas today to say we've arrived. What shall we say?'

'Well, we'd better not tell them about Mrs Sound forgetting to feed us, or Captain Sound being scatty,' I said, 'or they'll tell us to come home jolly quick. We shall have to concoct a letter with the utmost cunning.'

Ann said that when it came to diplomacy, cunning, and tactful documents she was streets ahead of me, so she would write the letter, and I could copy it.

In the afternoon Captain Sound insisted that we should take the three shod ponies out for a bit of roadwork, but I finally persuaded him to make it only two, the mauvey roan one which I had recklessly named Happy Dawn, and a cute little foxy-coloured one on whom needless to say we quickly bestowed the name Merry Night.

'All right,' he said, 'I'll go round to the small field and catch them while you two get ready.'

Five minutes later, Ann and I arrived at the small field to behold a sensational sight, Captain Sound leaping wildly about the field while the ponies gaily danced and kicked up their heels just out of his reach.

'I can't catch them,' he said crossly. 'I've never had this trouble before. It must have made them a bit wild when they went to be shod.'

I knew he was only saying this to save his face, because he must have had loads of trouble before.

Ann said, 'If you'll excuse me saying so, you should

never try to catch a pony by chasing it. You'll only scare and excite it, and then you'll never catch it. And honestly, you shouldn't wave the halter.'

'Well, what would you advise?' said Captain Sound. 'These are exceptional ponies.'

'It really applies to any pony with spirit,' I said. 'Push the halter down your coat and hold out an apple or a carrot and be very quiet until you've induced the pony to come to you. Then while he's eating the apple you can gently slip the halter on, and quietly lead him away. He won't mind coming a bit, because there's been nothing to startle him.'

'I ought to have tethered them,' he said.

'Oh gosh, no!' said Ann. 'They get all tied up in the ropes and go frantic. Shall Jill and I have a go at catching the two we want?'

Captain Sound was only too glad to let us have a go, but by now the ponies were thoroughly upset and knew what we were after, so we had no end of a job to make them interested in apples.

It almost felt like a rest cure when we were finally out on the road, Ann riding Black Boy and leading Merry Night, and I on Rapide and leading Happy Dawn. It was a pleasant, sunny afternoon with no wind, and we kept to the lanes of which there were plenty, letting the ponies use the grass verges as much as they could. The two wild ponies showed temperament all the time and we had to hold them closely, also our arms got very tired from keeping their heads up as their one idea was to stop and crop grass, but they were attractive ponies and we grew quite fond of them. Also, though I say it without boasting, they did recognise the hand of experience and didn't behave badly at all. When an unexpected lorry appeared round a bend Ann said, 'Now for it!' but nothing desperate happened. As you know, New Forest ponies do wander on the local roads and get used to seeing traffic.

'We might even make riding school ponies out of these,' said Ann cheerfully, 'in about umpteen years.'

When we got back, the pair of them walked in beautifully, Happy Dawn having a pretty natural action and Merry Night picking up his feet well.

'I say, they do look good,' said Captain Sound. 'We'll have those two saddled up in no time.'

(That's what you think! I thought.)

'Now what about a cup of tea, and then taking another pair to be shod?'

We groaned, not at the welcome idea of a cup of tea, but because we were aching already, but we didn't like to look unwilling.

We all went into the house, and there being no sign of Mrs Sound we made the tea ourselves, and then fled into our bedroom and ate a few of our biscuits. We then straightened our backs and prepared to take two more ponies to the farrier.

The two we took gave us a lot of trouble. If there is one thing I do not enjoy in the world of horses it is hanging on to the end of a rope with a dancing pony at the other end, doing his best to pull me up into the air. However, we stopped by a strip of common and let them dance until they were tired, and then proceeded to the village.

'What! Not you again?' said the farrier.

'Don't get excited,' said Ann. 'There are four more to come.'

'Coo!' he said. 'Somebody's gone crackers.'

We kept cool, and after a gruesome struggle that lot were finally shod, and we arrived back at Little Chimneys feeling like chewed string.

'I vote we call these two Mustard and Pepper,' I suggested. 'No romantic names for them.'

We turned the two into the small field with the other three shod ones, and took my ponies to the glorified pigsty where we rubbed them down and gave them a feed.

We were surprised to see no one about, and when we got to the house, though everything was open, there was nobody there. Then we saw a note on the table, 'Please feed chickens, gone to the pictures, your supper is in the oven.'

We thought it was a bit casual of the Sounds, just going off and leaving everything.

'I vote we get supper before we feed the chickens,' said Ann. 'I think it's a bit thick, Mrs Sound could at least have done that job before she went out. It isn't our work.'

When we looked in the oven we found a cheese and tomato pie, but Mrs Sound had left the gas too high and it was nearly dried up.

I said darkly, 'I don't believe they've gone to the pictures at all. I think they've gone out to get a decent meal. I can just see them now, sitting in front of roast beef and Yorkshire pudding and – '

'That's enough of that,' said Ann.

We ate the dry pie, and made a pot of tea, as there didn't seem to be any coffee in the house. Then we went and fed all the ponies, and the chickens, and put the chickens in for the night.

'We've still got to write those letters home,' said Ann.

It felt like the last straw. We got a writing pad out and Ann went into a sort of trance for about twenty minutes. Then she said, 'This is the best I can do. My brain feels addled.'

I read it.

It said:

Dear Mummy,

This is just to let you know that we have arrived safely. The country round here is lovely and just right for riding. We have nine ponies to look after as well as Jill's so we are kept very busy but it is out of doors all the time which is very nice. The grocer's shop in the village is called Webster's which is the same as ours at home, isn't that funny?

No more now, tons of love,

Ann.

'H'm,' I said. 'Sounds a bit gruesome to me. I don't know about your mother, but mine won't be exactly thrilled to get that. However, I'm too tired to do anything about it, so I'll just copy it and let's go to bed.'

By then it was nine o'clock and dark, and we wondered whether we ought to lock the door of the house before we went to bed. It really was a bit thick of the Sounds to leave us like this, not knowing what to do. In the end we didn't lock it, as we didn't want them banging us up after we'd gone to sleep.

We couldn't have baths as Mrs Sound hadn't thought of making up the boiler before she went out and the water was cold, so we rolled grumbling into bed. I may add that the bed was a feather one and you went down and down into a sort of tunnel among the feathers. Just as we tumbled in we heard the Sounds arrive back.

4   An awful lot of pony

The farrier refused to shoe the next four ponies until he got paid for the first five. Captain Sound grumbled like mad, but he finally paid up, and then said he didn't think he'd have the other four shod after all as it was all going to cost such a lot.

I told him that I thought he'd got too many ponies on his plate anyway. They were going to be an awful expense, and why not just concentrate on getting the five best ones into good shape?

'What about the other four?' he said.

Ann said, seeing that he'd bought the whole lot so cheaply, why not turn the other four loose in the forest again to join the herd before they got civilised?

He thought this over and then decided it was the right thing to do, so one bright morning Ann and I made a string of the four wilder ponies and led them off into the forest. As soon as we got into the glades they began to sniff the air of home and looked bright and happy.

'OK, girls and boys,' I said. 'You're going home and good luck to you.'

Soon we saw a small herd cropping grass under the ancient trees where as you know, or ought to know, the ancient kings of England used to hunt, and

William Rufus or somebody got shot by an arrow by mistake.

We loosed the four ponies and drew back to see what they'd do. They didn't hesitate, they just gave a little prance and trotted off to the others. There was a bit of nuzzling and a bit of neighing – doubtless the four were telling the others about their adventures on the brink of civilisation, so to speak – and off they all ran together.

'Golly!' said Ann, 'I wish we'd brought all nine,' and we both began to giggle.

We had both had letters from our mothers that morning. Mummy had written, 'You really didn't say very much in your letter. What is the house like? Are you being well fed? And you don't say a thing about Captain and Mrs Sound. I couldn't care less about Webster's the grocer's, so why drag that in?'

Ann's mother said much the same.

Ann groaned. 'Now I've got to concoct another diplomatic letter.'

'Oh,' I said, 'I'm just going to tell them that the Sounds are a little odd, but we're enjoying ourselves.'

So we drew a lot of funny pictures to show how we were enjoying ourselves and posted them off.

Captain Sound was very keen now that we should start training the ponies to the saddle, and five seemed very few to manage after all that crowd. By now they were getting to know us, and were quite friendly and manageable. Ann and I could do much more with them than Captain Sound could.

We started off by fastening blankets on their backs

and got them over the initial stages of not liking it very much. Then little by little we went through the business of the saddle and the bridle and the bit.

If you think this is easy you ought to try it. It takes endless patience, and we worked all day long, first on one pony and then another. The first time I mounted Happy Dawn it was like a rodeo, he put me off about five times. Mustard and Pepper had by now calmed down a lot, and the fifth pony we had named Rainbow because she was a skewbald.

Captain Sound was always very cheerful and seemed to think everything in the garden was lovely, but we weren't so sure.

I said one day, 'I suppose you realise, Captain Sound, that you're going to have an awful lot of expense if you intend to have a riding school with these ponies? It's going to be spring before they're ready to carry children, and even then I wouldn't trust them with beginners.'

Captain Sound looked a bit blank.

'Also,' I went on, 'you'll have to do something about building a stable for them, a big one. You can't have them out at grass till the spring. They've got to be clipped and groomed and kept clean. When they come in from rides they'll be wet and dirty and they've got to be got ready for next day's use. You'll have to lay in hay and straw and fodder. And harness and tack. At present you've only got two snaffle bridles and two saddles and one of those is coming to bits. It isn't safe. The girth gave way yesterday and Ann came off, and the saddle was under Pepper's stomach. I hope you don't mind me pointing all this out, but you'll need to get cracking on these things before long.'

He was obviously taken aback. You could tell that he didn't know a thing, and hadn't even considered what needed to be done.

'Oh, I don't know – ' he said vaguely. 'I hadn't expected to spend a lot of money. Surely – '

'You can't start a riding school without spending an awful lot of money,' said Ann, 'unless you're lucky enough to have a place with good stabling to start with, and can do all the work on the ponies yourself, and buy some really sound secondhand tack and saddlery.'

'Oh well,' he said, 'having gone so far I don't see why we should meet our difficulties halfway.'

'He really has got hopeless ideas,' I said, when we were in our room that night. 'I don't know what's going to happen when the weather turns bad. It's all right now in September but what about December?'

'I don't see why we should worry about the future for him if he can't be bothered to worry himself. Gosh, we're practically doing the housekeeping for Mrs Sound in any case,' said Ann.

This was true. We had taken to doing the shopping and ordering the food ourselves, in self-defence, and one or other of us usually did the cooking too, it was the only way to get anything to eat. Mrs Sound was awfully grateful and thought we were marvellous, but that didn't get us anywhere.

However, a month went by, and it happened to be a gorgeous sunny October, which didn't encourage Captain Sound to make any provision for the winter.

By now we really were getting the five ponies into shape by sheer hard work. We worked from about eight in the morning until it was dark, taking one pony in turn and working on it, not tiring it, but being patient and gentle and encouraging the pony's natural sense of fun so that it really enjoyed its training; then going on to another.

Each one of them would now let us ride it, and we would go out on the common with a pair of them, along with my two ponies. The novice ponies seemed to enjoy watching Black Boy and Rapide, and it helped a lot. Happy Dawn and Rapide got along particularly well together, and I would ride first one and then the other. Merry Night had always picked his feet up nicely, and Ann had got him quite well controlled and doing a pretty walk. It was very hard work but we felt it was worthwhile to see how the ponies were coming along because of our efforts. Mustard and Pepper both had too much sense of humour to be predictable, and were apt to get crazy. They could be very good if they liked, and they could also be terrible. Rainbow was actually the most docile of the five, but she wasn't very bright and was hard to teach, and she had the awful fault of rearing when she thought she had had enough.

Actually we couldn't see any of the five except Happy Dawn and Merry Night being any good in a riding school, but it was no good saying so to Captain Sound who didn't seem to like to hear common sense.

'After all,' I said to Ann, 'we're not paid to worry about the future.'

'Paid?' she said. 'Who's paid?'

'Gosh, yes,' I said. 'That's another thing.'

We had now been at Little Chimneys Farm for four weeks and nothing had yet been said about our wages, and we hadn't liked to ask.

'I'm going to ask him,' said Ann. 'You know how he is, he never thinks of anything unless he's prodded.'

So that evening while we were having supper, Ann said, 'By the way, I hope you don't mind me mentioning it, Captain Sound, but we haven't got any money left, and we haven't had our wages yet.'

'Oh, I say!' he said. 'It just slipped my mind. I'll give it to you after supper. Thanks for reminding me.'

Mrs Sound cleared away the supper things, and our employer carefully laid down one hundred and twenty pounds on the table and said, 'There you are.'

Ann and I stared.

'There's something wrong here,' I said. 'We've been here a month.'

'Well, yes,' he said. 'I've deducted ten pounds a week for your ponies' keep.'

'But my ponies are out at grass all day!' I said. 'And they get the same as the other ponies every night, and jolly few oats. And if it comes to that, my ponies are working for you all the time. We couldn't have done much without them.'

He thought for a minute and then said, 'Well, if you insist,' and put another fifty pounds down on the table very reluctantly.

'Excuse me,' said Ann, 'but that's only one hundred

and sixty pounds. We were to have forty pounds a week each.'

'Oh no,' said Captain Sound. 'Forty pounds between you.'

Ann and I were furious. fifty pounds each for a whole month's hard work and no square meals! We weren't mercenary, but this was just meanness.

We discussed it in our room, as we were getting into bed.

'I'll tell you what,' said Ann. 'We're leaving. That'll shake him. I don't see how he can do without us.'

'But how on earth can we go home, and tell everybody how we've been done?' I said. 'Our very first job too, that we got for ourselves. They'll think we can't look after ourselves, and they'll never let us do anything again. It'll be domestic science for ever and ever.'

'I don't care,' said Ann. 'Either he gives us the other one hundred and sixty pounds tomorrow, or we're leaving.'

'Well, I care,' I said. 'I've got pride. I'm not going home beaten, I'd rather starve to death in the snow.'

'That's what we'll both do if we stay here,' said Ann.

In the middle of arguing we fell asleep.

When we got up next morning we still didn't know what to do, but as we entered the living-room for breakfast Captain Sound came rushing in at the door.

'Where are the ponies?' he shrieked.

We stared.

'What have you done with the ponies?' he said.

'We haven't done anything with them,' I said. 'We fed them as usual last night and left them in the paddock.'

'You left the gate wide open,' he said. 'They've gone.'

'We did not leave the gate open,' said Ann. 'We've never done such a thing. People with our experience don't leave gates open. Actually I distinctly remember fastening it, because I caught my sleeve on the splintered bit on the top.'

'Yes, that's true,' I said.

'Well then, you didn't fasten it properly,' he said.

'Yes, we did,' I said. 'We always look to see if the gate is perfectly fast before we leave it. We've had that sort of training.'

He went on blaming us, and we were furious. Just then Mrs Sound came in with the boiled eggs and asked what was the matter.

When she was told she said, 'But you went down to the field yourself last night, George, after the girls had gone to bed. You took the torch, because you said you'd left your jacket on the hedge.'

Captain Sound went scarlet, realising that it was he who hadn't fastened the gate. He shrugged his shoulders and said, 'Well, that's neither here nor there. The ponies have got out and they've probably been gone for hours. When you've finished your breakfast you'd better go and look for them.'

'This is it,' said Ann, as we rode out half an hour later on my two ponies. 'The ponies have had a jolly good start. If you ask me, they're all back in their native wilds by now.'

First we made for the Common, thinking there was a possibility that the ponies might have settled down to crop grass there, but no. We asked in the village, and a man told us that he'd heard a number of ponies clattering madly down the street in the middle of the night.

'At the rate they were going,' he said, 'they're miles away by now, well out in the Forest. You haven't a hope.'

As you know, the New Forest is enormous. We rode about all the morning and saw plenty of ponies, but none of ours. It was like looking for five needles in a haystack as big as a cinema. Once back in those remote glades the ponies would joyfully decide that they'd had enough civilisation to last them for the rest of their lives.

We searched on until we were ready to drop, and finally turned into Lyndhurst at four o'clock and went into a café to get some sandwiches and tea.

'It looks to me,' I said, 'as if your comic job has packed up on us without any effort on our part. So what now? We just leave and go home.'

'Can't say I like that,' said Ann. 'Our first job that we've found for ourselves folding up like this, and we arrive home after one month – after all we've said about being independent. There'll be an awful lot of I-told-you-so.'

'But it isn't our fault.'

'Well, what are we going to tell them? That all the ponies ran away and we couldn't find them, so we gave up and came home? It sounds jolly fishy to me, and it will to all our friends.'

I said I couldn't see how a horsy story could sound fishy, and Ann said, 'Oh, don't be so difficult!' and we started squabbling because we were so fed up.

'Obviously,' I said gloomily, 'we shan't be staying on with the Sounds, so what do we do? If only we could find ourselves another job, and not have to go home in igno-what-do-they-call-it! Perhaps Captain Sound would give us some frightfully good references. He ought to, after all the work we've put in.'

'Work!' said Ann. 'I'm still black and blue with falling off Mustard until I got him to stop bucking. But I'm glad for the ponies' own sakes that they're gone, because I think they'd have had rather a miserable life – the Sounds hadn't a clue how to look after them – and we wouldn't have stuck it there for ever.'

5 The new idea

Suddenly a woman at the next table said, 'Excuse me, but did I hear you say you'd been working for Captain Sound? You must be the two girls I've heard about. What happened?'

She looked nice, and soon we had given her a short outline of our story.

'Oh dear,' she said. 'How hopeless. I agree with you, the ponies will never be found, and a good thing too. I don't know what would have happened to the poor things in the end, because the Sounds are hopelessly impractical people and always going in for wonderful-sounding schemes without any knowledge whatever. I know all about them, and this idea of a riding school was ridiculous from the beginning. I'm only sorry that you two got let in. We know all about you in the neighbourhood, and how good you've been – these things get round – and there certainly wasn't any future there for you. I'm jolly glad I've come across you. What do you propose to do now?'

'I suppose we'll just leave,' said Ann. 'We were going to, anyway.'

'And we'll be out of a job,' I said drearily. 'We'll have to go home, and it'll be an awful letdown, because we were so keen on getting our own pony job and being successful.'

'Would you want another job?' she asked. 'By the way, my name's Mrs York and I live at Pockett House, not far from where you've come from.'

'How do you do?' we said politely, and I added, 'I'm Jill Crewe and this is Ann Derry. We'd love to have another job, as long as it's the kind we like. We don't want another flop.'

'Listen,' said Mrs York, 'I may be able to help you. Could you come along to my house tomorrow and have tea? Anybody in the district will tell you where it is. I've got an idea which I'll explain to you when you come, and if you don't like it there's no harm done. What about it?'

Our spirits rose, and we said we'd come like a shot. It really sounded like a fairy tale where something always turns up just when you think that All Is Lost.

We rode back to Little Chimneys Farm, and reported to Captain Sound that it was everybody's opinion that the ponies would never be found, now that they had succeeded in getting back to the wilds.

He looked very gloomy and said, 'All that money just thrown away!'

We felt like saying, 'All what money?' but felt it might be cruel to mock him in his Hour of Despair, so we didn't say anything except that now the job had packed up, we'd be packing up too.

At this he went rather red and said we'd helped a lot and been jolly good, and if it hadn't been for the Fell Hand of Fate robbing him of the ponies like that he was sure we'd soon have had a smashing riding school going, and if he could think of something else perhaps we'd some day come back and help him with it because he thought we were absolutely terrifically good and very hard workers.

I could see the words, 'What About Our One Hundred and Sixty Pounds?' jumping up and down in Ann's throat, but she swallowed them down. After all, we had our pride and we weren't mercenary people.

Then Mrs Sound said, 'I've never liked anybody so much as Amy and Judy in my life, and it'll be awful to have to start doing the food again,' and practically wept. I mean she sniffed a lot and grabbed her handkerchief.

I tried to keep up the tone of the party by saying, 'Well, all good things come to an end,' but the whole evening was a bit dim.

In case any of you are wondering, none of the ponies ever appeared again, and somewhere in the New Forest there are five ponies called Happy Dawn, Merry Night, Mustard, Pepper, and Rainbow, who will have shed their shoes long, long ago.

If you are ever around that way and notice a very mauve one, that'll be Happy Dawn, and he'll have forgotten everything he ever learned by now.

The next morning we packed our things, and in the afternoon we set off on my two ponies for Pockett House. It turned out to be a huge red brick house with parkland all round it, and Black Boy and Rapide pricked up their ears at the sight of it and were all set for a gallop.

Mrs York saw us from the front window and came running out. She had a round face like the man in the moon and rather odd clothes consisting of a skirt, jumper, and cardigan, none of which remotely matched, but she was awfully kind.

'What adorable ponies!' she said. 'Are they yours?'

'They're Jill's,' said Ann.

'And wherever I go, they go,' I said firmly, so that she'd get the right idea at the start.

'They look to me as if they'd like a good canter round the park,' said Mrs York. 'Well, we'll have to see about that. Now do come in!'

She took us into an enormous drawing-room, with trestle tables in it, and sewing machines, and bits of sewing and knitting all over the place.

'I've had a working party here all morning,' she explained rather unnecessarily, 'and I simply haven't had time to clear up, in fact I hardly ever do, it doesn't seem worthwhile. Now what do you two girls say to some tea before we do anything else?'

We tried to look polite and not too eager, but I suppose our eyes glittered like the red eyes of famished wolves, as actually all we had had for lunch was a boiled egg each and a sardine between us.

'You look to me,' said Mrs York, 'as if you'd enjoy an enormous tea. I know I would, as I didn't have time for much lunch. I've a feeling you didn't get exactly what I'd call lavish meals at the Sounds'. Mrs Sound has a reputation for being a bit forgetful.'

'She forgets practically every meal,' said Ann. 'We started doing the catering in self-defence, but when we hadn't time nothing happened at all.'

'Good-oh!' said Mrs York. 'Let's have a terrific tea.'

She went out, and in about ten minutes came back followed by a beaming maid, both of them carrying trays with piles of piping hot buttered crumpets, sandwiches, and cakes, and even little sausages on sticks.

'Now get into that,' said Mrs York, 'and at the same time perhaps you'd like to tell me your life stories.'

We always enjoyed telling our life stories, so for the next half-hour we talked and ate like mad.

'And on top of all that,' said Ann, 'it does seem jolly hard luck that in our first job we should get all washed up. Of course we'll try and make our mothers and friends realise that Captain Sound wasn't very clever and he was the one who let the ponies escape, so that it won't sound in any way our fault, but I know what they'll say – "you'd better stay at home and do something sensible." Nothing's sensible without ponies.'

'So this is where I come in,' said Mrs York. 'I like you two girls very much, and I think I can help you and give you some fun while you do me a favour in return. Are you interested?'

'Rather!' we said, all agog.

'Well, now,' said Mrs York, 'I'm getting up a big bazaar in aid of the refugees. The bazaar is going to be held in this house next month. There are a lot of people in this district who ride, and I thought we could bring them into the affair by organising a treasure hunt and musical rides. They will all pay to enter, and the musical ride is something that everybody can go out into the park to watch, while the treasure hunt will cause a lot of interest and fun. If it had been summer I would have had a gymkhana, but it isn't summer and I think the two events I've mentioned will be suitable for the autumn weather. My idea is that you two girls come here and stay with me as my guests, and organise the two events. What do you think about that?'

'It sounds gorgeous to me,' I said.

'Me too,' said Ann. 'What should we have to do?'

'Have you ever organised anything of this kind before?' asked Mrs York.

We told her that we had organised pretty well every kind of event in the pony world.

'I shall want you to go round and visit all the people who ride,' said Mrs York, 'and get them to enter, and collect their entrance fee – say one pound each – '

'Two pounds fifty,' I suggested. 'Don't make it too cheap. They'll all pay two pounds fifty for so much fun, and I suppose there'll be prizes for the treasure hunt?'

'Oh yes, that's another thing. I'd like you to persuade the local tradespeople to give some prizes. And you'll have to make a list of things for the treasure hunt itself and train people for the musical ride, and take all that off my hands.'

We thought for a minute and then nodded at each other, having decided that this seemed just our kind of job.

'There's one thing, Mrs York,' I said. 'Shall I be able to keep my two ponies here?'

'Oh, but of course!' she said. 'That's no problem. We've got plenty of stabling at the farm and four horses of our own. The ponies will be useful to you, so count them in as our guests too. And by the way, I have a girl staying here just about your age, my goddaughter, who's helping me with the bazaar, so you'll have young company. Now when can you come?'

'We've only got to move out,' said Ann, 'so we could come tomorrow morning if you like.'

'Splendid,' said Mrs York. 'Now I know you're going to enjoy yourselves here. Work that's fun and fun that's work, and plenty of both, has always been my motto. Perhaps you'd like to see the room you'll have?'

She took us upstairs and showed us a very large bedroom with two beds and windows that looked over the park. Although there was plenty of furniture in it, there still looked enough space to give a party, very different from our cramped quarters at the Sounds'.

'It seems an absolutely smashing set-up,' I said to Ann as we trotted down the drive. 'Do you think there's a snag in it?'

'Oh, don't let's be gruesome,' she said. 'Mrs York seems a jolly nice person and at least she isn't scatty! I'm just wondering what we're going to say when we write home. Mummy may go off the deep end about me finding myself a job with a complete stranger.'

'Well, let's get settled in before we write,' I suggested, 'and then we can tell our mothers how nice it is and they'll be appeased. Isn't it marvellous that we haven't to go home after all?'

Next morning we said farewell to the Sounds. To our surprise, Captain Sound had a complete change of heart and pressed the missing one hundred and sixty pounds into our hands, and Mrs Sound really cried, and said, 'Goodbye, my darling Amy and Judy,' and presented us each with a half-pound carton of chocolates, so they really weren't so bad after all.

We rode to Pockett House, and the first thing Mrs York did was to take us down to the farm where my ponies were going to be stabled.

I was absolutely thrilled with it.

The whole place was most beautifully kept, and the farmer couldn't have been pleasanter. He showed us the stalls he had got ready for Black Boy and Rapide, and they took to him at once and started nuzzling his shoulder and whiffling at his hands, because they could tell he loved horses, so I felt very happy.

The floor of their stalls was of red brick laid in a herringbone pattern, and next door were the corn bins and running water, and there was a harness room for my tack, and a barn filled with hay and straw. It was a marvellous place. The other four horses on the farm consisted of three working horses, and a pony thirty years old which had been ridden by Mrs York in her youth, and was now enjoying its old age in perfect bliss.

Ann and I stayed among all these horses for ages, having the time of our lives until I realised it was nearly one o'clock and we ought to be getting back to the house. We went in at a side door and there was a lovely smell of lunch.

'Well, what did you think of the place?' asked Mrs York.

'Smashing,' I said. 'It's just the sort of farm I'd like

to have myself some day. I could stay there all day. Is it all right for us to ride in the park when we're off duty?'

'Of course,' said Mrs York. 'That's where you'll have to arrange your practices for the musical ride. I suppose you've seen one done?'

I said we'd both seen one at the Olympic Tattoo on television, and had got the general idea.

Mrs York told us to go into the morning-room, and lunch would be ready in five minutes. We washed first in a handy little cloakroom, and then went and stood warming ourselves in front of a gorgeous fire in the morning-room which was panelled in dark oak and had window seats.

Presently the door opened, and a girl came in.

'Now!' cried Mrs York. 'Here's my goddaughter who is dying to get to know you.'

I looked round.

'I bet she is!' I said sarkily, and Ann said, 'Oh golly!'

Mrs York's goddaughter was my cousin Cecilia.

6 It's Cecilia

Those of you who have read my previous books will know all about the ancient feud which had been waged between my cousin Cecilia and myself from my earliest years.

When I was young she was always held before me as the kind of model I ought to build myself up to, so to speak. Cecilia was never dirty, she was never rough, she never said 'Oh Gosh' or 'Blast' or 'Sucks' to you. She never yelled or got furious or broke cups or left the electric light on or lost her handkerchiefs or spilt ink or was late for school or couldn't find her atlas.

Cecilia, I had been told from my infancy, knitted beautifully from about the age of five, and passed the cups when her mother had people to tea without sloshing the tea into the saucers, and always wrote at once to thank people for things they'd given her. She also went to the dentist when she had to, without making a fuss.

Our mothers being sisters, I suppose they had always had a beautiful dream of Cecilia and me being loving friends, but what a hope! I had been to stay with Cecilia and Cecilia had been to stay with me. These visits had hardly been a howling success. Cecilia was a completely unhorsy person, and yet she pretended to know more about horses than I did. She was an awful show-off. She never read anything but books called *The Madcap of the Lower Fourth*, and so on. And she was a shocking fusser. I've known Cecilia wreck a whole picnic just because one wasp came buzzing around her plate, and everybody knows that if you don't bother a wasp it won't bother you, but if you get it excited what can you expect?

Oh well, I suppose there had to be a snag at Pockett House, and here it was, all dressed up in a pink tweed skirt and a matching twinset.

'Hello, Cecilia,' I croaked.

'Jill!' she said. 'I might have known!'

'I say, do you two know each other?' said Mrs York. 'How nice!'

'We're cousins,' I said.

'Only Jill is *so* horsy,' said Cecilia. 'But I should think just the right one for the job, Aunt Pat. She adores dragging ponies about, and backing them into things and so on, and she doesn't mind how wet she gets. And Ann's another the same.'

'Isn't that wonderful?' said Mrs York, quite missing the fact that Cecilia was being sarky. 'Now I'll go and hurry up the lunch.'

As soon as she was gone Cecilia gave a delicate sniff and said, 'Somebody's been around the stables.'

'Our clothes are perfectly clean, if that's what you mean,' I said, 'and we're not going to stand for that sort of remark! You dress like a lampshade if you want to, and if it's suitable to your job, and we'll dress suitably for ours.'

'I'm sure you will,' said Cecilia. 'Jodhpurs from morning till night!'

'Oh, call a truce,' said Ann. 'What sort of a life am I going to have with you two getting at each other all the time?'

'That's all right by me,' I said. 'Live and let live – as long as Cecilia doesn't try to teach me anything about ponies.'

'Oh, I gave up ponies long ago,' said Cecilia airily. 'They're childish.'

'Some poor pony will be relieved,' I said.

At that moment the situation was saved by the lunch bell.

Next morning Ann and I began our duties. The first thing was to get people to enter for the events, so Mrs York gave us a list and we sallied forth.

The first place we called at was a farm, and the farmer's wife said at once, 'Oh yes, mine would all love to join.'

'How many?' I said, and she said five, three girls and two boys.

'I suppose they've all got ponies,' said Ann, and the farmer's wife said that was the snag, they only had one and a half ponies between them, that was to say they had one pony of their own and part-time use of another which belonged to a girl who did part-time book-keeping at the hotel.

'But they're used to sharing,' said the farmer's wife. 'I mean, one gets off and another gets on.'

'I'm afraid that wouldn't be much use in a treasure hunt or a musical ride,' I said. 'What a pity, as we do want people.'

The farmer's wife said that the children might be able to borrow some horses from somewhere on the day, and we said we were afraid that wasn't much good as we wanted to start practices as soon as possible; and the farmer's wife said we could count on one of the children anyway; they'd just have to draw lots for which one, and it was pretty sure to be Josephine as she was born lucky, and we had to leave it at that.

Ann got out the list and wrote Josephine Pobley on the fair white sheet, and that was *one*.

The next place we called at was the doctor's house. As we approached we heard the sweet thunder of hoofs, and in the paddock next to the house a boy and girl were doing a racing gallop.

'Hi!' we shouted.

They pulled up, slid off, and came over to us.

'What do you want?'

We told them about the events and they were very keen.

'Have you ever done a musical ride?' I asked.

'I haven't,' said the boy, 'but I shouldn't think it's hard to learn. Nan was in one once, weren't you, Nan?'

'Yes,' said Nan. 'We got one up in the riding class and it was the most frightful mess. All the ponies either turned the same way, or crashed into each other. Miss Stocks was livid.'

'Well, that's encouraging, I must say!' I said.

'Oh, it wasn't so bad really,' said Nan. 'It only wanted a bit more organising. We only had two practices.'

'I'm all for the treasure hunt,' said the boy. 'I've always wanted to be in one.'

'All right,' said Ann, 'we'll stick your names down and we'll let you know when the first practice is.'

They said their names were Nan and Peter Bruce, and the person we ought to go and see was a girl called Dulcie Willow at Fuller's Cottage, as she had some riding pupils and would probably enter them *en bloc*, so to speak.

So we popped off to Fuller's Cottage. My idea of a girl called Dulcie Willow was somebody very fair and swaying and about eighteen, but actually she was very fat and brisk and had a voice like a foghorn, and she was quite old, about twenty-five I should think.

'I don't know who you are, but come on in,' she boomed as we approached the open door; and in we went to find her eating scrambled eggs with a grey pony.

That is to say, Dulcie was sitting at the table eating the eggs, and the pony was standing opposite to her eating cornflakes and bread out of a tin bowl on the table.

'I say,' said Ann, 'does she eat all her meals with you?'

'Of course she does,' said Dulcie. 'She's got better manners and is better company than most people I know. Who are you and what can I do for you?'

I told her that we were staying with Mrs York who was getting up a bazaar, and our job was to organise some pony events.

'We were told that you had a riding school and that

you'd be just the person to get us some people to enter for the events,' I said.

'If anybody told you I've got a riding school they're up the pole,' said Dulcie cheerfully. 'I take a few pupils, but I'm jolly particular who I take. I can't do with these Know-All kids, and I haven't the slightest use for people who only want to ride so that they can win things.'

'I couldn't agree more,' I said. 'When you go to gymkhanas nowadays half the people aren't there for fun or good riding but only to win, and they glower at the other competitors and are beastly to their ponies if they lose. My friend and I are only interested in good horsemanship.'

'Then you're the sort of people I like to know,' said Dulcie. 'Pour yourselves some coffee, it's on the gas. I can give you the names of some decent kids for your ride and treasure hunt. Move over, Susannah.'

The pony obligingly moved over, and from a drawer in the table Dulcie took a writing pad and a pencil and began to jot things down, while we took her at her word and helped ourselves to some coffee.

'There's Pamela Shooter,' said Dulcie. 'She's got a pretty pony with lots of sense. What would you say to a palomino? Or do you want the ponies paired, two grey, two chestnut, and so on?'

'I don't think so,' said Ann. 'We don't want it to look too formal. It would be very colourful to have a palomino, and a few piebalds and skewbalds if we can come across them.'

'Rightio,' said Dulcie. 'That'll be John Hicks on his

palomino, and – now let me see, who's got a piebald? – oh yes, Janet and Pam Watts on two piebalds, though Janet's an awful person for falling off, and that wouldn't look so good in a musical ride. We'll have to glue her to the saddle or something. You'd better go and see the Fosters. They both ride awfully well and have lovely ponies, and they'll give a lot of tone to your show, but they've got one of those fussy mothers who only likes them to ride in the very best events. You'll have to convince her that yours is one of the very best events.'

'I don't know,' I said. 'I don't feel that I and the Fosters would click.'   'OK,' she said. 'Wash out the Fosters, but if they come to you of their own accord and ask to enter, have them. Now there's the vicar's son, Noel Shaw, he'll make a leader, but you can't have him without having his brother Tony, and Tony's an absolute clown and always playing for laughs.'

'I say!' said Ann. 'I didn't know there were so many snags in getting up a musical ride.'

'If I were you two,' said Dulcie Willow, 'I'd get all the kids round and try them out, then winkle out the ones you really want for the ride.'

'I don't know if that would do,' I said. 'We need a lot of entries because of the two pounds fifty for the bazaar, and if we hurt people's feelings by telling them they're not good enough they'll sheer off in disgust, and Mrs York will get hardly any money at all.'

'Oh, I don't think you need worry,' boomed Dulcie. 'They can all go in for the treasure hunt, there's no limit. I should hand-pick about sixteen for the ride and take a collection from the spectators.'

'That's an idea,' I agreed. 'Coo, I feel like Napoleon planning a campaign.'

We went round and visited the people whose names she had given us, and a few more, and told them all to turn up the following morning at Pockett House for a practice in the park.

Mrs York was pleased with what we had done, especially when next day she saw the people and the ponies arriving.

I suddenly got cold feet and said, 'Oh help!'

'What's the matter?' said Mrs York.

'I just wondered how all these people would take to being told things by Ann and me, when we're only about their own age and they don't even know us.'

'Oh, I'll go out and make them a speech,' said Mrs York. 'It'll be all right. What are you going to do, Cecilia?'

Cecilia said she would watch us from the window and make tea cosies, or dainty doilies, or something, for the bazaar.

I don't know about Ann, but my knees were knocking together as we went out and faced twenty people with ponies who all stood staring at us in a glazed sort of way.

Mrs York stood on the steps and said, 'I'm so glad all you people have turned up and I'm sure you're going to have fun.' She then introduced Ann and me to them, and said a lot of their names which I felt I hadn't a hope of remembering, and went on, 'Jill and Ann are going to be in charge of the training and organisation, so you do as they say. Agreed?'

Nobody seemed to object so Mrs York pushed off and left us to it. The first thing I asked was whether anybody had ever done a musical ride before. Blank silence. Ann said, 'Has anybody ever seen a musical ride?' and about twelve put their hands up, and one boy said, 'On television and it looks jolly easy.'

'That's what you think!' I said.

A girl said, 'It's possible if you're a competent rider, but some people hardly know their left rein from their right, and the music puts you off a bit, anyway.'

'Well, let's have a shot without any music, because we haven't got any yet,' I said. 'All get into line and walk a circle, and I'll watch your performance and see how the ponies match up.'

Although it was early November it was a lovely, mild, sunny day and the grass was sparkling and the sky blue. As soon as the ponies began to walk round I felt fine. It was a wonderful feeling, as only horsy people can understand.

'Do we match the colours of the ponies?' said Ann. 'Or do we mix them up?'

I said I didn't see how we could attempt to match the colours, or the heights and comparative performances would be all wrong, so we'd study the performance first and then see how the heights went.

The performances were, needless to say, pretty mixed. A few people were good, experienced riders, and a few looked as if they had been in the saddle about three times in their whole lives.

'Gosh!' I muttered to Ann. 'This'll take some

sorting out.' As I said it, one girl fell off for no apparent reason at all and her pony went lolloping away across the park. Everybody stopped while the girl chased her pony, and when she got back another girl called Althea Something said she was bored stiff already, and in any case we'd have to pick out the best people for the leaders and it was obvious who the best people were.

'Noel Shaw and I had better be the leaders,' she said. 'Our ponies are the same height and have much the same pace.'

Several people began to mutter at this, and a girl said, 'It isn't fair. Althea and Noel seem to think they have to lead everything. Why can't Judy and I lead? We're as good as they are.'

'Don't be silly,' said Althea. 'You're too little and fat to lead anything, and Judy rides on the rein all the time. That's no example to people.'

Judy started shrieking at this, and I said, 'I haven't seen enough of any of you to decide anything yet. I'm going to pair you off myself, on performance, and we'll see what happens.'

I felt that Althea wanted taking down a peg, so I picked out a quiet-looking boy and girl for the leading pair and followed them up with Althea and Noel, and Judy and the little fat girl who was called Lucille. Eventually Ann and I arranged the ten pairs, but the grumbling nearly shook the leaves off the trees, people saying that they couldn't possibly ride with the people I had partnered them with.

'All right!' I yelled, 'It's only temporary, can't you grasp that? I've got to make a start somewhere.'

At last I got the pairs riding round, and it was obvious that the leaders I had chosen were a bit too quiet, and very slow, and held up the rest.

'There you are,' said Althea. 'You'll have to let me and Noel lead after all.'

I was afraid she was right, so we tried it that way, but the spacing proved frightful as the leaders rode much too fast for the pair behind, and the third pair crowded the second, and so on right down the line.

I told them that they simply must keep an equal distance apart, and some managed this and some didn't.

'It's having all these inexperienced kids in,' said Tony Shaw in disgust. 'We shall look a motley gang, with a few good riders in front and a trail of hopeless kids behind.'

'Don't worry,' I said coldly. 'The kids will probably be better than you when I've done with them. In any case I shall put a good pair at the end to finish the team off.'

'Well, I hope it won't be Alec and me,' said the boy.

'It'll be the ones I decide it will be,' I said.

Meanwhile Ann was changing a few people's places, and then we tried them again and it was a bit better.

'I'm bored with this already,' said Althea. 'It's going to be pretty dull just forming twos and fours and eights when I could do it without any practice at all. I don't think I'll come any more.'

I could see the musical ride falling to bits if I wasn't careful.

'Oh, be a sport,' I said. 'People will be paying to watch you ride on the day, and it's all in aid of the refugees, and we can't have it at all if the best riders won't take part.'

'That's right,' said Noel, unexpectedly coming to my aid. 'I think we jolly well ought to do it, Althea.'

'That's right,' I said. 'Somebody back us up. It's all in a good cause, and I think you might try a bit harder. Look, Ann and I will do a demonstration.'

So Ann and I rode up in single file, and at the top I turned left and Ann turned right. Then we rode up as a pair and turned left.

'There you are,' I said. 'And surely the second pair can remember to turn right. Just *try*.'

After that it was a bit better, though some people like Tony Shaw – whom I could cheerfully have murdered – thought they were there to act the fool and clown about. There always are some people like this, I don't know why. I hope nobody who reads this book is one.

At last we decided they'd had enough for one day and sent them off home. A few said they'd enjoyed it, and some didn't say anything at all. I was beginning to wonder whether, after all, this wasn't going to be as bad as training New Forest ponies.

7 Wasn't it murder?

'Phew!' said Ann. 'Wasn't it murder?'

I said I was sure the thing would sort itself out when the people got more used to us, and to riding in formation with each other, and Ann said she jolly well hoped I was right.

'You certainly worked hard,' said Mrs York, 'and some of them didn't seem very helpful.'

'The whole point is,' I said, 'that they're not getting much out of it except hard work and being bossed around. Althea was right, it isn't much fun for them, they'd be far happier having a country ride or practising something they enjoy doing. Some of the older ones are prepared to do it to be sporting, but others just aren't as sporting as all that!'

'And they've got to groom their ponies and come out here on their school's free afternoon and Saturday morning,' said Ann. 'I feel as if we'd got to offer more inducement or they'll just fade away.'

Mrs York looked quite upset and said, 'You're right! I ought to have thought, and now I feel awful about it. I let them go off this afternoon without even offering them a biscuit and a drink of Coke, and if they never come any more it's my fault.'

'Oh, don't worry,' I said. 'They couldn't be as unsporting as that.'

'Jill seems to think everybody ought to be so sporting!' said Cecilia. 'Oh, these horsy people!'

'Well, you're not one, so kindly keep out of it,' I said, in my sweet, cousinly way, and Mrs York looked a bit shaken.

However, she recovered and said, 'In future I'll see to it that they get Cokes and cakes whenever they come, and of course there will be a present for everybody who takes part in the ride on the day.'

'Goody!' said Ann. 'We'll tell them that.'

'Really?' said Cecilia. 'Fancy having to bribe people!'

'Oh, shut up,' said Ann, who also knew what Cecilia was like. By now Mrs York looked quite agitated, and to stop her from going into a complete flap Ann and I went on talking hurriedly about our team until gradually she got interested and calmed down.

At the next practice, four of our original twenty didn't turn up, the boy called Alec and his partner Tony Shaw, the girl who had fallen off her pony, and one of the younger kids, and when we asked about them it appeared that Alec and Tony didn't want to come any more as they thought it silly, and the mother of the girl who had fallen off wouldn't let her come any more because she said it was dangerous, and the small kid had got measles.

'None of the other sixteen must fall out,' I said, 'or we shan't have a team. We'll have to butter them up a bit.'

'Team or no team,' said Ann, 'I'm not taking anything from that bossy Althea.'

However, Althea ceased to be bossy and was quite pleasant when it was finally decided that she and Noel should be the leaders. Nan and Peter Bruce were also very good, and so were Pamela Shooter and her partner, and we started matching the rest of the people for ponies and height. Judy and Lucille yelled like mad when we separated them, but we had to convince them that they looked hopeless together, and at last they agreed to ride with other partners. Judy settled for Janet Watts because she liked Janet's piebald, and Lucille said, 'In that case I'll have John Hicks because I want to ride with his palomino,' and John said, 'Oh help, I want to ride with another boy!'

'Oh, come on, John, be a sport,' I said. 'At this rate we'll never get matched up,' and to my relief he said OK.

The Coke and cakes arriving at that moment brightened things up quite a lot.

Fortified by this, we thought we would have a go at the actual ride. Most of you must have seen a musical ride, and our idea was quite simple, everybody to ride up in single file, the ponies to turn left and right alternately, then up in pairs, left and right again, up in fours, and eights, and finally the whole sixteen abreast.

We marked out a sort of arena with poles, and hauled the sixteen riders into position and set them off. They were supposed to keep a pony length apart, but of course this didn't happen, the first few were all right but after that there was chaos.

'Walk, Janet!' I shouted. 'Don't trot.'

'Breeze won't walk,' Janet shrieked. 'She's fed up with walking, she wants to trot.'

'My Russian rabbits!' said Noel Shaw, turning round. 'Hasn't the girl got any control over her pony?'

'You look after your own pony,' I said, 'and never mind what's going on behind you.'

'It sounds like a stampede going on behind me,' said Noel.

'Use your legs!' shouted Ann. 'We've got to have a balanced pace.'

'Oh, let's try the turns,' I suggested, 'and look after the pace later.'

The ragged file rode on, one or two excited ponies dancing sideways, and others trying to pass the one in front. Indignant remarks flew through the air.

'Never mind!' I shouted. 'Come on up the centre. First pony left, second pony right.'

The first four ponies, ridden by Althea, Noel, Nan, and Peter, did it correctly, but Janet Watts instead of turning left followed Peter to the right and after that it was wild confusion.

'Get yourselves sorted out,' I said. 'We'll have to go on doing this until you get it right.'

We tried again and things improved, until one child's pony at the back suddenly broke into a smart canter, careered past all the rest, and went galloping across the park. The child shrieked, four people set off in pursuit, and the pony finally came to a stop with his saddle under his tummy and the child clinging upside down under his neck. It looked so funny that everybody burst out laughing, and strangely enough it put everybody into a good temper and they did better after that.

Next we tried the pairs, and of course there were any amount of collisions.

'Oi!' shouted John Hicks. 'When my partner gets ahead do I keep my place or keep up with her?'

'Keep your place,' said Ann, 'and Lucille, you *must* keep the right length whatever happens.'

Lucille grumbled, 'That's not very easy when people behind are shoving into you.'

In the end Ann went and fetched Black Boy and Rapide and she and I rode alongside the most feeble ones and showed them, and pushed them, and even hauled them about.

'Crumbs!' I said. 'Wouldn't you think it would be simple to watch the pair in front and just turn the opposite way?'

'Well, it isn't,' said a girl called Cherry Johnson, 'because the people in front start turning one way and then realise they're wrong and turn the other way, and by then you're up the pole.'

So Ann and I rode with each pair in turn and at last we got them straightened out. By the time we got the twos into fours the turning was simplified, but we could not get the person on the inside to pivot while the one on the outside took the wide turn, and the place looked like a battlefield.

'Somebody said this would be easy!' I said bitterly.

'I did,' said Noel, 'and so it would be if we didn't have to cope with all these beginners.'

'Don't exaggerate,' said Ann, 'even if they're not all as clever as you. I'll tell you what, let's get the music out and see what happens. It'll make things more fun.'

Mrs York and the gardener brought out the enormous record player, and we put on a march and turned it up to full strength. The effect on the ponies was atomic. The few who were used to hearing bands at shows didn't bother, but the others went mad, bucking and prancing, side-stepping and rearing, and soon they were cantering away in all directions, half the riders shrieking, 'Stop, stop!' and the other half yelling with laughter. This brought the practice to an end, and we decided that next time we should have to start off with some nice, soothing music.

'You've no idea how funny you two looked,' said Cecilia when we went in. 'All that pandemonium over a simple thing like a musical ride.'

I could have thought of a few things to say, but instead I walked upstairs with terrific dignity. In my room was an approving letter from Mummy. I had written to tell her that we had left Little Chimneys Farm because all the ponies had got lost and Captain Sound had given up the idea of the riding school, and that now we were staying with Cecilia's godmother and having a wonderful time. The fact that Cecilia was staying there too seemed to give Mummy a lot of unnecessary joy.

In the afternoon Mrs York took us in the car to Bournemouth to look at the shops and have tea. The shop-window gazing wasn't too successful, as Ann and I couldn't find a horsy shop so decided we

wanted to look at horsy books in a bookshop, while
Cecilia wanted to get some new ideas for tea cosies
at an arty-crafty shop, and we were all so frightfully
polite and self-sacrificing to impress Mrs York that
we nearly blew up.

The tea, however, put us all in a good humour. It
was supersonic. While Mrs York was paying the bill
we decided that we'd like to buy her a present, so
Ann and I being very noble said that Cecilia could
choose it, and we each gave her two pounds, and
she went off into the department store where the
café was. But when she came back we realised we
had been a bit too noble, as what she had bought
was a chiffon square in washy mauve with peculiar
brown cacti printed on it. While wondering how we
should apologise for it, we realised that Mrs York
was gushing over with thanks and admiration, and
she promptly tied it round her neck and wore it all
the way home, looking horrid. She never had it off
after that, and Cecilia looked smug, and Ann and I
were able to answer the question we had often asked
ourselves, Who buys all the gruesome things in shops
we feel sick to look at?

Mrs York then decided that it would be a good
thing if we went round and asked a few people to
give us prizes, as we should need a lot for the bazaar
competitions and the treasure hunt.

We felt a bit dim about this, as it was hardly in our
line and we weren't very good at asking people for
things.

'I'm sure Cecilia will go with you,' said Mrs York.
Our eyes nearly popped out with horror, we felt that

would be the last straw, but Cecilia was all for it; and, surprisingly, we were soon glad we had taken her because she proved to be a wizard at getting things out of people. You would think she had been doing it all her life, in fact she probably had.

We sailed into the grocer's shop where Mrs York dealt, and Cecilia began to make a lovely speech all about The Cause, etc., and the grocer fell for it like one o'clock and promised Cecilia some tins of chocolate biscuits.

Then we went into the draper's and out came Cecilia's little speech again, and the draper was practically weeping with emotion as he promised some boxes of handkerchiefs. At the confectioner's we landed two iced cakes, and at the china shop some glass dishes and ashtrays, and at the fancy shop some arty calendars and wooden owls with pencils through their noses.

So it went on, everybody falling over themselves to promise masses of prizes. Quite honestly, Cecilia had done it, we had hardly said a word.

'There!' she said. 'That's how it's done. Of course you have to have the right manner, and somehow horsy people never do.'

Ann and I could have slain her, but on the other hand she had done our job for us in a terrific way, which proved that everybody is good for something, even a person like Cecilia; and Mrs York was so excited at the forty-seven prizes we had amassed that she praised us like mad, and I must say Cecilia was sporting enough not to say that she'd done it all herself.

Ann and I were now back at the game of struggling with the musical ride.

'The trouble,' said Cecilia, giving us her unasked advice, 'is that half those kids can't really ride. The onlooker sees most of the game.'

Ann said it was a pity that the onlooker was so clever as to keep one eye on the game and the other on the tea cosy, and the onlooker would soon be developing a squint and dropping a few stitches, and I said sarkily that perhaps the onlooker would like to do the training herself?

'Nothing simpler,' said Cecilia. We gasped.

'Done!' said Ann. 'You flipping well take them this afternoon.'

Without turning a hair Cecilia said it was a bore but she'd show us for once, and we said OK get on with it, and she said, thanks I will, and we said good luck to you, and she said don't mention it.

So when the sixteen riders arrived that afternoon – and very glad we were to see sixteen, because we wouldn't have been surprised if about eight had fallen out and we would have found ourselves with no ride, no nothing – instead of Us greeting them, there stood Cecilia in her pink jumper and skirt, and lipstick on, and believe me or believe me not, they all looked at her as if she was the crowned queen of Hickstead. There wasn't a grumble out of any of them, they were so impressed, and Cecilia twiddled her pearl beads – yes, she actually had some on – and said, 'Heads up, knees up, and hands down, and when I say it I mean it, and keep like that; and ride with your knees and not your reins, and if I see anybody sawing at the reins they'll get sent off, and if anybody but ME says anything *they'll* get sent off too.'

Ann and I wouldn't have dared to talk to them like that in case any of them did go off, but they took it from Cecilia. She got them into pairs, and two, not one, pony lengths between each pair, and then said, '*Now* don't tell me you can't see what the pair in front are going to do!'

She bossed them like I've never in my life heard anybody bossed, and they took it! They rode in a silence that was uncanny, and even the kids at the back did it right.

Cecilia said, 'We'd better have somebody good to bring up the rear or it'll look like a sick snake,' and she ordered Nan and Peter to go to the back.

They went without a mutter. If I'd told them there'd have been a scene.

When she had put the team through the whole performance – singles, pairs, fours, eights, and finally the whole sixteen – Cecilia calmly said, 'You can have your break now,' and while they were clustering round Mrs York's tray of cakes she walked over to Ann and me, still twiddling her pearl beads, and said, 'There you are – positively easy.'

We hadn't a word to say. Cecilia strolled into the house and left us to carry on. Humiliating as it sounds, from that moment we had hardly any trouble with the team. We couldn't understand what had happened until we heard that a story was going round the village that the girl in pink

was really Ann Moore! I mean – Cecilia! And all
she actually knew about riding was what I had
managed to din into her when she was staying at
my home.

8 Brushing up the team

'What dear Cecilia didn't take the trouble to notice,' said Ann, 'is that only about four people out of the sixteen know how to put on a pony's tack. What with tight girths and loose bits it's a disgusting sight. Do you think we dare tell them?'

I giggled. 'They'll probably appeal to Cecilia if we do. Let's say we're going to have a tack inspection.'

We made everybody stand by his or her pony's head, and went round the lot. Hardly a buckle was right, and by the time that Ann and I had slackened or tightened the lot we never wanted to see a buckle again and were thoroughly unpopular, except with Althea, Noel, and the two Bruces who were very smug when we couldn't find a thing the matter with their ponies.

We made everybody unsaddle, and then we found out the sort of grooming that lazy people do!

'You're a horrid lot,' said Ann. 'What do you think a pony feels like with dirt and sand under the saddle? I'd like to fill all your shoes with grit and make you run in them.'

The people she was referring to looked shame-faced, and Lucille who was one of them said, 'I've only left it once, I was in a hurry so I just groomed the part that shows, but I won't do it again.'

'I should think not,' I said. 'Take your pony round to the farm behind the house and ask them to lend you a dandy brush – and you too, Vincent. And if ever I find a sore or a girth gall on either of your ponies I'll have you eaten alive by my tiger.'

'What tiger?' said Lucille, and I replied, 'The tiger I keep specially for people like you. Leave your saddles here, and bring your ponies back clean.'

The two of them set off at a run, and everybody else laughed, and somebody said, 'They believed you about the tiger.'

'At least you'll all have your tack on properly,' I said. 'Don't the people who teach you tell you this sort of thing?'

Several people hung their heads and muttered that of course they were taught, but since they stopped having regular lessons they hadn't bothered so much, and I said heatedly, 'What do you think you were taught for? So that you'd do things properly for the rest of your life, and be able to show other people, and be a credit to horsemanship. Next time you feel lazy about putting on your tack properly, think of it from the pony's point of view, and think how awful you feel if you've got your coat buttoned in the wrong buttons, or the left shoe on the right foot, or something too tight round your middle.'

'That sank in all right,' said Ann, as we watched people very carefully checking their tack. 'We could do something about making them sit straighter. I've noticed that they don't all have their stirrup leathers dead straight. Even Noel pushes his back a bit.'

'Well, what's the matter with that?' said Noel when we mentioned it to him. 'I'm used to it.'

'Your seat can't be as firm as it should,' I said. 'You'd find that out if you did any cross-country jumping. Why not get it right once and for all? All the books say that the stirrup leather must be perfectly perpendicular.'

'I'll have a try,' said Noel. 'There, is that right? . . . It feels jolly awkward to me.'

'Get used to it,' I said. 'If your weight is right in the saddle you'll soon feel perfectly balanced. Come a bit further forward – that's better.'

'Yes, it is better,' agreed Noel. 'Thanks for showing me.'

By now everyone was looking down to see if their stirrup leathers were straight and very few were, so they all began to adjust rapidly, and said how weird the correct position made them feel.

'But I expect it's the same as in playing golf,' said Althea. 'When you hold the club properly it feels terrible, but as soon as you realise it's the only way to hit the ball a lovely bash you wonder how you ever managed to hold it wrong.'

Soon we had them riding in a circle and all the stirrup leathers were dead straight. The difference it made to everybody's appearance was remarkable.

'There'll be sure to be people here on the day,' said Ann, 'who'll make rude remarks about the riding if they get the chance. Don't let's give them the chance.'

'I say,' said Nan Bruce, 'couldn't we do some of that weaving in and out riding?'

'You can try it if you like,' I said, 'but I'm afraid some of the younger ones will get woven into a solid mass.'

They did try it, but it turned out a frightful mess, though it caused a lot of fun and people were good-tempered about it. We decided that we'd better concentrate on getting our ordinary programme perfect. They all had the idea of the simple figures by now and weren't making many mistakes.

'But there hasn't to be one – not one single mistake on the day,' I pointed out, 'because only one would ruin the whole thing.'

'The riding looks very, very much nicer,' said Mrs York when we went in to lunch. 'I don't know an awful lot about it, but they all look smarter somehow.'

Cecilia smirked and said, 'I did my best with them, Aunt Pat.'

Ann and I exchanged glances, and Ann said, 'It's funny, Cecilia, that you didn't notice that half the saddles were too tight and most of the bits practically hanging on the ponies' front teeth, and that everybody's stirrup leathers were at a different angle. Jill and I spent half the morning putting that right, that's why they look better.'

Cecilia said, 'The two kids next to the back looked a scream. They had their tongues hanging out and their hands up nearly under their chins. They looked as if they were begging for biscuits.'

'We were concentrating on legs this morning,' I said in a snooty sort of way. 'We'll see to hands next time.'

Ann giggled, and as we went up to our room she said, 'Cecilia nearly got us that time. I was looking at the legs so hard I honestly never noticed the hands, and evidently you didn't either. Gorgeous sort of teachers we are, I must say!'

Next time the team met we looked hard at the two kids Cecilia had mentioned, and there was a lot in what she said.

'It's Rose and Arthur,' I said. 'They look like two poodles asking to be taken out.'

We thought it was unfair to single out these two kids, so we made the whole line stop and told everybody to check the position of their hands. Immediately Rose and Arthur went scarlet and brought their hands down with a bump, and then looked round anxiously to see if anybody had noticed.

'That's better,' I said, 'only some people's elbows are now sticking out at the sides. Rose, get your fists out of your tummy and relax your hands. Goodness, Lucille, don't wave your elbows – '

'Are mine all right?' shouted Judy. I told her that her wrists and fingers were too stiff. Eventually I managed to get everybody's hands on a level with the reins, and we did a bit of stopping and starting in that position, some of the lazy ones complaining that it was all a frightful effort, though the more sensible ones realised that it made things easier and the ponies appreciated it.

Unfortunately, after this practice the weather broke

and we had gales and torrents of rain, so we had to miss several practices. Mrs York was worried in case the day of the bazaar should be bad and the musical ride washed out of existence, and Ann and I were more worried still lest we should have to carry out the ride without sufficient practice and it would be a mess.

Meanwhile we started planning the treasure hunt in which we hoped that practically every rider in the district was going to join.

First we collected a huge number of cocoa tins and mustard tins and other small tins which had held coffee powder, nutmegs, and so on. Then into each tin we put a slip of paper on which was written either Prize or Bad Luck. There were twenty prizes, and all the other papers were bad luck ones. Then we made a plan of the park and marked the spots where we were going to bury the tins when the weather cleared up, and we wrote out the clues, such as, 'South-south-west of the big chimney stands a tree that looks like a parrot. Find a spot with no moss and dig,' and 'Follow your nose from front door to three rabbit holes in a row. One of them may prove your goal.'

This took a jolly long time to do, as you can imagine; in fact we spent days over it, all through the bad weather, and for once Cecilia was quite helpful and thought up some ingenious clues.

'You ought to have been jolly well wrecked on a treasure island in the Caribbean in the days of the buccaneers,' I said. 'I bet you'd have got to the treasure first.'

Cecilia pointed out, quite rightly, that it was a lot easier to make up clues than to follow them.

'Don't be too ingenious,' said Mrs York, 'or nobody will find anything and then they'll all be wanting their money back, and what we need is the money.'

Then the weather cleared up and was sunny and mild and not like November at all, so three days before the bazaar we went out and buried the tins with the help of the plan we had made. Each clue was now in a sealed envelope with one pound written on the outside, which was what the competitors had to pay for it, and as the prizes were jolly good it was worth it.

In a way the break from practices had been a good thing, because everybody turned up keen and anxious to make up for the lost time. By now all the ponies had got used to the record player, even when it was on full blast, so we didn't think there was anything to fear from the local band who were going to play on the day. The tunes we had chosen were *Colonel Bogey* and *Blaze Away*, because they are jolly and have the right beat and somehow all ponies seem to like them; though Cecilia was rather disdainful and said, 'Gosh, what taste! Some people don't know anything about music. Couldn't you have had *Swan Lake*?'

We hastily pointed out that this wasn't a ballet but a pony ride, and Cecilia said she was afraid that that was going to be only too obvious.

Ann and I were shaking at the knees by now, because we felt that if the musical ride wasn't a success, although Mrs York would be too kind to criticise, we should go home with our heads in the dust, so to speak. Our professional reputation and the whole prestige of equitation seemed to be at stake.

'I'd feel happier if it wasn't for Rose and Arthur,' I said gloomily. 'I dream about those kids every night, it's a sort of nightmare.'

'I'm more worried about Lucille and John Hicks,' said Ann. 'He hates riding with her and he doesn't bother to help her to keep level. He keeps the pace and length himself and leaves her to muddle along. It's jolly selfish of him.'

'I suppose I'd better have a word with him,' I said. 'I'll put it down in my book under *Things I have Got To Do*, and there are twenty-two of them already.'

'What's the first?' said Ann, and I said it was Grooming and Tack Cleaning On The Day.

As we felt this was terribly important we gave the team a special lecture on it, and it seemed to sink in.

'Nothing but perfection will do,' I said, and Ann said afterwards that I sounded like our late lamented headmistress at school.

'What are we going to wear?' asked Althea. 'It'll be too cold for white shirts and jodhs.'

'I vote for black coats,' said Nan Bruce. 'We might as well look terrifically high-class.'

There was a shriek at this, as it turned out that only about four of the sixteen had got black coats.

'But we can't all wear different jackets,' said Pamela Shooter. 'We shall look so odd.'

'Jackets are dull, anyway,' said Judy. 'Let's all wear turtleneck jerseys, all different colours.'

'Jerseys,' said Ann, 'sound right, but help! Not all different colours!'

'What colours have you got?' I said.

It turned out that everybody could lay hands on either a yellow or a white jersey, so we suggested that they should bring the jerseys on the day and we would pool them and put each pair of people into the same colour.

'And just see,' I added, 'that everybody's jodhpurs are clean and fit properly.'

I put that bit in because I know from my vast experience that when a show day comes some lazy people have forgotten to get their jodhs cleaned, so they hastily borrow their sister's, which either hang down in swags or are so tight that the wearer looks like a wooden doll.

'Can I wear my new yellow gloves?' asked Janet Watts.

Everybody howled.

'No, she can't!' said Nan Bruce. 'We haven't all got new yellow gloves.'

I then rubbed it in about shoes being polished, and no revelation of luminous pink socks or anything like that.

John Hicks said in disgust, 'Crumbs! Is this a riding practice or a mannequin parade?' He said that for two pins he'd take himself and his palomino out of it, and because we wanted the palomino so much because it gave tone to the team, we managed to calm John down.

At last everybody went home, and Ann said after all that arguing she felt like a shadow that had lost its body.

I said that, talking of shadows, it was nice to feel

we had a good lunch to go to instead of one of Mrs Sound's meals which weren't there.

After lunch we gave ourselves a treat by going for a long ride on my ponies, across hill and down dale. Cecilia came too, on her bicycle, and criticised our riding most of the way. When we had had enough of this we turned into some woods where she couldn't follow us on her bike, and thus lost her. It sounds a bit mean, but she brought it on herself.

9 The Usefull Charmes

'Just listen to this,' said Ann.

It was a pouring wet afternoon and we were sitting in the morning-room, Cecilia madly making pincushions out of pink felt, me just as madly darning my only decent pair of tights, and Ann reading a funny old book which she had dug out of a cupboard.

'This is comic,' she went on. 'It's a chapter called *Usefull Charmes* and here's one called "a charme for good weather on the Festal Daye".'

'What festal day?' asked Cecilia who has no imagination.

'Any festal day, you dope,' I said. 'The day you dance round the maypole, or the day the beautiful village maiden gets married, or anything you want a fine day for. Like the bazaar.'

'I don't see why we need a fine day for the bazaar particularly,' said Cecilia maddeningly. 'It's all in the house, anyway.'

'What about our little equestrian show?' I said coldly.

'Well, really, Jill, you can't say it's important,' said Cecilia. 'I mean, the bazaar wouldn't conk out without it.'

'Come off it!' said Ann. 'People will want to look

at something decent and exciting when they're sick of gazing at your beastly pincushions. And I think you've got a nerve and a half saying that our show isn't important. Mrs York must think it's important or she wouldn't have bothered to have us staying here all this time.'

'She's got you there!' I chortled. 'Go on about the charm, Ann. You were saying something.'

'It tells you what you have to do,' said Ann. 'You get some horse hairs and tie one tightly round each finger of your left hand. We could manage that. Then you wash your hands carefully in a "brew made of clover picked by ye light of ye moon". Gosh, do you think there's any clover around in November?'

'There's some in the kitchen garden. I saw it,' I said. 'In fact the gardener was just going to root it out, but it'll be on the rubbish heap. How do we brew it?'

'Just in a teapot in the ordinary way,' said Cecilia sarkily.

'No, you don't, chum,' said Ann. 'You pour boiling water over it, and let it simmer. Well, OK, we've got our hands washed, and next we have to go into the woods and find a latch tree – '

'A what tree?' I said.

'It says a latch tree.'

'She means a larch tree,' said Cecilia. 'The girl can't read.'

'It says a latch tree,' said Ann, 'and if it says a latch tree it jolly well means a latch tree. This is a sensible book. Don't tell me in all the woods round this house there isn't a latch tree.'

'You've got my permission to go and find one,'

said Cecilia. 'I shan't stop you. I couldn't care less.'

'What do you do when you've found the latch tree?' I asked.

'You walk round it three times with your eyes shut, and say, "Sun, Sun, come if you may, shine upon our festal day." That's all.'

'Let's do it,' I said. 'It'll be fun. Let's put our macs on and go and get the horse hairs out of Black Boy's tail, and find the clover and get it brewed while there's nobody in the kitchen.'

'How childish can people get?' said Cecilia.

'That's what I thought when I saw you making those silly pincushions,' I said, and felt very pleased with myself, because it was the first time in my whole life I had thought of the right thing to say at the right moment. One usually thinks of it about twelve hours too late.

Ann and I got the scissors and went down to the farm and cut ten hairs carefully out of Black Boy's long tail, though he looked at us as if he thought we were mad, and I expect we were a bit.

Then we went to the rubbish heap, and sure enough there were heaps of wet green clover. The charm didn't say how much to use, so we got two good handfuls. There was nobody in the kitchen, as Mrs York's maid always had a lie down on her bed between two and three in the afternoon, and so did Mrs York.

We put the clover into a pan and poured boiling water over it, and let it simmer on the gas ring for about five minutes. Then we washed our hands in it.

It felt a bit funny and messy, and we were glad when it was done. We poured the water away, threw the boiled clover in the bin, and thankfully dried our hands.

'What's the next thing?' I asked.

'Oh murder!' said Ann. 'We ought to have tied the horse hairs round our fingers before we washed our hands! Now we'll have to do it all over again.'

'You absolute clot!' I said. 'Well, you can jolly well get some more clover and boil it. Let's tie the hairs on each other.'

This took ages. I don't know if you've ever tried tying horse hairs round somebody's fingers – I don't suppose you've ever done anything so batty – but having started this we simply had to go on. The horse hairs were stiff and kept coming untied, it was a frightful business. However, at last it was done, and Ann got some more clover and we went through the whole washing and tidying up process again.

'Now we've had it!' I said. 'It's going to be dark before we can get into the woods and find this latch tree.'

At that moment Mrs York came into the kitchen and said, 'What on earth are you girls doing?'

We told her, and added, 'I expect you'll think we're bats.'

She began to laugh, and said, 'I think it's rather fun.'

'We've left it a bit late,' I said, 'because now we've got to go into the woods to find a latch tree and we don't even know what it is.'

'Do you think it means a larch?' said Ann. 'And

even if it does, I don't know how we're going to find one.'

'Oh, it's easier than that,' said Mrs York. 'A latch tree is what the local people call a tree in the park that has a fence round it to keep the cattle from rubbing against it. There's one right outside the side door.'

'Why, that's marvellous,' I said. 'Come on, Ann, bring the book and let's get it right.'

Mrs York was so intrigued that she came with us and we all crept out of the house giggling.

'Now shut your eyes,' said Mrs York when we got to the latch tree, 'and feel your way round it, and I'll tell you when you've gone round three times.'

'Wait,' I said. 'Let's learn this comic poetry off by heart first. If we say it wrong we'll probably bring down a hurricane.'

It wasn't hard to learn, and Ann and I went groping our way round the tree saying, 'Sun, Sun, come if you may, shine upon our festal day.'

By now we were all pretty wet, and Mrs York said that she thought some tea and hot buttered buns would meet the case, so we helped her to make these and took them into the morning-room.

'You don't mean to say you've been doing that silly rubbish?' said Cecilia, looking at our wet hair. 'You want your heads examining.'

'In that case,' said Mrs York, 'I must want mine examining too, because I've been doing the silly rubbish with them.'

You never in your life saw anybody so completely squashed as Cecilia. She couldn't say a word, and then in the end she gulped, and said, 'I do hope the charm

works because we do want a fine day on the day.'
Which was quite a climb-down for Cecilia.

To make a long story short, the charm worked! On
the day of the bazaar we woke up to see the sky a lovely
clear pale blue, and soon the sun came up and it shone
all day. The grass in the park sparkled, it was going to
be just right for the ride and the treasure hunt. Ann
and I spent the morning inspecting our 'props', while
Mrs York and some of her friends and Cecilia got the
stalls ready in the drawing-room and dining-room,
and laid the buffet tables for tea in the hall and the
morning-room.

Everything went well, and Mrs York laughed and
said we had better try a few more charms as we were
so good at it. When the preparations were finished,
we had sandwiches, coffee, and bananas in the kitchen
as it was the only room that wasn't full of bazaar, and
then Ann and I went upstairs to get dressed.

We had decided to wear our white turtlenecks, and
light jodhpurs, as we thought this would match the
team and also look a bit glamorous, but when I opened
my drawer to get out the jersey I gave a scream of
horror.

The day before I had thrown in my red silk head
scarf and it was damp with rain, and the red had run
all on to my beautiful white jersey in streaks.

'Gosh!' said Ann. 'That's torn it. Now what are
you going to do?'

'I've simply had it,' I wailed. 'Now I've nothing to
wear but my old blue one, I shan't match, and I shall
look like a tramp and it's all my own fault. I never
thought of the red running.'

I was miserable too because I knew I was to blame. Mummy had told me ten million times about throwing things into drawers wet because I couldn't be bothered to hang them on the rack and dry them, and now I was well and truly caught out.

Just then Cecilia passed the open door and heard my shrieks of anguish.

'What on earth's the matter?' she said.

'Jill's ruined her white jersey,' said Ann, holding it up.

'Well, she shouldn't have thrown a wet red thing on it,' said Cecilia.

'Do you think I don't know that,' I yelled. 'I could murder you!'

'I'll tell you what,' said Cecilia. 'I'll lend you mine, as it's all in aid of the bazaar.'

I nearly fell down dead.

'You don't mean your new one?' I said. 'You've only worn it once.'

'It's OK,' said Cecilia. 'You can wear it.'

As this was the most noble thing my cousin had ever done in her life I was completely overcome.

'I say, that's terrific of you,' I said. 'Thanks very much, Cecilia.'

'I'll get it for you,' she said. 'And perhaps you won't be such a careless idiot in future.'

So when Ann and I were ready we really did look magnifique. Then our pony people began to arrive, and all our fears were at rest because they looked magnifique too. One kid's mother had tied a pink scarf round its neck in case it got a sore throat, but we soon had that off. We stood them all in a row and made them give a final rub to their boots and put their hats straight. Then we inspected the ponies, and believe me, they were decently groomed too, except for one or two minor items which we soon put right.

Of course everybody had butterflies, and Janet moaned, 'I know I shan't pivot properly in the fours,' and her partner said, 'If you don't you'll wreck the whole thing;' and Noel said, 'If she wrecks the whole thing I'll absolutely pulverise her,' and Janet said, 'What's pulverise?' and her partner said, 'Something absolutely beastly.'

'For goodness' sake shut up,' I said, 'and don't put everybody else off.'

Crowds of people rolled up for the bazaar which started off with a whack, everybody madly buying things from Mrs York's stall. Ann and I felt we must do something for Cecilia after she'd been so atomically decent about the white jersey, so we went to her stall upon which sat all those revolting-looking tea cosies and pincushions which weren't selling too well, and I said I would like to buy a tea cosy for Mummy, and deliberately chose the most hideous one which I knew nobody else would be mad enough to buy, and Ann cottoned on to the idea and bought a pincushion for her mother.

Cecilia beamed and said, 'Thanks frightfully. There's nothing like a thing of beauty, is there?'

I could have said that my idea of a thing of beauty wasn't pea green with yellow squiggles, but I was noble enough not to. After all, I had on the white jersey in all its pure unsullied beauty.

By now the tea provided by Mrs York was going

with a swing, like tea at bazaars always does. You wouldn't think people wanted tea at three o'clock in the afternoon, but at bazaars they always do, and I must say the sandwiches and cakes looked out of this world. Looking at them was about all that Ann and I got, because by now the people who were riding in our team had begun to drift around the tea-room, eating cakes, and saying, 'I say, what time do we start?' and we were afraid we should never get them rounded up.

I said to Mrs York, 'Please do you think you could tell everybody that the Musical Ride is just about to take place, or they'll go on eating for ever, and so will our team.'

'Right ho,' said Mrs York, and she clapped her hands, and a hush fell. It sounded funny when everybody stopped rattling cups and jabbering.

'The Musical Ride is about to start,' said Mrs York, 'and I can assure you it's going to be good. Whatever you do, don't miss it. Jill and Ann, here, have been training the boys and girls for ages, and when you see them you'll be just thrilled. So please will everybody go out to the front of the house.'

'I wish she hadn't laid it on so thick,' I murmured to Ann as we crawled away. 'It makes me feel more wobbly than ever.'

There waiting outside was the local band in red uniforms. When everything was ready and the riders drawn up and the crowd assembled, they started to play *Colonel Bogey*, and we were off.

Oh, how careful everybody was! After a while, when we saw that it was going properly and that nothing awful was going to happen, Ann and I started breathing again after holding our breaths till we nearly burst.

I can't say it was perfect, but the spectators seemed to think it was, especially the mothers of the riders; and after it was over they asked for it to be done again, and a photographer from the local paper took pictures, and Mrs York's helpers picked up a huge collection of money.

Then the fond mothers clustered round Ann and me and said what marvellous teachers we were, and we went very red and murmured, 'Oh, not really!' and modest mutterings like that, and the photographer said, could he have a photo of us two together?

(The pictures appeared next day in the local paper, and Ann looked really glamorous and about nineteen, and I had my eyes shut and my hat had slipped, and I looked about twelve. This is the sort of thing that happens to me.)

The next item was the treasure hunt in which absolutely everybody in the neighbourhood who could dig up a pony had entered.

Three of the Pobley children who had only one pony between them were in it, sharing the pony, and Dulcie Willow turned up on the most beautiful grey mare you ever saw, and a woman who looked about ninety and had been hunting all her life turned up, all smiles and cracking jokes and riding side-saddle.

Ann and I sold the envelopes with the clues, and the money fairly rolled in. There was some confusion while people read their clues and tried to make out what they meant, then somebody would go streaming away across the park, only to discover a tin with a blank paper in it. Then he or she would come back to pay another pound for another clue.

The first home to get a prize was Dulcie Willow, and her prize was a pair of glass jam dishes for which I wouldn't have thanked you, but Dulcie thought they were super.

Josephine Pobley won a large iced cake which – believe it or not – she and her two brothers devoured in about five minutes, and the Ancient Huntress, as Ann had christened her, won a lipstick in a case.

Then to our surprise Cecilia appeared, and said, 'You patronised my stall so I'll have a go at your show, a girl has lent me a pony.'

I felt a bit doubtful, as Cecilia on a pony has to be seen to be believed, and is apt to spread death and destruction around, but who was I to argue, so I took her pound; and the last thing I saw of her, she was mounted on a pony and cantering off into the misty stretches of the park where it was now beginning to go dusk. I never gave her another thought until the girl whose pony she'd borrowed came and said she wanted to go home, and where was her pony?

'Hasn't Cecilia come back?' I said, and the girl said, 'She must be at Southampton by now.'

I thought, if Cecilia was never seen again, her mother, my aunt, would blame me for letting her go off like that, as if anybody could stop Cecilia from doing anything she wanted to do!

Then Mrs York came out and said that Cecilia had rung up. The pony had galloped for about three miles before she could stop him, and a nice woman whose cottage she had nearly bashed into had asked her in and given her a second cup of tea and let her sit by the fire, and had kindly rubbed the pony down. And would somebody come and fetch them?

Mrs York sent off the farmer with the horse van, and Cecilia and the pony arrived back without a hair out of place.

'Gosh!' I said bitterly. 'What luck you do have. If it had been me I'd have got into a frightful scrape.'

By now everything at the bazaar had been sold, and Mrs York was dizzy with bliss over the money she had got for the refugees. All the sixteen riders in our team were given boxes of chocolates for their hard work, and went home very thrilled.

'The whole day has been the most terrific success,' said Mrs York, 'and a lot of it has been due to you girls. It certainly was a lucky day for me when I met you, and darling Cecilia too.

'As none of you had a chance to win any prizes for yourselves,' went on Mrs York, 'I am going to give you each one.'

She put a small parcel into each of our hands, and when we opened them we found in each of them a lovely blue enamel bracelet.

We stuttered our thanks, and said, 'We've simply loved being here, and we wish it was all beginning instead of ending.'

This was true, as we had already realised that our job at Pockett House had ended now the bazaar was over, and we couldn't help wondering what was going to happen to us next. What did happen was that we both had letters from our mothers, saying that Christmas was coming and we must both be home in time for it. Of course we wanted to be home for Christmas.

'But we don't want to stay at home for ever,' said Ann to Mrs York sorrowfully. 'We'd love to have another pony job, but they're not easily come by and we don't know where we'll find one.'

'You'll find one,' said Cecilia, who was also preparing to go home. 'I never saw anybody like you two for falling on your feet.'

'I might even be able to hear of a job for you,' said Mrs York. 'If I do, I'll ring you up after Christmas.'

We said that would be marvellous, and after thanking her again for all the fun we'd had at Pockett House, we set off home for Chatton with a terrific store of adventures to tell.

10 Lucky again

Mummy said she hoped I was cured of going out into the wide, wide world in search of adventures, and I said on the contrary I was looking forward to more. She roared with laughter over all our mishaps at Little Chimneys Farm, and was excited about the lovely time we had had with Mrs York, and then began to see my point of view.

'Only don't count too much on Mrs York finding you a job,' she said. 'She may not know of anything or she may forget.'

'Whatever it is,' I said, 'I don't suppose it will be as good as it was at her house, but it would be fun to see what turns up.'

But I wished Mummy hadn't said that about Mrs York forgetting, because it struck chill upon my beating heart. (This poetical phrase I got out a of a book, but I really did feel like that.)

I asked Ann, did she think Mrs York would forget? And she said that even if Mrs York did we couldn't do anything about it because we should be making a nuisance of ourselves, and *her* mother would be livid if we did that.

We decided that we wouldn't start worrying until after Christmas and New Year, but on the second of January we would start worrying. We went into Ryechester to buy Christmas presents for our nearest and dearest, and as usual I wished I was a millionaire as I turned the few sordid coins over in my purse. Talking of purses, I bought Mummy a very nice one made of red leather, and Ann bought her mother a scent spray.

Ann and I decided that for once we wouldn't give each other horsy presents, so I bought her a diary – blue with gold edges – and she bought me a bottle of bath essence called Dew of Lotus, because I couldn't imagine what this scent would be like and I had to try it. It sounded too glamorous for words, but the first time I used it Mummy came rushing upstairs shrieking, 'Is something burning? There's a most ghastly smell all over the house.'

It is funny that dew of lotus should smell of burning socks, but it did.

Well, Christmas was over and we took down the paper chains and the holly, and put away the balloons and the silver fir cones and red ribbons for next year, and put the Christmas cards into a box so that we shouldn't forget anybody next time, and finished the last of the chocolates and the last bit of the Christmas cake, and I wrote all my thank-you letters.

I had had a Christmas card from Mrs York and so had Ann, so she hadn't forgotten us, but as the days went by we came to the sad conclusion that she wasn't going to do anything about another job for us.

When the first of February came I sensed a change in the home atmosphere. Mummy began muttering darkly that it was time I did something, and I myself felt that it was, because the holidays were over, but Mummy's ideas of 'Something' and mine were so gruesomely different.

The crisis came that very afternoon when Ann arrived and announced that her mother had put her down for a course in Flower Arrangement so that she could Take It Up Seriously, and get a job with a very good florist in Ryechester.

I told her I didn't know she was any good at Flower Arrangement, and she said she wasn't, but her mother thought she ought to be, and she had to go to this place on Monday morning and they would teach her all about chicken wire and pinholders and things.

'If only Mrs York would phone!' said Ann. 'Even if she didn't know of any job, at least we'd know she hadn't forgotten about us.'

She sounded desperate. I was very blue. It was a hopeless prospect, you must admit, and I could see poor Ann being swept away into the jaws of this flower arranging place and me into something equally sordid. Of course we couldn't hang about doing nothing, we realised that, and we wanted to work, but it was sad to see our beautiful dreams coming to naught.

That very afternoon I had just come into the kitchen from feeding the ponies when the telephone rang. Mummy answered it and said calmly, 'It's for you, Jill. It's Mrs York.'

I rushed to the phone, so breathless and excited that I could only stutter.

Mrs York said, 'Is that you, Jill?' and I said, 'Yes, it is,' and my voice came out in a squeak like a day-old chick.

By the time she had finished talking and rung off I was in a pink-coloured trance, but I soon came out of it when Mummy started telling me off for going straight from the stable to the sitting-room without changing my shoes.

About half an hour later I was charging up to Ann's house on my bike. She saw me from the window and rushed out.

'What on earth is it?'

'Shhh!' I said. 'Mrs York has phoned.'

Ann's house is the kind of place where you have to say Shhh! otherwise everybody wants to know why you've come and join in your private conversation.

'Come on up,' said Ann, nearly bursting with excitement and we went up to her room and flopped on the bed.

'It's a job!' I said,

'No kidding?'

'Absolutely not. I can hardly believe it myself. She rang up about half an hour ago. The job is with somebody called Miss Day. She's an old, old friend of Mrs York's, and she has a large farm with lots of room, and knows everything there is to know about pigs and chickens, but nothing about ponies and – '

'Oh Christmas!' shrieked Ann. 'Don't tell me we've got to go and teach somebody about eighty, who's a friend of Mrs York's, to ride a pony?'

'Will you shut up and listen till I've done?' I said. 'Miss Day has two nieces from Australia staying with her, and she thinks it would be nice for them to learn to ride and also have some young companionship – that's us – so would we like to go, and we'll stay at the farm and she'll pay for the use of my ponies, and pay us a salary too. Can you imagine? Isn't it super?'

'I don't know,' said Ann, biting her nails. 'That young companionship bit gets me. Are these nieces dotty, or something? Why can't they be young companions to each other?'

'Oh, don't you go all cautious and prudent!' I said. 'What's the matter with you? Don't you realise our lives are saved? Or do you *want* to go and stick flowers into chicken wire for the rest of your days? I think you're the depths.'

Ann said she didn't mean to be the depths, but somehow the job wasn't exactly what she'd visualised. She had pictured something much more glamorous and promising in the world of equitation.

I bounced on the bed and a spring gave way with a loud ping.

'What's the matter with you?' I said. 'Beggars can't be choosers.'

'We haven't begged for anything,' said Ann, 'but as for teaching two little kids to ride – Going all the way back again to the dreary "Mount like this" and "Sit like this", and leading them round on a rein. I thought we'd done with that for ever. If only we could have had a job exercising hunters!'

'Well, we haven't had one offered,' I said crossly. 'And we have had this job offered, and I thought you'd have been running round in circles, yelping hurray. You'd better go and arrange your beastly flowers.'

'Oh, not likely!' said Ann. 'We'll try the job, but you must admit it sounds gruesome, being stuck on a farm with two kids and some pigs and chickens, and a woman called Miss Day who isn't horsy and knew Mrs York a hundred years ago.'

'If we don't like it,' I said, 'we can always come home.'

'No, we can't. They'll laugh at us and say we can't keep a job.'

'Look,' I said, 'are we going or not? Because if we are, don't beef about it,' and she finally said OK.

Then we went downstairs to tell Mrs Derry, who had been hoping all along that Mrs York wouldn't ring at all. However, the one thing that pleased Mrs Derry was the fact that this job sounded so dull and tame, because she had been afraid that somebody would offer us a job in a circus, so she said that Ann could go if she liked, but she'd soon be bored stiff and glad to come home.

So a week later we landed at Mayside Farm, complete with our luggage and Black Boy and Rapide. It was a pretty farm and very well kept, and the house itself was all chintzy, and the weather was spring-like and pussy-willowish, and Miss Day was the fussy kind. She seemed to spend her whole life dreaming about pigs and chickens, and she looked at my ponies as if she expected them to grunt or peck.

'I don't know the first thing about them,' she said. 'But I've got a nice stable that has never been used, and I've told the corn shop that you're to order just what you need for them.'

This sounded promising, and actually the arrangements for the ponies were even better than I could have wished. We were then shown what looked like thousands of white chickens and pink pigs and we said we thought they looked jolly nice, and Miss Day beamed. She was very small and had on an enormous pair of dungarees, and her hair was in little screwed-up curls.

Then she took us in the house and gave us each a glass of milk, and opened a huge tin of chocolate biscuits, and said, 'I know what little girls like;' which was the right idea, though we weren't very sold on being called little girls when we were sixteen, and we would rather have had tea than milk but didn't like to say so.

'The children are out somewhere,' she said. 'They love playing in the woods, I expect it's being Australian, all those wide open spaces, you know.'

Ann looked at me and made a face, and I glared at her.

'You see my idea, don't you?' said Miss Day. 'Go on, have some more chocolate biscuits. All the children about here seem to ride, and I thought it would be nice if my nieces could learn too, it would give them something to do, so I asked them if they'd like to, and they said they didn't mind trying.'

My spirits sank a lot. The 'children' began to sound pretty grim to me, what with playing in the woods and saying they didn't mind trying to learn to ride. I daren't look at Ann.

We then went up to our room, a very nice one, and sat down on our beds, and Ann said, 'We've had it! Milk, and pink pigs, and two little woodsy kids from the wide open spaces who've never ridden on a pony and think they'd like to try. My Russian rabbits!'

'Oh shut up!' I said, which wasn't clever, but I just

felt bad. 'You go home if you want to,' I went on. 'Probably with a most terrific effort I might even teach these kids all by myself. I seem to remember having done similar things in my youth.' I thought this last bit sounded frightfully grand and sarky.

'Oh, I'll stick it out,' said Ann. 'We'll review the position after a week. By then we'll know if they're possible or hopeless. But I won't read fairy tales to them, or nurse their teddies.'

'Girls! Girls!' came from below.

'There she goes,' I said. 'We'd better go down.'

The 'children' had come home. From the way that Miss Day had treated us, as though we were six, I suppose we ought to have realised. Our new riding pupils were twins, and about our own age, in fact a bit taller than either of us.

11 Two duds

'This is Norrie,' said Miss Day, 'and this is Dorrie. And this is Jill, and this is Ann.'

'Hello,' we said.

'Hello,' said the twins without enthusiasm. They looked a bit glum.

'Now you four get to know each other,' said Miss Day, 'and I'll buzz off.'

When she had gone I said, 'We've got to teach you two to ride.'

'That's the idea,' said one of them, I don't know which.

'Do you want to?' said Ann.

'We don't mind,' said the other one. 'It'll please Auntie and it won't hurt us.'

'It might hurt us,' I said. 'I like teaching people who really want to learn.'

'That's all right,' said one of them. 'We'll have a go. I don't suppose you want to start now. We don't. Let's give it a miss till tomorrow, we've been out all afternoon and we've had enough fresh air to last us for ages.'

'I thought you came from the wide open spaces,' said Ann, 'where you never get anything else but fresh air?'

'Actually,' said the other one, 'we come from Sydney, but that wouldn't mean a thing to Auntie. She thinks Australia's one big dustbowl full of sheep.'

I began to giggle, and one of the twins said, 'What's on your mind?'

'We thought you were little kids,' I said. 'We thought you played in the woods and we'd have to read fairy tales to you.'

Later on, Ann said to me, 'I don't see this job lasting long. These people are practically grown up, like us. They'll learn to ride well enough to satisfy Miss Day in about two weeks. Then she'll have to hire or buy ponies for them, and we shall go home.'

But it didn't turn out like that. I have met some duds in my time. In my long and chequered career I have taught people who didn't know which way round a saddle went on, and were absolutely incapable of understanding simple orders like Hands Down and Knees Up, and did the wrong thing instinctively, but never, never have I encountered such supercharged clots as Norrie and Dorrie when you tried to put them on a pony.

I led out Black Boy as he was used to beginners, and had the sweetest nature and really tried to help people, and was so patient.

'Now come on, Norrie,' I said. 'I'll help you up so that you can get the feel of sitting in the saddle.'

I helped her up, and she promptly fell off the other side. I did it again, and she did it again.

'How *do* you keep on, anyway?' she said helplessly.

'Have you ever heard of balance?' I said sarkily. 'Have you ever sat on a chair? Well, just *sit*!'

Norrie said she'd have another try, and this time she clung on as if she was sitting on the top of a peak with a hundred-foot drop on all sides. Then she said she was giddy and could she get off!

By then I was worn out, so I told Ann to have a go with Dorrie. It took ages to get Dorrie up, and when she was up somehow she was facing backwards. It sounds incredible, but she was and had to begin all over again. The second time she got her arms round Black Boy's neck.

'Let go and *sit up*!' yelled Ann.

'I daren't,' shrieked Dorrie.

Ann mopped her brow and said, 'This is killing me.'

I agreed. In all our wide experience, with all the kids we had taught, we had never never come across such duds. It took us one hour to get Norrie and Dorrie even to sit in the saddle like pokers.

Norrie said, 'If ever the pony moved I should die.'

I said, 'You two are the depths,' and Dorrie said they thought we were too tough with them, which struck us dumb.

When we went in for lunch Miss Day said, 'Well, how did the pupils get on?' Ann and I said nothing, and Dorrie murmured that it was harder than they'd thought, and Miss Day said, 'Really? Quite little children seem to do it so easily,' which didn't add to the gaiety.

We lammed into the food.

I know I say a lot about food in my books, and Mummy puts a pencil through about half of what I have written, but I think it is interesting.

I don't know if you have ever stayed on a pig and poultry farm like Miss Day's, but it is logical to suppose that one would get nothing to eat but chicken and pork. We had chicken and pork in every shape and form, and mostly the lopsided bits that didn't go down well with the buyers. At first Ann and I adored it, but to make a long story short, by the time we left Mayside Farm we never wanted to eat those two things again as long as we lived.

However, apart from never seeing any other animal on the table, as though they didn't exist, the meals were always very good, and Miss Day had the right idea about puddings, which were spongy, jammy, and supersonic.

After lunch we expected there would be another pony lesson, but Norrie and Dorrie just announced that they were going out, and proceeded to disappear. On bikes.

'Do you see that?' I said to Ann. 'Bikes. And they can't sit on a pony.'

'I expect they're made wrong,' she said. 'Gosh, I do like those tapered black trousers they've got, and those super mohair sweaters.'

'Never mind their sweaters,' I said morosely. 'They'll be the death of me. After I'd had Dorrie on a leading rein for five minutes, shrieking her head off, I tell you I could have gone into orbit.'

Ann said she would rather teach two-year-old babies any day, and it struck me we had quite a job on our hands. At this rate we would be at Mayside

Farm for years. I suppose there are some people who are incapable of learning to ride, but I didn't think that I should ever come up against any! I even began to wonder how soon it would be fair to tell Miss Day that she was wasting her time and money, and that her beauteous dream of seeing her dear nieces on steeds of fiery disposition was all washed up.

However, the girls had gone out and Ann and I didn't seem to have anything to do, so we asked Miss Day if it would be all right for us to go for a ride, and she said, 'Do, dears, do.' So we did. We had a wonderful ride on my ponies, and found some heathland to gallop over, and thoroughly enjoyed ourselves. The country around was marvellous, and Ann said, 'Well, even if we do work ourselves to death in the mornings and nearly break our horsy hearts, it's worth it for rides like this.'

Norrie and Dorrie came back about six, without saying where they'd been. After supper I felt I ought to do a bit for my living, so I told them that we'd have a session on The Care of the Horse, round the dining-room table. They didn't seem very keen, but I did my best, and if they didn't take it in that wasn't my fault. We ended up by playing Scrabble.

Next morning I felt in the mood of a slave driver, so I led them to the stable and made them muck out, groom the ponies, mix the feeds, give water, etc., etc., all under my eagle eye and supervision. They were very ham-handed and took ages. I said sarkily, 'Well, well! We'll just about be done in time for lunch. How on earth would you manage if you wanted to be out early or go hunting?'

Norrie said that she couldn't imagine them ever wanting to be out early, and they were never likely to go hunting, and Ann said, 'You're telling me!'

Eventually we got them out into the paddock, and led them round on leading reins. Imagine, at their age! As soon as we left them alone they slid round the ponies' necks or got their feet tangled in the stirrup leathers.

At lunch Miss Day again asked for a progress report, and Dorrie said, 'I think we're getting on.'

It was more than Ann and I thought, but we let it pass.

In the afternoon we tried again. How we worked! The ponies must have been as fed up as we were, but by tea time Norrie and Dorrie could actually ride a slow and wobbly circle, all by themselves.

'I've got hopes,' I said to Ann. 'I should think about another two years and they'll be able to enter for the under-tens showing class. I suppose we can't expect much from the poor little things. They're only sixteen.'

We laughed it off. The only thing you could do with Norrie and Dorrie was to see the funny side. I wanted to show them how to rub down the ponies, feed them, and put them up for the night, but Ann said if I did we'd still be in the stable at midnight, so we did it ourselves.

In the evening I got out the horse book and showed them pictures of the various kinds of tack and taught them the names, or tried to, and told them what everything was for.

'Are you trying to work us to death?' said Dorrie. 'I just can't *hold* any more.'

'You haven't held anything yet,' said Ann brutally. 'Tomorrow we're going to teach you to mount properly, and you've got to know the various parts of the tack we're referring to.'

Norrie said they'd rather learn as it came, and as both Ann and I by then felt like bits of chewed string we gave up for the rest of the evening.

The next day, the girls' idea of 'learning as it came' may have been amusing to the onlooker, but I assure you it wasn't to us. When I said, 'Take the reins in your left hand,' they promptly took them in the right. When I said, 'Take hold of the saddle with your right hand', they grabbed the crownpiece of the bridle. When I said, 'Put your left foot into the stirrup', they put the tips of their toes in, and I said, 'Right in for, goodness' sake.' And Norrie somehow got her foot upside down and sat down on the ground with a thump.

'Give me strength!' said Ann.

Dorrie said, 'Well, everybody's got to learn, haven't they? Even you had to learn.'

'What you're learning now,' said Ann, 'I learned in five minutes when I was three. Norrie! For goodness' sake, *spring* into the saddle, you're not climbing the Alps, and sit down – don't bounce – oh, my gosh!' Ann shut her eyes as Norrie thudded into the saddle and grabbed the reins for dear life. 'Honestly,' she went on, 'it isn't fair on the ponies. I know Black Boy's angelic, but it's too much to ask.'

Well, in the end Norrie and Dorrie learned to mount

a pony. This doesn't sound much – but oh boy! It took about a week. And we never did teach them to dismount properly, off they would slither, so we gave up.

We sat them straight in the saddle, nicely forward, and then shoved their heels down, their knees up and in, and their hands down.

'Now that's all right,' I said. 'Off you go, and stay like you are now.'

Off they went. Gosh! In three minutes their hands were under their chins and their knees sticking out a mile. They looked like two taxis with the doors open. Then Miss Day came out.

'Oh,' she said, 'they can ride! Isn't that splendid! You *have* done well!' Ann and I didn't know whether to laugh or scream, but we decided that the only way to cope was to laugh.

'It's no good taking these two seriously,' I said to Ann, 'or we'll break our hearts. Miss Day is satisfied, and we're having fun here, so let's make the best of it while it lasts.'

Yes, we were having fun at Mayside Farm. Hopeless as Norrie and Dorrie were when they came in contact with ponies, they were very good company. When the morning lesson was over they used to say, 'Thank goodness, we've had our daily dose now, so let's go out and really enjoy ourselves.'

We felt guilty about this, as it didn't seem to be giving Miss Day good value, but all she said was, 'Yes, run along and enjoy yourselves, girls.' So we took her at her word.

We used to go on the bus to the nearest town where

there was an ice rink, and then it was the twins' turn to laugh at Ann and me. They were both wonderful skaters – which again stunned us, as they seemed to have mastered the art of balance on everything but a pony – and they were awfully decent about teaching us and hauling us round until we could go under our own steam. Soon we were enjoying it tremendously. After an hour at the rink we would have ice cream and then go to the pictures, and come back for supper.

Norrie and Dorrie were both very good at indoor games and taught us some new and riotous ones to play in the evenings, and they also had lots of imagination and made up smashing stories which they used to write out, and read us one instalment every night to keep us guessing.

Ann said, 'Well, honestly, you can't call this a *job*. We're having much too good a time. I think we ought to ask Miss Day if we can help on the farm.'

So we did, but she only said, 'No, no, no! You're here to be company for the girls, that's all I ask, and I'm quite satisfied.'

It was funny really, because when we wrote home we never knew what to say, as we didn't want to give our parents the impression that we were simply playing about, as we should have been promptly dragged home to do something more serious. As it was, every time Mummy wrote she would say, 'Haven't you taught those two girls to ride yet? You seem to be taking a very long time over it.'

I then wrote and pointed out that we really did a lot of chores, and so we did, as the four of us managed the cooking and so forth between us without any great effort, and actually that rather pleased Mummy as she is great nuts on girls being domesticated, and Ann added, 'P.S. Jill makes the most super cakes.' I certainly did make cakes, though I don't know about them being super, but Mummy was appeased.

12 Mysterious

We had a Mystery on our hands. Three afternoons a
week Norrie and Dorrie disappeared. I don't mean
they melted into thin air before our very eyes or
anything like that. They just said nothing, got on
to their bikes, and went off and didn't come back
until nearly supper time.

'It's jolly odd,' I said to Ann. 'Where on earth do
they go to?'

'Search me!' she said. 'You'd think they'd say.'

But they never did.

Once I said to them in a casual, nonchalant way,
'Where are you off to?' and Norrie just said, 'Out,'
and sprang on her bicycle.

'I suppose it's just that they don't want us around
all the time,' said Ann.

'But you'd think they'd say!'

'P'raps they want to go to the rink on their own.'

'But they ride off in the other direction.'

'P'raps that's to put us off.'

'Oh blow Norrie and Dorrie,' said Ann. 'At least
it gives us a chance to have three jolly good rides a
week on the ponies, which we couldn't have if they
were sticking around all the time.'

This was true, and Ann and I were enjoying our

rides very much. It was glorious riding country all around, even better than at home, and we explored every inch of it, galloping the ponies over great open stretches of common and weaving our way through woodland glades.

'You don't know what you're missing,' we said to Norrie and Dorrie as we washed up the supper things. 'If you'd only pull your socks up and learn to ride properly Miss Day would hire you two ponies – she said so – and you'd love it.'

'We've been here a month already,' said Ann, 'and in spite of our positively gruesome efforts on your behalf, all you two can do is amble round the paddock. It's time you were out on the road, but we daren't take you. You'd fall off if you saw a motorbike!'

'Well, we can't help that,' said Dorrie. 'Riding isn't everything.'

'We think it is,' I said. 'And we're supposed to be here to make you think it is. We've got a hope!'

'If we don't want to go out on the road, we don't want to go out on the road and we're jolly well not going to,' said Norrie. 'So that's that.'

We pointed out that Miss Day would be disappointed, but actually she didn't seem to bother. Then one evening she said she had seen a film of some girls jumping in a gymkhana, and she would love to see Norrie and Dorrie doing that, and did I think they'd be able to by the time the summer Shows came along? Did I? I ask you!

I had to say truthfully that at their present rate

of progress they wouldn't be jumping in competitions much before they were fifty, and she said, what a pity.

I said to Norrie, 'You two jolly well ought to learn to jump, it's awful not to be able to.'

'OK,' she said. 'We'll have a try.'

'I would like to draw a veil over the twins' first jumping lesson. We only put a pole on two bricks in the paddock, the sort of thing you'd do if you were teaching the under-sevens, but from the way those two went on you'd think we were asking them to jump Becher's Brook at Aintree.

At last we persuaded Norrie, who was the more daring of the two, to try. Black Boy gave me a look as if to say, 'Blimey! Am I reduced to this?' He then carried Norrie over the pole without the slightest jerk.

She finished up with her hands tangled in his mane, looked back, and said, 'Did I really jump it?'

'No, you didn't,' said Ann. 'Black Boy did it entirely unaided by you. Gosh, that's the sort of jump we give to three-year-old kids.'

'I'll have a go now,' said Dorrie.

She was up on Rapide, and I wickedly didn't change her over to Black Boy. I knew Rapide's little tricks, and I thought it was time Dorrie had a real lesson. I gave her a few brief, elementary jumping instructions and let her go.

Rapide has always been incapable of jumping less than four feet. He's a bit dim in the head that way. Even a pole three inches off the ground is a four-foot jump to him, and so he made it this time. Up he went in his best showground manner, flicked his heels, and pretended he was doing a triple bar.

I shut my eyes, expecting to find Dorrie's corpse thudding at my feet.

'OK,' said Ann dryly. 'She's still on.'

Yes, Dorrie was still on. She had her mouth wide open and looked stunned.

'Did I jump?' she said. 'I thought I was in a helicopter.'

'You jumped,' said Ann. 'You jumped about four-foot-six. I could see four counties between your legs, which isn't done in the best riding circles, and you looked like a sack of oats being chucked over a wall, but you jumped. Now do it again, and try and stay in the saddle this time.'

'Don't, Dorrie, don't,' shrieked Norrie. 'It was awful. That pony's crackers. He thought he was jumping a wall that wasn't there.'

'That's only Rapide's little way,' I said. 'He's all right.'

But Dorrie said she'd had enough.

'Well, try on Black Boy,' I said. 'He'll step over the pole, you won't feel a thing.'

'No thanks,' said Dorrie. 'Let's go and have our elevenses. I want to forget it.'

'Oh, you two are feeble!' I said. 'Another week of teaching you and I'll nearly go into orbit.'

This made them a bit huffy, and after we had washed up the lunch things they went out without a word, mounted their bikes, and set off.

'There they go,' I said. 'I wish I knew what they were up to.'

'Well, let's pretend we're great detectives and follow them,' suggested Ann.

'Don't be silly,' I said. 'We've nothing to follow them on but the ponies, and we should look like sleuths, shouldn't we, clattering along behind them and pretending we weren't there?'

'I expect they just go for a bike ride,' said Ann, 'like we go for a pony ride.'

'Well, why don't they ask us to go with them?'

'I suppose because we haven't got bikes.'

'We could hire bikes.'

'Oh, stop nattering,' said Ann. 'I couldn't care less where they go.' But it still remained a mystery, and mysteries always irritate you until you know what they're all about.

'How did the jumping go on?' asked Miss Day at supper.

'I jumped four-foot-six,' said Dorrie calmly. Ann and I began to giggle.

'Is that good?' asked Miss Day, turning to me.

'Oh, frightfully good,' I said sarkily. 'They'll be riding at Richmond and Hickstead in no time, at this rate.'

Miss Day looked bewildered.

'Richmond is a very nice place, dear,' she said, 'I have some cousins living there, only I don't see why the girls should want to ride there, and I never heard of Hickstead.'

Ann and I tried not to shriek.

Strangely enough, from then on Norrie and Dorrie did begin to make an effort, and improved quite a lot.

'I don't think they tried before,' Anne said to me, 'but now they're getting interested, and they both sit quite decently and don't fool about any more.'

This was true. We even got them on the road, and on the Common, and when we asked Miss Day she hired two ponies from a local stable and the four of us had a ride in the woods and came home feeling pleased with ourselves.

'You're doing us credit at last,' I said to Norrie and Dorrie. 'We've got our professional reputations to think about, and it was getting us down, thinking that we couldn't do anything with you. It would have been awful to go home feeling that we'd failed.'

'Oh, we're sorry,' they said. 'We never looked at it that way. We'll try harder.'

They did try. We got them doing easy jumps and they sat well and looked very nice. We put up four two-foot-six jumps in the paddock – if you have read my other books you will remember that I can make jumps out of practically anything – and the girls learned to do this little round in a way that I had to admit was quite passable.

Then to my horror they began to get big-headed about their riding. This was awful.

At lunch one day Norrie said to Miss Day, 'We're getting jolly good at riding *and* jumping. I should think we could enter almost any competition.'

'What!' I yelled.

'Well, so we could. We were absolutely faultless this morning over the jumps, both of us were.'

'Gosh!' I said. 'Faultless over two-foot-six jumps, and you're sixteen years old. Two-foot-six jumps

are what you get in the juniors. You're just beginners.'

'Rot,' said Dorrie. 'Once you've mastered the
principles of jumping the height of the jump doesn't
matter, you told me that yourself.'

'Are you suggesting,' said Ann, 'that you've mastered the principles of jumping? Don't make me
laugh.'

'You're just discouraging,' said Norrie. 'We're
better than you think, in fact we're jolly good.'

'All right,' I said. 'You go on thinking so. Perhaps
in the summer after we're gone you'll be able to
enter for a competition, and then you'll learn. It's
the only way.'

'Well, push the jumps up this afternoon,' said
Norrie, 'and we'll have a go.'

So we went out and put the four jumps up to four
foot. Norrie had Black Boy and Dorrie had Rapide
and they both managed to get over the jumps; then
they changed ponies and did it again.

'There you are!' said Dorrie. 'We can jump
anything.'

'Give me strength!' said Ann. 'Don't you realise that
Jill's ponies are trained to show-jumping, and they've
been doing it for years? It was the ponies who jumped,
you just stuck on. You didn't do a thing.'

'Yes, we did,' said Norrie indignantly. 'We gave
them the aids like you taught us.'

'They'd recognise those aids if they were jumping
in their sleep,' said Ann. 'I'd like to see you try on
strange ponies.'

'As a matter of fact,' I said to Ann when we were

alone, 'they've both developed a bit of style lately. Have you noticed?'

'Absolutely,' said Ann. 'And Norrie's timing surprised me this morning. P'raps they've got hidden talent which our noble efforts are at last bringing into bud. But we mustn't let them think we think so, they're impossible when they're big-headed, and they've nothing to be big-headed about. P'raps after we've gone they'll enter for a few competitions in the summer. That'll show them!'

By now Norrie and Dorrie were being more co-operative in their lessons, and doing exactly what we told them, but I couldn't say they were taking any great interest, and they always seemed glad when the morning lesson was over, which wasn't very flattering to Ann and me.

I'd say, 'Well, I think we'd better knock off now,' and one of them would say, 'thank goodness', and it annoyed me very much.

'Anybody would think it was an arithmetic class,' I said to Ann. 'Fancy being glad when a riding lesson was over! Gosh, when I was at the stage they're at I used to nearly weep when the lesson was over. I wanted it to go on for ever.'

'It's just that they're not keen,' said Ann, 'and it's no good pretending they are. Miss Day's wasting her money, though I must say, she doesn't seem to mind.'

There was now no question of an afternoon lesson at all. Norrie and Dorrie took it for granted that by lunch time they had done their duty to the ponies, and in the afternoons we either went off together to the ice rink or to town, or they did their famous disappearing act.

One thing I will say for them, they were very good about mucking out, feeding the ponies, and cleaning tack.

'As a matter of fact,' I said to Ann, 'they seem to like that better than riding, aren't they bats?'

We both decided that Norrie and Dorrie were mild cases of lunacy and left it at that.

It was now the end of March, lovely spring weather and gorgeous for riding. Ann and I came home about five after a wonderful ride, rubbed the ponies down, and sat on the old mounting block in the yard, drinking lemonade. It was one of those afternoons when the girls had vanished, but we had given up bothering about that particular mystery as we didn't seem to have any opportunity for being detectives.

'How long do you think we ought to stop on here?' said Ann. 'I had a letter from Mummy this morning and she's getting restive. Says I've been away two months, and it's time I came home and did some serious thinking. Gosh! As if I didn't do some serious thinking every day of my life.'

'I know,' I said. 'It's jolly nice here – in a way, we're having a smashing time – but it's a bit of a dead end. We're not getting anywhere ourselves, and we're not learning anything. And between you and me, I don't think Norrie and Dorrie are going to get any further than they are now, not in a million years. P'raps we'd better tell Miss Day we're leaving. We don't want to miss our summer riding in Chatton.'

We decided that we would take the first opportunity

to suggest leaving and see how Miss Day took it. Perhaps she was just waiting for us to go but didn't like to say so.

But life still had a shock in store for us.

13 Shock after shock

Norrie and Dorrie came in that particular evening looking pleased with themselves, and when we sat down to supper Dorrie said, 'What's a point-to-point?'

'It's a race meeting for amateurs,' I said. 'Usually over hurdles, and it's usually got up by the local hunt at the end of the hunting season.'

'Can anybody go in for it?' asked Norrie.

'If they're good enough,' I said. 'But the standard's very high.'

'There's going to be one here on Friday week,' said Dorrie. 'As a matter of fact, we've entered. We thought it would be fun.'

I have been stunned, knocked for six, and poleaxed in my time, but this was the lot. I looked at Ann and she looked at me, and our mouths dropped open, and we sort of yammered at each other.

'That sounds nice, dear, why don't you all enter?' said Miss Day.

'To begin with,' I said, finding my voice, 'Ann and I don't consider ourselves good enough to ride against the best local riders, and as for Norrie and Dorrie – well, I can't imagine what they're thinking of!'

'Oh, don't be stuffy!' said Norrie.

'If you think,' I said, 'that you're going to ride on my Black Boy and Rapide in the local point-to-point, I can tell you now you've had it. It's fantastic. They're not racing ponies. They've never raced in their lives, and they're not going to start now with you two up!'

'Not to worry,' said Dorrie, calmly eating sausages. 'We're being lent two horses by a friend.'

'She wants her head examining,' said Ann. 'Has she ever seen you *ride*?'

'Now and then,' said Dorrie.

'Look, Miss Day,' said Ann desperately, 'we don't want to look like spoilsports and I expect you'll think it isn't our business, but you oughtn't to let the girls do this. It's absolutely beyond them, honestly.'

Miss Day looked bewildered and said, 'Well, I'm no judge, am I, dear? But if they think they can, I don't see why they shouldn't try. After all, we never know what we can do till we try, do we? Or so my mother used to say to me.'

'This is hopeless,' I said, gritting my teeth. I went on, 'As a matter of fact, Miss Day, Ann and I were thinking that it's about time we went home. We've taught the girls all we can and we can't do any more, and we think we ought to get on with some other job now.'

'Well, that's just as you wish, dear,' said Miss Day, smiling amiably. 'But I think you must really stay for another week or so and watch them ride in this point-to-point. It sounds so interesting. Then you could go home on the Saturday.'

'The Saturday!' moaned Ann as we went upstairs

later. 'So we're to stay and watch Norrie and Dorrie make fools of themselves and perhaps break their necks, and at best foul all the other horses, and everybody will say that *we* taught them to ride! This is the end.'

'It may not be so ghastly,' I said. 'After all, there'll only be one under-eighteen event, and they'll probably just trail along at the back and come in last, and if somebody is idiot enough to lend them ponies that's their business. Let's write to our mums and say we're coming home. That'll be something to look forward to.'

From then on we might just as well have been at home for all we saw of Norrie and Dorrie. They were always going off to their 'friend's' to practise for the point-to-point.

'Say, who is this friend?' murmured Ann. 'Why haven't we heard of her before? And is she the one they've been popping off to in the afternoons?'

'Search me,' I said. 'It's the most fantastic thing. This is the silliest job we ever had, Ann, and I wish we'd never come – only don't let's breathe that at home.'

'At least we've learned to skate,' said Ann.

The next afternoon we thought we'd go for a ride and forget everything. We went a new way, and found ourselves passing some enclosed parkland, and on the edge of the park alongside the road was an enormous notice board with a huge poster stuck on it.

POINT-TO-POINT MEETING
IN THE PARK

ON FRIDAY MARCH 25TH
FIRST RACE AT 2 P.M.
ENTRIES INCLUDE BEST-KNOWN
COUNTY RIDERS
REFRESHMENTS

And then something else caught our eye. In red
letters.

SPECIAL ATTRACTION
EXHIBITION OF PAIR JUMPING AND
RACING
BY THE FAMOUS CANNON TWINS
(NOREEN AND DOREEN CANNON)
AUSTRALIA'S GIRL RIDING CHAMPIONS
NOW ON HOLIDAY IN THIS COUNTRY

To say that Ann and I were by now staring at each
other is an understatement. Our eyes were practically
sticking out and meeting. We had often read about
the Cannon twins, and how they were supposed to
be coming to England in the summer for the big
Shows.

Cannon! Noreen and Doreen Cannon! Our brains
were clicking like mad and we just couldn't believe
it, but it was all falling into place.

We were remembering that we had never once
heard Norrie's or Dorrie's surname. Nobody had
ever mentioned it. If we had thought of it at all,
we had taken it for granted that it was Day, like
their aunt.

'It can't be!' gasped Ann. 'It must be! Are we going mad? And what on earth does it all mean? How did we come into it?'

'Come on,' I said grimly. 'Let's go home and find out.'

Norrie and Dorrie were cheerfully mixing food for the chickens when we got in. Norrie was sitting on the kitchen table singing 'Waltzing Matilda', while Dorrie doled out the meal into the bucket which Norrie held.

'Hello, you two,' sang out Dorrie. 'Coming to watch us workers?'

'Oh yes?' I said. 'Would you by any chance ever have heard of the Cannon twins?'

Neither of them turned a hair, and Norrie said, 'I suppose you had to find out some time. But it was fun while it lasted.'

'But what's it all in aid of?' Ann burst out. 'What on earth have you been playing at? And why on earth all these so-called lessons? It's fantastic, it's absolutely bats, isn't it, Jill?'

'Somebody's bats,' I said. 'I've got to the stage when I don't know who.'

'It's quite a story, really,' said Dorrie, giggling. 'I'd better spill the entire thing. It didn't start as a racket, it just grew and grew, didn't it, Norrie?'

'We got so far in, we couldn't get out,' said Norrie. 'Go on, you tell them, Dorrie.'

'Well, it was this way,' said Dorrie. 'Aunt Maud isn't actually our aunt, she's our mother's cousin, and ever since we were born she's been on at Mother to let us come over and stay with her.'

'Over from Australia?' I said.

'That's right. Well, we'd never been to England and we were due here this summer for the Shows, so Mother suggested that we should come over for Christmas and stay with Aunt Maud here until it was time for us to go down south. We'd just got through a heavy two years' riding at home, and with the prospect of an exciting and quite strenuous summer, we all thought a quiet holiday here in the country would be rather good.'

'Quiet is the right word,' said Norrie. 'We'd had a hectic time, and we did need a rest.'

'I bet you did,' said Ann. 'Jill and I have read all about you for ages, and we still can't believe you're actually the Cannon twins.'

'I'm afraid we really are,' said Dorrie. 'Well, let's go on with this gruesome tale. We arrived here at Mayside Farm full of peace and good intentions, only to find that Aunt Maud didn't know who we were, because she didn't know the horsy world existed, if you get me.'

'You mean to say, she didn't know you were the famous Cannon twins?' I yelped.

'Just that,' said Norrie. 'To her we were just her dear little nieces from Australia, and she wanted to find something to amuse us, so one day she saw a jumping competition on a film, and she got the bright idea it would be nice for us to ride like other kids. She suggested this, and just for the joke of it we let her have her way.'

'She was so thrilled at her bright idea,' said Dorrie, 'that we hadn't the heart to spoil it for her. And another thing, we didn't want her to know that we were experienced riders already, because if it once got round the neighbourhood who we were, we'd have been bothered to death by people wanting us to ride for them, and do this and that for them – you can imagine it – and we shouldn't have got any rest from competitive riding at all, and that was what Mother wanted us to have, so that we shouldn't be stale when the British season started. Of course we didn't know what Aunt Maud's ideas would lead to; when we did know we got quite a shock.'

'One day,' said Norrie, taking up the story, 'Aunt Maud came in with a face like the rising moon and told us that she'd heard of two girls who wanted a pony job – preferably to teach riding – and she was going to invite them to come and stay here and TEACH US!'

'We nearly fell flat on our backs,' said Dorrie, 'but we didn't like to say we didn't want you, so we thought we'd wait and see what happened. Then you arrived and we liked you and thought it would be fun to have you here. We talked it over in bed, and decided that we'd play the game Aunt Maud's way and let you jolly well teach us, and we'd be as slow and clottish as we could.'

'Gosh!' said Ann. 'If we'd known what you were really up to we'd have murdered you.'

They rocked with laughing.

'Oh, it was a scream, pretending to be so thick-headed,' shrieked Dorrie. 'And you two were so marvellous. At night, when we got to bed, we used to have the most ghastly pangs of remorse for the trick we were playing on you, but then we were in it up to our necks, and we couldn't give the game away.'

'I don't know how you kept it up,' I said. 'I mean, doing all the wrong things.'

'It was frightfully hard,' said Norrie. 'Once I automatically reined back, and then remembered that you hadn't "taught" me to do that! Fortunately you hadn't noticed me!'

'By that time,' said Dorrie, 'of course we *couldn't* give ourselves away. The explanations would have been too ghastly.'

'I'll say they would,' I said helplessly. 'But now perhaps you'll solve a mystery for Ann and me. *Where did you go in the afternoons?*'

They looked at one another and grinned.

'We went,' said Dorrie simply, 'to a friend of ours a few miles away who keeps a hunting stable. We met him when he was riding in Australia. He let us exercise his horses and get the practice we wanted to keep us in form, and of course he kept our secret.'

'And he persuaded us,' said Norrie, 'to give a show at the local point-to-point. He felt we owed it to the neighbourhood before we went south.'

'Well, that's terrific!' said Ann and I together.

Suddenly I saw Miss Day coming across the yard to fetch the chicken food.

'What are you going to do about *her*?' I asked. 'Tell her?'

'Oh, we couldn't – we couldn't possibly,' gasped Dorrie. 'She'd be furious to think we'd played such a trick on her.'

'I don't think she'd be furious, so much as miserable,' said Norrie, looking blue. 'I begin to feel so low I could crawl under a blade of grass.'

'Never mind,' I said. 'Let's just wait and see what happens at the point-to-point. She'll probably be so thrilled at your riding that she'll forgive you anything.'

14   The point-to-point

What happened at the point-to-point was that Miss
Day was so thrilled with the girls' riding that she never
even asked any questions, and had nothing to forgive.
Instead – but I must tell you what happened.

You should have seen the girls, immaculate in
white cord breeches, shining boots, black coats,
snowy stocks! In contrast, and not to make ourselves
conspicuous seeing we weren't taking any part in the
proceedings, Ann and I wore skirts and jackets.

'Now I wonder what Miss Day is going to say about
these rigouts?' I said to Ann.

Miss Day didn't see anything extraordinary. She
simply looked at the dazzling twins and remarked,
'Very nice, my dears. I suppose that's what people
wear for riding. What a pity Ann and Jill aren't riding
too, and wearing such nice clothes.'

We nearly went into hysterics.

The car came round and we all set off for the park.
There were crowds of people there, and the first thing
we did was to go and have a look at the course, which
was a snorter as the ground was heavy and some of
the hedges high enough to be tricky. All the same,
Ann and I would have rather liked to have a try at
it, but we hadn't had the practice. Dorrie and Norrie

were chortling with glee as they said it was just right for them, in fact they'd been working out on similar ground for weeks, unbeknown to us.

Very soon some of the rather grand committee members came and swept them away from us, as of course they were the star attraction of the afternoon, the Cannon twins, and had to be introduced to the local Master of Foxhounds and the united hunts president, and Lady Something-or-other.

Ann and I slunk into the background and went into the refreshment tent to have a sausage roll or two, and there we were found by Miss Day.

'Oh, have you lost the girls?' she said frantically, and we said, no, they'd just gone to get ready for their event.

Meanwhile the first race got under way, and there was a good deal of falling off, and riderless horses roaming about with a grin on their faces, and the usual things that happen at a point-to-point where the winner is always the one who manages to stick on longest. As we didn't know any of the people riding, or in fact any of the people milling about, we weren't terribly excited, but Miss Day was dancing up and down and thought it was supersonic, and asked, 'When are the girls coming on?'

Well, the girls came on all right, and you should have seen them, on a pair of perfectly matched, gleaming-coated chestnuts lent for the occasion, and so spirited that they fairly danced.

'Golly!' I breathed. 'Don't they look *smashing*?'

They certainly did, and the way they handled those

horses was smashing too. They were first-class and showed it.

First they gave an exhibition of pair jumping and it was out of this world, as the horses moved in step and every action of the riders was synchronised. They were just like one rider and its shadow, and as they sailed over the hedges the crowd went mad with cheering.

Then came the main race of the day, for the President's Cup, and of course all the best riders were in it because they wanted to say that they had raced with the Cannon twins. It was terrific, and as the horses came thundering up and took the last hedge, almost flying, there were Norrie and Dorrie and two fine men riders practically neck and neck.

I thought Miss Day was going to have a fit, shrieking, 'Come on, girls! Sock 'em, bash 'em, leave 'em behind!'

In the end Dorrie won by a neck, with Norrie and a man dead-heating second. I was so excited I could feel my eyes sticking out like organ stops.

'Hurray, hurray!' shrieked Miss Day. Then to our amazement and horror she suddenly turned to Ann and me and flung her arms round our necks.

'You clever, clever girls!' she yowled. 'You marvellous girls! To think *you* taught them!'

I've had some shocks in my time, but this was the tops. That poor woman actually thought – well, Ann and I were dumb.

'Oh, don't!' yelled Ann. 'Please, Miss Day! We didn't – I mean – we weren't – I mean, they – oh *gosh*!'

Meanwhile the President was coming on to the course to present the Cup, and as was the proper thing Dorrie and Norrie just shook hands with him, and stood back so that the man, who was a member of the Hunt, could have the Cup, and everybody cheered.

'Why aren't they getting the Cup?' demanded Miss Day. 'Why's that man getting it?'

We muttered something about the girls being just visitors, but she wasn't a bit pleased and rumbled on darkly about it being unfair, and we were so terrified that somebody would hear her that we dragged her off to the refreshment tent to get a cup of tea. She still kept saying, 'I don't understand –' and we felt that any minute she'd go and complain to the Committee.

However, another embarrassment arose for us. In came some people that Miss Day knew, and before we could get our breath she was introducing us to them as 'the two clever girls who taught my nieces to ride'. As these people were local riders of some repute, they looked at Ann and me with their mouths open.

'Taught the Cannon twins to ride?' somebody gasped.

'Yes, indeed,' said Miss Day, smiling like a pussy cat. 'Jill and Ann are so clever. Wonderful teachers. Dorrie and Norrie couldn't do a thing until these two took them in hand.'

By now a few more people were gathering round and staring at us. We felt awful, and wished we could crawl under a table or something. Worse was to follow. Along came a newspaper reporter and a cameraman.

'Where are the girls who taught the Cannon twins to ride?'

'It's all a mistake – ' began Ann in a sort of strangled voice, but it didn't do any good, because the next minute they were pulling us out into the open and arranging us, and the newspaperman was saying, 'Smile, please – get a good, full picture of them, Bill.'

There was a ring of people all round us, watching. I don't know what we looked like, but we were shaking like jellyfish, and I'm sure neither of us looked like the sort of bods to teach a three-year-old kid to ride, let alone the Cannon twins.

'Now we'll have one with our famous riders in it,' said the cameraman, and along came Norrie and Dorrie giggling at us and nearly having hysterics.

'Did these girls really teach you to ride?' asked the newspaperman.

'Sure they did,' said the awful Norrie, winking at me.

'Too right, they did,' said Dorrie.

'I say, this is a scoop,' said the newspaperman. 'Cannon twins were taught to ride by two unknown British girls.'

So they got us in a row and took another photograph. Norrie and Dorrie grinned from ear to ear.

'Come on, you two,' muttered Norrie. 'Look as if you were enjoying it.'

'Can they put us in prison for this?' murmured Ann.

'If *you* didn't teach us,' said Dorrie, 'I don't know who did.'

The twins linked arms with us, the camera snapped, a lot more people came along and everybody clapped.

Miss Day was so happy she was fairly dancing about. Everybody else guessed there was something peculiar going on, knowing who the twins were, but they were all enjoying themselves so much that nobody asked any awkward questions, and the next minute – believe it or not – Ann and I were invited, along with Miss Day, to go and have tea in the Committee tent.

By now we were seeing the funny side of it too. While we nibbled gorgeous sandwiches and cakes amid the great and famous of the riding world, people kept coming up to us and winking and saying, 'Some teachers!' and things like that. And there was darling Miss Day talking to the Master of Foxhounds and we could hear her voice above everything else saying, 'And do you know, two months ago the dear girls couldn't even mount a pony! And look at them now!'

'Marvellous!' agreed the Master.

'And it's all owing to Jill and Ann,' went on Miss Day, 'so if you know of anybody else who wants to learn to ride – '

'It's all turned out wonderfully,' cried Dorrie, seizing a tray of ices and pressing them on to Ann and me. 'Aunt Maud is happy, it's the day of her life, and we've enjoyed every minute of it, and the only black spot is the thought that you'll soon be going away. It's all been such fun.'

'Yes, it has,' I agreed. 'It's been a super job for us,

and everything is going to feel awfully flat after this, when we get home.'

Somebody grabbed Norrie and Dorrie and took them away, and Ann and I were left alone.

'I must say, we do get into some thrilling situations through no fault of our own, don't we?' she laughed.

'What's all this?' said a stern voice behind us.

We whizzed round, and there stood our old friend Captain Cholly-Sawcutt, the famous British rider, who had been such a help to us in the past as you know from reading my previous books.

We couldn't believe our eyes.

'Is it really you?' I gasped.

'Yes, it's really me. I'm told to come and have a look at the two wonderful girls who taught the even more wonderful Cannon twins to ride, and who do I behold but my little Chatton friends Jill and Ann! I've come across you two in some comic spots, but this beats all. How come?'

'Come over here,' said Ann, 'and we'll tell you the whole story.'

We piloted him into a corner and poured it all out. He laughed his head off.

'If your mothers knew the sort of things you get yourselves into!' he chortled.

'It's just these pony jobs,' I explained. 'They always turn out unexpected. But this one's all over now, and we're going home tomorrow.'

'And we don't know what we'll do next,' said Ann sadly. 'You see, our mothers expect us to do something with a future in it. We're getting rather old now.'

Captain Cholly-Sawcutt looked serious.

'Yes, you are. Too old to play around any more. You've had lots of fun and I agree with your mothers it's high time you settled down.'

'But what are we going to *do*?' I asked. 'Because we don't know.'

'I'll tell you what you're going to do,' he said. 'You're going to get yourselves seriously trained for some proper job, and you're going to keep up your riding for a hobby. You'll always enjoy it, but you can't be kids for ever, playing around with your ponies. Now you two get back to Chatton and tell your mothers what I say, and jolly good luck with whatever profession you take up. Agreed?'

'I do think you're right,' I said. 'And whatever Mummy suggests I'll get down to it. I'll learn shorthand and typing and French and German.'

'So will I,' said Ann. 'It's a deal. This is our very last fling, and now we're going to be grown up.'

'Coo!' I said. 'I feel as if I was secretary to the Prime Minister already. Let's go and have another ice to celebrate.'

The Jill pony series by
Ruby Ferguson

All Hodder Children's books are available at your local bookshop or newsagent, or can be ordered direct from the publisher. Just tick the titles you want and fill in the form below. Prices and availability subject to change without notice.

Hodder Children's Books, Cash Sales Department, Bookpoint, 39 Milton Park, Abingdon, OXON, OX14 4TD, UK. If you have a credit card you may order by telephone – 0235 831700.

Please enclose a cheque or postal order made payable to Bookpoint Ltd to the value of the cover price and allow the following for postage and packing:
UK & BFPO: £1.00 for the first book, 50p for the second book and 30p for each additional book ordered up to a maximum charge of £3.00.
OVERSEAS & EIRE: £2.00 for the first book, £1.00 for the second book and 50p for each additional book.

Name...

Address ....

....

....

If you would prefer to pay by credit card, please complete:
Please debit my Visa / Access / Diner's Card / American Express (delete as applicable)
card no:

Signature...

Expiry Date...